SUMMER
STORM

SUMMER
STORM

SUSAN C.
MULLER

Summer Storm
Copyright © 2017
Susan C. Muller

Published in the United States of America by
Stanford Publishing Company

Cover design by
Najla Qamber Designs
http://www.najlaqamberdesigns.com

Interior Design and Formatting by:

www.emtippettsbookdesigns.com

Books By
SUSAN C. MULLER

This book is dedicated to all my fellow writers. From those who win awards and hit lists, to those whose words will never be seen by another human. For those who write in the early morning hours or late night silence, who scribble on a yellow legal pad while on their commute to work or write in a perfectly organized office with an ergonomically correct desk chair. From those "plotters" who know every scene before the first word is written to those "pantsers" who have no idea what the next chapter will hold or how their story will end.

We all, every one of us, hold a candle in the darkness. Never give up on your dream.

CHAPTER ONE

WARM WATER BUBBLED against the back of Madlyn Gwinn's neck. *Dammit, Wade. You lowered the temperature again.* This was supposed to be a hot tub, not a tepid bath.

The July night was hotter than the water.

She reached behind her for the bottle of expensive cabernet, refilled her glass, and placed the empty container on the pebbled decking.

Another little soldier bites the dust.

The warmth of the wine combined with the gurgling of the water made her drowsy. Or was it the Xanax? Didn't matter. This was the best she'd felt all day.

A constant stream of worriers, complainers, nitpickers, and fear mongers trooped into her office every day. They fretted about this. They were concerned about that. But none of them turned down the money and walked away.

Ungrateful parasites, feeding off her hard work.

The air jets slowed and the bubbles stopped. She reached over and slapped the timer again. A third twenty minute sequence wouldn't hurt. Not at this temperature.

The unending array of fireworks last night had lit up the sky with an ostentatious display of fake patriotism and sent her indoors before she'd had time to relax. *Crack. Boom. Bam.* Over and over. All night long. Not to mention the continual clamoring of every dog in the neighborhood.

Especially that yippy little monster next door.

Even inside, the noise set her teeth on edge and kept her up until dawn.

Didn't those people have to work?

Why did they put up with such a blatant waste of their tax dollars?

She eased lower into the water until the back of her head rested on the lip of the spa and her feet touched the facing seat. She locked her knees. This position would prevent her from slipping under if she fell asleep. And she needed sleep more than she needed the wine.

Well, as much, anyway.

Wade had asked if her conscience contributed to her insomnia. The fool. Another one who didn't turn down the money. No, her conscience was fine.

The stress of holding everything together with her fingernails was all that kept her mind swirling until dawn. Given time, the wine, the Xanax, and the soothing water took care of that.

Down the street, some kid set off a string of leftover fireworks with a *pop, pop, pop.* Nearby, a dog voiced his objections, but the Xanax was working. She closed her eyes and let the warm water do its work.

Tonight she would sleep.

Her eyes half opened at the sound of footsteps. How long had the air jets been off? That must be Wade, coming to bring her inside.

Her eyes closed and the corners of her mouth eased. Not a smile, but no longer a frown as she waited for his voice.

He did love her.

Detective Noah Daugherty tried to avoid looking at the body still floating in the lukewarm water. God, he hated drowning cases. "When can you give me a time of death?"

The M.E. didn't bother to look up. "You'll get it when you get it. The condition she's in, I won't know until after the autopsy. Even then, it'll be a crap shoot. I'll have to work backwards from the time she last ate and unless she went out to dinner in public…"

Yeah, yeah. Asking the only person known to be with her when she died was like asking the fox to show you how he got into the hen house. "Can you at least tell me if it's a homicide?"

Eyes warm as snowcapped mountains pinned him from under a shock of white hair. "You know better than to ask me that, Detective. This isn't the only suspicious death the city of Houston's had in the last twenty-four hours. As I said—"

"I know, *I'll get it when I get it.*"

Noah forced himself to study the body. Hard to tell with all the bloating, but her driver's license listed her as forty-six. Much too young to die, although neither of his parents made it past forty.

A shiver ran down his spine. If he lived four more years, and that was a big if, he'd be older than his parents ever were. That didn't seem fair.

But then, nothing in his life had ever been fair. Not dealing with the murder of his father. Not dropping out of Julliard to take care of his dying mother. Not raising his sister alone a year later. Not losing his wife when their life together was just beginning.

Time for a mental head slap. This was a murder investigation, not a pity party.

He pivoted and searched the increasingly crowded patio for his partner, Conner Crawford. The July sun bounced off the pastel stucco walls of the four-story townhome and the reflection from the water in the Olympic-sized swimming pool glared into Noah's eyes, giving him a horrendous headache.

Or had he reached his quota of dead bodies for the month? The year? His attitude had certainly changed since his own errors in judgment had forced his partner to shoot a kidnapper in the back as he drew down on Noah.

Some mistakes were hard to forgive. Especially your own.

His eyes landed on his partner's familiar profile. Conner had found a slice of shade under a red and gold striped umbrella. He sat at a wrought iron table making notes in his ever-present memo pad.

The textured decking around the pool was great for avoiding falls, but hell to stand on for an extended period of time. Noah eased himself onto the comfortable chair facing his partner. "You solved it yet?"

Conner blew out a deep breath and sagged against the cushions. "The only good piece of news is that the pool guy threw up in the landscaping instead of the hot tub."

"What about hubby?" Noah consulted his notes. "Wade, isn't it? What does he have to say for himself?"

"Had no idea anything had happened to his wife until the pool guy beat on the door, screaming."

"Where the hell did he think she was all night and this morning?" Rich people. The more time he spent around them, the less he understood them.

"Can you believe it? They didn't just sleep in separate rooms, they slept on separate floors."

"By George, I think we have our first clue. Nothing says happy marriage like sleeping in separate areas of the house." It couldn't be that easy, could it? Sure, statistics said the husband was the most likely suspect, but Noah tried to keep an open mind. At least longer than the first hour.

Every marriage was unique. After twelve years in the department, Noah was well aware of that, but even with crazy hours and midnight call-outs, no force on earth could have kept him from sleeping next to Betsy. Only in the last few weeks had he stopped spraying her perfume on the pillow next to his head.

Conner finished his log of personnel present at the crime scene and the time they arrived. He glanced at Noah. The wheels turning in his partner's mind were almost visible as he drew a sketch of the area.

The two of them were as much alike as they were different. Noah topped him by a good two inches and twenty pounds, with hair and eyes a couple of shades darker than his own. They tended to come at a problem from opposite directions—Conner plodding from point A to point B while Noah let his gut point him in the right direction—yet they usually ended in the same place if for different reasons. This made them not only close friends, but excellent partners.

"Ready to knock on some doors?" he asked when Noah set his pen down.

"Might as well. I haven't had my fill of crass materialism for the day."

He couldn't argue with Noah on that. As he looked around the gated enclave, each townhome was bigger, more elaborate than the next. These weren't the homes of your everyday, garden variety millionaires. These people had *money*.

He and Noah stepped out the front door and looked both directions. Silence. They were practically in the shadow of the Galleria and only a block off San Felipe, yet the traffic noises were muffled by extensive landscaping. "All this green space and not a kid out playing."

"You're joking, right? These people don't send their kids out to play. The older ones are in private school and hired nannies have taken the younger ones to some type of organized activity."

With Jeannie due in less than a month, was that what he had to look forward to, play dates and baby yoga and someone else watching every milestone? When Jeannie first became pregnant, she insisted she wanted to start back to teaching in September. As she'd grown larger and larger each day, she hadn't mentioned it again.

Noah's prediction was right. At the first house they checked, only the maid was home, a middle-aged woman wearing a salmon-colored smock. She held a mop in one hand and a freshly groomed Shih Tzu in the other. Conner had trouble telling them apart except that one barked and the other looked wet.

"Sorry, I only come in four days a week, so I wasn't here last night. The Mister has gone to work, and Missus had one of her luncheons today. Simone, the nanny, took Master James to school. She'll take the baby out somewhere and bring her home in time for lunch and a nap."

"Are there any windows that look down on the Gwinn's yard next door?"

"Is that their name, Gwinn? The only window on that side is upstairs in the bathroom, and it's made out of frosted glass. You can't see through it and it doesn't open. I don't think you could see anything through the fence, either."

No, the fence was eight feet high and solid stucco. No price was too high for complete seclusion.

"I'd like to check out that window if you don't mind. May we come in?" Conner believed her, but never marked anything closed until he'd seen for himself.

The maid twisted the edge of her shirt around one roughened hand. "I'm not comfortable with that. The Missus will be home by three. Come back then."

He'd had doors shut in his face before, but they weren't usually two-story carved mahogany with gold inlay and worth more than his entire house.

"Well, that was fun. Shall we try another one?" Noah grinned, but his partner didn't seem to find humor in the situation. They both trudged to the mansion on the other side.

The lady of the house was in, but even less welcoming than the maid with the dog and mop. "I can only give you five minutes. I'm presiding over a murder trial in an hour. I suppose I shouldn't worry. It's not like they can start without me, but I demand punctuality in my courtroom so I try to set a good example."

That wasn't all she demanded. Noah had never testified before her, but he knew others who had and they'd quaked in their boots. She was sometimes known as Hard Ass Hargity. But not to her face.

Noah was only half through explaining why they had knocked on her door when the judge held up her hand in a *stop* motion. "I'm sorry, Detectives. Last night I worked on court filings in my office on the far side of the house until past midnight, after that I went to bed. I'm not in the habit of wasting my days—or nights—spying through windows at my neighbors. I did not see or hear anything unusual except a few leftover fireworks and dogs barking, something that has been going on all week. If I did have any ideas or suspicions, which I don't, they would be hearsay and inadmissible. Now, if you'll excuse me, I can't help you and I need to get to court."

He and Conner were out the door and standing on the sidewalk before he had time to protest.

Two more houses, two more closed doors. Noah would give anything to kick something—a pinecone, a tin can, a twig—but nothing was out of place on these manicured lawns. He swung to face Conner, disgust bubbling up from somewhere deep inside like a Yellowstone geyser ready to erupt. He'd rather interview drug dealers any day. At least they were honest about their dishonesty. "I'd like to do some real police work before this day is over. Let's leave the grunt work to the uniforms. See how the upper class like having a squad car parked in front of their house."

"What'd you have in mind?"

"I want a list of every resident, visitor, and serviceperson who came in or out of that gate between noon yesterday and ten o'clock this morning. Plus a copy of that video," he nodded toward a camera set discreetly in a tree beside the entrance, "before someone has time to erase or copy over it."

"Might not be that easy. You know how these people guard their privacy. I put a call in to the security company when we first got here. The owner insisted we show him a warrant."

Noah muttered a few choice profanities but they didn't make him feel any better. Conner rolled his eyes. The choirboy.

"I've got Earl Sparks working on drawing up the warrant. It should be ready by the time we reach the office."

A smile struggled to break through and Noah decided not to fight it. As soon as he did, his headache subsided. Why let some miserable moneyed misers ruin his day? "I wouldn't wish a blow to the head like Earl got last spring on anybody, but having him on desk duty is like having our own private secretary."

"It would be if he could spell. I don't know if that concussion jumbled something in his brain or if he was always phonetically challenged, but I have to proofread everything he prepares."

"I think he always had a problem. I remember a case we worked on when he sent a warrant to a judge explaining how we chased a guy because he was running from the scene wearing a bloody shirt. Only he left the *r* out of shirt. The judge demanded we take the suspect to the hospital immediately to check for internal injuries."

Conner shot him a *good try* look. "That's an old story and I've heard it about everyone on the squad, even you, but I'll double-check the warrant before I send it in, just in case."

Maybe that story was one of those urban legends. That didn't mean Earl knew how to spell or could type. "Before we leave, let's go back to the crime scene and check the perimeter. I'd like a good look at that fence."

"The pool guy and the lawn company enter the backyard through a gate on the side, but it's kept locked at all times and requires a passcode to open. The pool cleaner swears it was locked when he got here this morning. So, if this does turn out to be murder, how did the perp get to her?"

"He opened the back door and tiptoed out to off his wife before heading up to bed, a wealthy widower?" A twinge of guilt tapped Noah on the shoulder. Did he hate all rich people or did Wade Gwinn just rub him the wrong way when he met them at the door wearing silk pajamas?

"Very possibly, but if so, we'll need to prove it. Or at least prove no one else could have gotten in. Which, I assume, is why you want to check the perimeter."

Noah stomped across the flagstone entry toward the Gwinn condo. "Yeah. Sometimes it sucks to actually have to do your job instead of simply calling the boss and telling him who you think did it."

The day hadn't cooled any, but Noah and Conner stood on the grass rather than the pool decking, so the heat didn't reflect up their bodies. Instead, it bounced off the stucco fence. The glare was like a spotlight boring into Noah's eyes.

Hidden in a far corner, behind a storage shed that was itself masked by ornate landscaping, a plastic post stood two feet above ground. The post and the shed were both further camouflaged by being painted the same color as the fence.

Noah kicked the post. "What the hell is this?"

"Cable box, I think."

"It looks like a giant condom."

Conner tilted his head. "It does, kind of. Think somebody balanced on top of that to get in or out?"

Noah put a hand on Conner's shoulder and hefted himself on top of the post. The curved top only left room for the ball of one foot. He grabbed the fence for support as he wobbled unsteadily. "I'm six two. I can see over this wall, but barely. Not sure I could muscle my way onto it, and if I did, then what? There's nothing back here I can see."

He pushed off the wall and jumped down, landing awkwardly. Pain encircled his ankle as he fought to maintain his balance. The palms of his hands stung and showed red, pockmarked spots from gripping the rough stucco wall. "No one came over this fence without something to climb on and walking down the street carrying a ladder at midnight is a little suspicious."

Conner gave the storage shed a shake. "This isn't sturdy enough to use and doesn't offer any footholds. Let's go out and see if there's any way to get in from the other side."

By the time they followed the fence around the outside of the complex, Noah was dripping with sweat. He could taste the salt when he licked his lips. The heat had traveled through his sport coat, making his skin feel like cheese left too long under the broiler.

He glanced at his partner. Conner looked cool as ever. How did the guy do that? He must have an ice bag in his pants. There wasn't any other explanation.

A park ran along one side of the enclave. The smell of fresh cut grass was at odds with the sound of freeway traffic two blocks away. Leafy trees lowered the temperature by fifteen degrees. Swings, slides, and plastic tunnels waited for nonexistent children to play, but it was a wrought iron bench that called to Noah. Ten minutes sitting in the shade and he'd be a new man.

But he'd never admit that to Conner.

He crossed behind the bench. "How much do you think this thing weighs?"

Conner lifted one end by the arm rest. "Not that bad. One person could probably move it."

Noah bent his knees and hefted the bench. It banged him on the shin. He changed his grip and lifted it again. It banged him on the other shin. Shit. There had to be a better way. Between his ankle, his palms, and his shins, he'd be lucky to make it home in one piece.

Conner used one hand to lift the right end of the bench. He swung it toward the fence and moved to the left side, doing the same thing. "Sometimes finesse works better than brute strength."

Dickhead.

The back of the bench was a foot and a half higher than the cable post. Once it was in place next to the wall, Conner climbed up and peered over. "It's like you said. I suppose I could make it up onto the wall, but I'd have to jump down eight feet into these people's yard, hope they don't own a dog, cross to the other side, somehow climb that fence, jump down, cross that yard and do it again before I got to the Gwinn's."

"What about walking down the top of the wall?"

"Maybe if you were a tightrope walker. The wall's less than three inches wide. Your foot would hang off on each side. You'd have to travel half the length of a football field and trees droop over in some spots. In the dark? No way. Crawling would be worse. This stucco stuff kills your hands."

Yeah. Tell me about it.

Conner brushed the pink-tinged stucco dust off his hands, but a gritty residue remained on his pants. "Let's see if we can work our way directly behind the Gwinns' place."

That plan sounded good, but ten minutes of walking took them to the front of a company specializing in outdoor statuary, antique benches, and lawn ornaments. The business was surrounded by a sturdy chain link fence topped with curls of razor wire. A sign warned the area was protected by guard dogs. The sight of a horse trough-sized water bowl, half-gnawed T-bones, and several impressively large piles of dog poo removed any doubt.

"No one got into the Gwinns' backyard unless it was through the front gate. Let's head to the office. You can see if your warrants came through." Noah was ready to be finished with the Gwinns and their affluent neighbors for the day.

"What's on your agenda while I battle Lady Justice?"

"We can't do anything more on this case until we know if it was murder, suicide, or accident. Meanwhile, we have two others we need to work on plus one coming to trial next week. I want another shot at talking to the girlfriend in the Redden homicide. She admits to being drunk the night in question. I don't think she has any idea if Junior slipped out while she slept. She just doesn't want to believe someone she loves could kill his own parents."

"Would you? Imagine trying to close your eyes at night knowing the person next to you was capable of cold-blooded murder."

The partners stepped up their pace and circled back to their motor pool car. A beat-up Nissan Sentra, its once red paint faded pink, was parked on the curb beside the entrance gate. At the sight of the two detectives, the driver hopped out, waving a memo book similar to the one Conner kept. "Detective, a moment, please. May I have a word with you?"

The man's clothes looked like he'd slept in them. Only his face showed more wrinkles, as if someone had wadded up the newspaper he worked for and straightened it out again.

"Step on it. That's R.J. Perry from the *Chronicle*. How did he find us? The bosses won't like this." Noah hated TV reporters with a passion most people reserved for IRS agents. Their perfect hair and gleaming white teeth made you look like a slob and they edited what you said into something unrecognizable to fit their story.

But newspaper reporters were worse. They actually dug for that nugget of truth you were trying to hold back. And like a dog with a tug-toy, they never let go. This was compounded by the fact their news cycle lasted longer than fifteen minutes.

Conner double-tapped the key, unlocking both doors. Noah slipped inside and his headache returned with a vengeance. After several hours of sitting in the Texas sun, the interior was like entering Hell. Literal Hell. With fire and brimstone and Satan laughing at Noah's attempt to fasten his seatbelt without blistering his fingers on the metal buckle.

"*Oouuchh*," Conner groaned as he grabbed the scalding steering wheel and pulled away from the curb.

Noah flipped the AC to high, but it blew in steamy air from outside which wasn't any help. By silent mutual consent, they drove the first several blocks with the windows down until a trickle of cooler air seeped through the vents. It smelled like rancid cooking oil, but lowered the temperature inside a few precious degrees.

"Let's drop this mother off at the motor pool and I'll drive Lola out to the trailer park to see if I can break Junior Redden's alibi." His love affair with his truck had suffered a serious setback when she was nearly totaled in April, but her heat and air conditioning worked with a flip of a switch and she smelled like Heaven compared to the wreck they were driving.

"You think the girlfriend will be there this time of day?" Conner eased across two lanes of traffic into the station parking lot.

"I don't know, but if I call ahead to check, she definitely won't be."

Noah slipped out of the hunk-of-junk motor pool loaner and into Lola. She was hot when he opened the door, but comfortable before he was out of the parking garage. He turned the fan to high and aimed the vents toward his face. His headache disappeared immediately. Yep, she still had it, repairs or not.

Driving east away from the downtown area and the Travis Street headquarters, the sky was an unending expanse of blue, broken only by a lone contrail left by an invisible jet, high above the city. A feeling of kinship swept over Noah at the thought of the unseen pilot. Both of them speeding along, cocooned in a metal tube, with plenty of backup, but basically alone, shouldering heavy responsibility.

Shit. He'd let his guard down and the black dog of despair was nipping at his heels again. It was the damn Gwinn case. He tried not to jump to conclusions, but six weeks short of one year since Betsy died and he still had trouble dealing with a husband who didn't cherish his wife while he had the chance.

But he wasn't really alone. He had a warm, if tiny, body

waiting at home and he had family: his sister, Rachelle, and his two nieces, Emma and Iris. Not to mention Conner and Jeannie and their soon-to-be baby.

He shook his head, trying to dislodge those thoughts like a mutt shaking off water after a rain storm. Action. That was the only cure when the cursed dark cloud got too close. He needed to close as many cases as possible before Conner took off on family leave.

A light flipped on inside his head. That was the problem, not the Gwinn case. The thought of Conner and the life waiting for him. A life denied Noah because some son-of-a-bitch long-haul trucker decided he could drive eighteen hours without taking a rest. That a deadline was more important than a life. Two lives.

How old would their baby be if Betsy had lived? Three months?

Not walking, he knew that much, but sitting up, teething? Would he be bitching about lack of sleep like he'd heard other new parents do? Or realize how fortunate he was?

What did it matter the cause? The answer was the same. Get busy. Break Junior Redden's alibi. Then, God help Wade Gwinn if he discovered the guy had killed his wife.

CHAPTER TWO

NOAH EASED LOLA around a refrigerator-sized pot hole and past a sign that read *Land of Lost Pines*. It should have read *Land of Lost Hopes and Dreams,* or, more accurately, *End of the Road,* because the trailer park was situated at the bottom of a dead end street.

The steps to Junior Redden's single-wide sagged under Noah's weight and he grabbed the roughened railing, worried more that his foot might plummet through the rotten wood than about splinters in his hand. The door swung open before he knocked, and Junior's girlfriend's face fell at the sight of him.

She wore tight jeans and an off-the-shoulder lipstick-red blouse. Her hair gleamed as if freshly washed and the scent of cheap perfume floated out the door and hit him in the face. Who had she been expecting?

He needed to wrap this up fast if Junior was on his way home.

Her gum cracked as she heaved an exaggerated sigh. "I

thought you were finished with us. Don't you have anything better to do?"

Yeah, two more murders to solve, but a guy who sets his parents on fire ranks pretty high on my list. "I only have a few more questions. I thought it would be more convenient to talk here than to bother you at work."

He could have miscalculated on that. Being pulled aside to talk to him might be more inviting than waitressing at Cooter's.

"I don't have anything to say to you that I haven't said ten times before. Why can't you believe me?" She waved her arms in exasperation and Noah caught a glint of sparkle on her left hand. Junior hadn't spent any of his parents' money on his home, but he'd blown a wad of cash on his girlfriend. It looked like Kelly Manus had been promoted to fiancée. He'd have to check with the DA's office to get the exact law on spouses testifying against each other, but the rules wouldn't matter.

Once they tied the knot, he'd never get her to admit she lied.

Kelly stepped aside to let him in. "I won't be working there much longer. Junior says as soon as you get off his back and he can collect the insurance money, we're going to buy us a high-rise condo in Kemah, overlooking the water. He's going to invest the money and be one of those real estate mongrels."

Junior might have dreams of becoming a mogul, but Kelly was closer to right than she realized. He'd never be more than a mongrel.

Noah forced a smile he didn't feel. If only he were better at dealing with people. He had been at one time, but that was too long ago to remember. Too bad Conner wasn't here. He had the knack of knowing the right thing to say. What had he said earlier about falling asleep?

"I'm starting to believe you, Kelly. You wouldn't lie about a thing like that if you're planning to marry Junior. Can you imagine spending your life with someone who knows your testimony could send him to jail for the rest of his life? Every time you had the least little disagreement or fight, you'd have to wonder if he still trusted you. How would you close your eyes at night if you didn't know for positive he hadn't slipped out after you went to sleep that night? I only wish I had some proof."

Kelly's red hair and creamy white skin reflected her Irish heritage and Noah didn't think she could look any paler. He was wrong. "I cut my head."

"What?"

"That night. Junior and I were cuddling on the sofa, watching TV and drinking beer. Two's usually my limit, but he was so sweet. He brought me a third one and insisted I drink it. I think he was feeling a little…frisky." The slight flush to her cheeks wouldn't have been noticeable on anyone else. On Kelly, it looked like a neon sign.

"Is that when you cut your head?" He didn't have any idea where this was leading, but if she thought it was important, so did he.

"When the movie was over we started back to the bedroom. It must have been that last beer because I felt so dizzy. I stumbled and hit my head on the corner of the table. Over there." She pointed to a scarred end table. "Blood poured out. Junior hates blood, but he cleaned me up and bandaged my head. He even helped me into my jammies. He held me until I went to sleep and had his arms around me when I woke up. Would he do that if he was planning to kill his parents?"

Yep, that's exactly what he'd do. "What did you do with the bandages?"

Her brows knitted together in confusion. "They're probably still out there in the dumpster. We're so far out in the country, the garbage truck only comes by every two weeks."

"What'd your bags look like?"

"My bags?"

"Your garbage bags. Are they white? Black? Yellow?"

She took three steps into the miniscule kitchen and opened the cabinet under the sink. "They're white with a blue pull-tie."

He sped out of the trailer and down the steps, ignoring the ominous creaking when his foot hit the rotten boards. Two dumpsters were located off the road and across a winding creek. He shucked off his suit coat and tie and tossed them in the back of the truck bed as he raced past Lola.

His phone chirped and he thumbed it on, shouting over Conner's greeting. "Get a warrant for Junior's trailer. Kelly Manus may have been drugged. She cut her head and bled on the end table and rug. Meanwhile, I'm going dumpster diving for the bandages. The cans are located on public property so it shouldn't be any problem, but tell Lieutenant Jansen what's going on and GET ME SOME HELP."

"Got it," Conner said, and disconnected.

How would he ever manage six weeks without his partner?

And that was if Conner came back to homicide after his family leave time. There was always the possibility he'd decide to transfer to a department with regular hours and less stress.

Other detectives had.

Ten days in the Texas sun had done a number on the contents

of the two dumpsters. Whatever garbage men made, they should be paid twice as much.

Noah wrestled a wooden pallet between the dumpsters to use for a ladder as he threw back the covers. A swarm of flies rose in unison as the rancid odor of spoiled meat, dirty diapers, old tampons, almost-empty cat food cans, and wet cardboard assailed his nose and made his eyes water.

The jar of VapoRub he used to mask the smell of decaying flesh at crime scenes was resting safely in Lola's glove compartment. He'd take a quick look over the edge before deciding if he should go back and retrieve it. Balancing precariously on the pallet, he peered over the sides.

About half of the contents of both containers were white bags with blue pull-ties. The local dollar store must have run a sale on that particular brand.

He was figuring the logistics of climbing into the first dumpster when a rhythmic pounding sounded behind him. He snapped his head around in time to see 250 pounds of flab in the form of Junior Redden running full speed over the footbridge crossing the creek. The guy was bigger, badder, meaner, and madder than Noah. Not a good combination when he was standing balanced on his toes, three feet in the air.

He reached for his Glock, but the pallet wobbled at the sudden movement. His arms windmilled, sending his weapon flying. It crashed against the dumpster lid with a resounding *clang* before plopping silently onto piles of neatly bagged garbage.

Noah grabbed the metal edge of the container to steady himself, but succeeded only in ripping a gash out of his hand. The makeshift ladder teetered and fell from under him.

He toppled to the ground, tangling one foot in the wooden

slats of the pallet and landing in a heap in the dirt. Before he could right himself, Junior was on him, fists swinging, head butting, kneeing, kicking, cursing.

Spittle flew in every direction and Noah had no idea if it was his or Junior's, but the guy was close enough to smell the beer on his breath. Noah couldn't place the brand, other than cheap, but he knew Kelly had wasted her time shampooing her hair and spritzing on perfume. Junior was beyond noticing.

Junior opened his mouth and leaned in to bite Noah's shoulder. It took everything Noah had to push the big man back. If he failed, would he have to worry about AIDS? Rabies?

One arm was pinned to his side by Junior's bloated body. He needed the other to protect himself, but what was more important, his face or his balls? Junior reared back to head butt him again. Noah swung his elbow up and connected with Junior's eye.

A *crunch* and a *pop* sounded simultaneously. Junior rolled in the dirt, screaming incoherently. White-hot pain shot through Noah's leg as he struggled to sit up. Junior's knee had sent Noah's foot smashing through the pallet, splintering the slats and slicing his shin to the bone.

He needed to get cuffs on Junior before the tub-of-lard recovered. Blood covered the pallet and he couldn't see what had a death grip on his ankle. The only thing messier than his foot and leg was Junior's face. The sticky red stuff flowed from his bad eye into his good eye and he shook his head, trying to clear his vision as he patted the ground for a weapon of any kind.

Noah crab-walked the two feet between them, lugging the pallet like an anchor. Junior's ham-sized fist closed on a tree branch as Noah slapped the cuffs on one arm.

Junior bucked and fought, but Noah held on. Lose his grip and he was sure to die. He dragged himself an inch closer. Two. Three. He twisted Junior's arm behind his back and held it with his shoulder while he groped for the other wrist. Junior tried to twist away. Big mistake. The move brought his free arm closer to Noah.

With a *snap*, the cold metal closed, but Junior didn't give up. He tried to wiggle away, pulling Noah and the pallet with him.

When the first sheriff's deputy arrived fifteen minutes later, Junior had slithered halfway over the footbridge. Noah clung to the size fifty-two jeans that had worked their way down to Junior's thick ankles but wouldn't pull over his size twelve work boots. The pallet, with Noah's foot trapped inside, was firmly wedged sideways between the railing on each side of the bridge.

Neither man could move an inch in any direction.

Noah cracked one eye open at the *scrape* of the curtain opening. Conner stood at the foot of his bed, hands on his hips. "How many times am I going to have to bring pants to you in the hospital?"

"You never have. Rachelle brought them last time. You were too busy chasing a hit man without me to care if I was trapped in this hellhole, pantless."

Conner tossed him the gym shorts that usually resided in Lola's back seat. "Well, this time you got the guy and he's resting four floors above us. Handcuffed to his bed. You happy?"

"Extremely. How's his eye?" His words didn't sound right even to his own ears. His tongue felt twice its normal size and his mouth couldn't have been dryer if he'd spent the afternoon chewing on a wool sweater. He stretched out his arm for the plastic cup on the rolling hospital tray, but couldn't reach it.

Conner stepped to the side of his bed and poured water from the Styrofoam pitcher into the cup, but didn't hand it to him. "Don't know. Don't care."

Had Conner actually said that? Conner, who worried if any suspect sustained a scratch?

He held the cup inches outside of Noah's reach. "Because of the two of you, I missed Jeannie's ultrasound."

Impending fatherhood must be doing a number on Conner. He wasn't usually this grouchy. Jeannie'd already had two or three of those things. They weren't invasive or painful from what little he knew.

"The guy's screaming for a lawyer, so I couldn't question him, but his girlfriend busted his alibi. She admits she has no idea if he got up during the night. If the lab tests come back showing she was drugged, we'll have him. Until then, he attacked a police officer. He's not going anywhere."

Why wasn't Conner happier? That was one case to worry about. "You going to keep complaining because I wrapped up a case or give me a ride home?"

"You can't go home. You're attached to an IV." Conner nodded toward the pole beside the hospital bed and the tubes connected to Noah's arm.

He eyed the cup of water in Conner's hand. He'd be damned if he'd beg for it. "That's an antibiotic. It'll be finished by the time you get me signed out of here. Tomorrow, we start on the Gwinn case."

"We? Don't you need to take it easy for a few days?"

"Naw. It's nothing but a couple of stitches." Noah nodded to the bandage on his shin where a rusty nail ripped down his leg. No one would ever need to know how many it had actually taken to close the gash. "I'm fine if I don't have to chase after anybody. And if I do...I'll let them go and catch them another day."

Conner handed him the cup of tepid water and he gulped it down like he'd run a marathon. "What about the warrants for the front gate passes and video? They come through all right?"

"No problem. You should have seen how eager the security company was to cooperate once I got the warrants."

Noah studied Conner's face. Why did he look so relieved? Was he afraid Noah's injury would impact his upcoming family leave time?

He held out the cup for more water. He couldn't blame Conner. Given the chance, he'd feel exactly the same.

His partner hesitated, the pitcher poised above the plastic cup. He lowered his voice as he poured. Noah strained to hear him over the background hum of the busy ER.

"You realize you could've been killed three times this year. Must I keep worrying about you taking reckless chances? Haven't you learned anything? Can I count on you to stop playing Lone Ranger and wait for backup? I refuse to be the one who has to tell Rachelle she's lost her only brother or Emma and Iris their Uncle Noah is gone. I won't do it. I can't."

Noah took the cup from Conner and pretended to drink, but couldn't swallow past the fist-sized lump in his throat. He wasn't the only one worried about losing his partner.

CHAPTER THREE

LOLA SAT IN Noah's driveway when Conner dropped him off. As he hobbled up his front steps, he sent out a mental *thank you* to whoever brought the truck back for him.

The key hung in the lock and Noah jiggled it while cursing under his breath. Not today. Not after all he'd been through. He didn't have the strength to go down the steps, up the driveway, and around to the back. He never came in or out the front door. That was the problem.

The front door was for visitors. And he didn't have visitors.

He held his breath and tried again. The key turned and he let himself inside. Tomorrow he'd graphite the lock. Tonight he wanted to crash. But first he had chores to manage. He pushed into the kitchen to find five pounds of Yorkshire terrier complete with red, white, and blue Fourth of July hair bow ready to attack whoever had the nerve to invade her territory.

"Everything's fine, Sweet Pea. I know you don't like surprises, but I came in through the front this one time only." He couldn't blame her. He wasn't too crazy about change, either. Was there any such thing as a good surprise? He'd never come across one.

The little Yorkie was queen-of-the-castle until Noah showed up three years ago and usurped her place in Betsy's heart and bed. She had only begun to accept him when Betsy left for work one day and never came back, leaving her in the care of an angry, grumpy man. Things were better now, but he had no doubt she still considered him on probation.

The dog looked skeptical as she circled him, sniffing.

He scratched behind her ear, exactly the way she liked. "I know, I smell like a hospital." Veterinary or human, not her favorite scent.

After a thorough investigation, she allowed him to put out fresh piddle pads and feed her, but kept her eye on him while she ate.

By ten o'clock, she was willing to curl up on Noah's chest while they both watched the news. Madlyn Gwinn's death was the lead story. Trumping even an off-duty officer being shot at a rundown bodega.

Money always mattered. Of course, the officer survived. Madlyn didn't.

Early morning shots of the sun peeking around oatmeal-colored townhomes with wrought iron balconies and intricately designed topiaries made good TV. Add in ten foot high monogramed security gates and a flagstone entry the width of an airport runway and who wouldn't rather watch that than a beer-bellied drunk with only half his teeth being hustled into a patrol car?

The fact no one had any idea if Madlyn's death was murder, suicide, or accident didn't slow down the pretty-boy newscasters.

Vultures. They fed off any tragedy like the carrion-eaters they were. At least they did if it was photogenic.

Ugly was out of luck.

Feeling sorry for himself wasn't getting him anywhere. Time to call it a night and start fresh tomorrow. He flicked off the TV and let Sweet Pea out the back door to make one last circle of the yard, checking for intruders, two legged or four. With tails or boots. Fur or clothes. No one crossed into her domain without permission. She stopped long enough to take care of her business and he whistled her inside.

If all went well and he didn't get any new cases—low odds of that in a city the size of Houston—he had the Gwinn case and one other to solve before Conner went on family leave.

The idea of working alone, or worse, with whoever happened to need a partner that day, was more than he could handle. He had plenty of vacation time waiting. With a clean slate, he could take his holiday the same time as Conner.

He'd been thinking of adding a deck in the backyard, something he probably should have done before summer hit in full force.

But he didn't mind sweating. Sometimes he thought it might be the only way to get rid of the evil lurking inside him.

What was this, déjà vu all over again? Noah resisted the urge to swat at a snickering Lefty Bob as he hobbled into the squad room using his mother's antique cane. At least this time his sore hand was on the opposite side.

How many times this year did he have to drag into this room all beat to shit? Much as he hated to admit it, Conner was right. He needed to exercise better judgment or the date of his departure wouldn't be up to him.

He'd already given up on his self-imposed tally for the number of true bad guys he needed to put away, but October twenty-sixth, fourteen months after Betsy's death, remained circled in red on his calendar.

If he chose to go ahead with his plan.

Today, he was still here and he had work to do. He sneered at Lefty Bob and plopped into his chair, startling Conner who was concentrating on his computer screen.

"So, you decided to honor us with your presence. I was hoping you had come to your senses and stayed home to recuperate."

Noah had considered that for about five minutes, when he tried to get out of bed and discovered he hurt in places he didn't know could hurt. An extra-long, extra-hot shower would have gone a long way toward easing the stiffness, but the doc had warned him not to get his stitches wet. He wrapped his leg in a plastic garbage bag and settled for an awkward, one-legged rinse-off.

An extra cup of coffee helped convince him he'd be better off working than sitting home feeling sorry for himself. He swiveled his chair toward his partner. "We have too much on our plates to consider playing hooky over a couple of stitches." Closer to a couple of dozen if you counted the ones on the inside, but Conner didn't need to know that. "Did we find out anything from the M.E. or Crime Scene on the Gwinn case?"

"Not a word. And before you ask, no, I won't call and nag them. I swear those glorified ghouls move a case down a notch in their stack every time you dare disturb their private domain."

Yeah, he'd learned that the hard way on other cases, but it was so damned frustrating. "What about the warrants? You get anything there?"

"Funny you should ask. You know that camera footage the security company was so keen to protect? There was no footage. Camera wasn't hooked up to anything."

Noah banged his head on the desk. Why had he bothered to come in today? A rich snob murdered by her rich snob of a husband and other rich snobs who would never deem to talk to them. This was one time Conner seemed more upset than he was.

His partner tapped some papers into line harder than necessary. "Wait until the residents learn they were scammed. And they *will* find out. If we can't arrest anybody else, maybe we can charge the guy with running a con."

"Don't need to. Once word gets out, he'll be buried in lawsuits so deep he'll never see the light of day. I'll bet that enclave has more lawyers per square foot than the courthouse. Did he at least have a record of who came and went during the day and who buzzed in visitors?"

Conner stepped over to Noah's desk and slapped down the stack of papers he'd been manhandling. "Right here. You take the *came and went,* and I'll take the *buzzed in visitors.*"

Noah mentally measured the two drastically uneven piles and raised his eyebrows.

"Don't get all bent out of shape. When I finish this list, I'll have to call all the visitors and service people. Plus, if something comes up, I can do the leg work while you finish the desk work."

"If something comes up, we'll both do the leg work and Earl can do the desk work." Noah glanced at Earl, struggling to fill in a duty roster form. A form he'd filled in every day for years. Maybe his old friend hadn't completely recovered from that blow to the head.

For the next hour, Noah lowered his head and tuned out the squeaking chairs, ringing phones, raised voices, printers, pagers, copy machines, and text messages. He did his best to make nice with citizens who didn't appreciate being asked to account for their whereabouts.

When he looked up again, Conner was drawing a line through the last name on his list. "And you're sure you didn't see anyone loitering outside? Wouldn't have to look suspicious. Could be anyone who might have slipped in behind you before the gate closed."

Conner nodded and said, "Uh huh," a couple of times before disconnecting.

"Finished?" Noah rolled his head from side to side and his neck sent out a series of *snaps* and *cracks* in protest.

"Two I couldn't reach, even on their cell phones. I'll try them later. So far, no one saw anything or anyone hanging around, trying to get in. You?"

"Same thing. Nobody saw nuttin' and what right did I have to call and bother them? I have several call-backs to make, but I don't expect any different result."

"I hate to spend the time on this case until we have a definitive answer from the M.E. but if we wait, no one will remember what they saw when." Conner drummed his pen against the edge of his desk, the rhythm off enough to make the musician in Noah cringe. "We sure could use a break. What do you think the chances are this will turn out to be an accident?"

"Too slim to figure the odds. And that husband… Why don't

you see what you can dig up on him while I finish these calls?"

Conner rubbed his forehead. A sure sign he was preoccupied. "Be nice if we could wrap this up by tomorrow."

Tomorrow? Was he crazy? They had nothing. Nada. Zip. Zero. Noah glanced at his partner, whose eyes stared blankly across the room. "Sorry I made you miss Jeannie's test yesterday. Will she forgive me?"

Conner pulled his eyes back to Noah, but his focus was glazed. "You? Always. Me? Not so much. Not today, anyway. Speaking of—"

"Crawford. Daugherty. My office." Lieutenant Jansen stood in his doorway and motioned with his chin. Conner opened and closed his mouth but no sound came out. He pushed his chair back and started for Jansen's office.

Noah followed, reluctantly. This couldn't be anything good, but what choice did he have?

Jansen swung to face them as they crossed the threshold. "What the fuck are you two doing on the Gwinn case? I've had calls from the DA, the Mayor, the Chief. I'm surprised I haven't gotten complaints from the meter maids. How many toes can you step on in one day?" The door was open and his voice loud enough to carry across the squad room.

What the hell? This wasn't like Jansen at all. The Lieu hated posers more than he did, and never reprimanded anyone with the door open. He should know.

Conner didn't answer, leaving it all to him. "We're trying to pin down who opened the security gate and at what time so we can figure out how a stranger might have gotten in. We don't suspect the residents of doing anything wrong. If we gave them that impression, it was in error." Was he supposed to call everyone back and apologize? He'd eat dog turds before that happened.

"See to it you're more careful in the future." Jansen's voice boomed past his ear. The Chief must have really reamed him out.

"Yes, sir." Noah kept his voice a notch below the Lieu's but loud enough to rattle the glass panes.

Jansen's face twisted like he'd developed some sort of tic. Was the guy having a stroke? The Lieu put his hand on Noah's shoulder. One eyebrow descended a quarter inch, like a caterpillar breakdancing, while his eyelid closed. *A wink?* His voice dropped to a whisper. "Good job on the Redden case. Now wrap up the Gwinn case before I have to listen to that air-bag blow-hard excuse for a mayor defend his pampered playmates from the country club. Asshole calls here and tells me how to do *my* job. That'll be the day."

"Yes, sir," Noah said again. Only this time he meant it.

Noah was in the twilight zone between asleep and awake in front of the TV. A baseball game droned in the background and Sweet Pea dozed on his chest. He'd piled two sofa cushions under his leg for elevation. The only instruction from that quack doctor he'd followed.

Even Pea recognized the irregular sputtering of Rachelle's car in his driveway. When was that sorry excuse for a brother-in-law going to fork over the money for a tune-up? He didn't like his nieces or his sister riding around in something undependable. People got hurt that way.

Five pounds of excited Yorkie dug her nails into his stomach and jumped to the floor. She ran to the back door, and did her happy dance—leaping, turning, barking, tail wagging—waiting for her favorite visitors.

Emma and Iris had the door open and were petting Sweet Pea by the time he reached the kitchen. Rachelle was wrestling something out of the backseat of her Kia. "Hey, Brother. I thought you might be hungry so I brought you something to eat."

Oh no. Not one of her famous—or was it infamous—tofu casseroles. He'd have to actually eat it if she stuck around.

She held up a large square box. "A Margarita pizza. I didn't have time to cook for you."

Thank the Lord. He'd kill for some pepperoni or Italian sausage, but as long as he wasn't trapped into eating her cooking, he was gold. "Thanks, Sis. You didn't need to do that. But I'm glad you did. Come on in. Can you stay awhile?"

"Only a minute. The girls have homework and our own pizza is in the car, getting cold."

"Aww, Mommy, can't we stay here?" Iris threw herself at Noah and he almost lost his balance.

"Careful, Uncle Noah has a sore leg. Why don't you take Sweet Pea out back and play toss with her for a few minutes? I'll bet she didn't get a walk today."

Noah found Mr. Squeaky Man and gave it to Emma as both girls scrambled to be the first outside. The sound of giggles faded as the door slammed shut behind them.

Rachelle bustled around his kitchen as she set out a paper plate, napkin, and a glass of iced tea. She kept her eyes averted from him and he knew a pizza wasn't the only reason she'd dropped by.

He tried a preemptive strike. "Your car sounds like a locomotive struggling uphill. When are you going to get it fixed?"

She swung to face him, her eyes, almost as dark as his, burned through him. "Frank made me an appointment yesterday, but I canceled it because my brother was in the hospital."

"That wasn't necessary. Conner brought me home."

"Yes, but I wasn't sure how badly you were hurt and I couldn't take a chance you might need me. How often must I go through this? Don't you know what it would do to me, to the girls, if something happened to you? Can't you see how much they love you and count on you to always be there? They'd be devastated if they lost you." Her eyes teared up and she turned her back on him.

She slammed the silverware drawer hard enough to rattle the glasses that were rinsed and waiting to be loaded into the dishwasher. "I've come to terms with the fact that you've chosen a dangerous profession. I'm proud of you, really I am, for wanting to help people. I even understand why you feel the need to protect strangers. But look at Conner. He doesn't end up in the hospital on a regular basis. Do you have a death wish? Is that why you take such foolish chances?"

Noah's throat tightened. He hobbled closer and put his hands on her shoulders. "This was a freak accident. I lost my balance while looking into a dumpster. I promise I wasn't taking a senseless risk. I wouldn't do that to you and the girls." Hell, Rachelle had lost as much as he had.

Well, almost.

He had some serious thinking to do. Decisions to make that didn't affect him alone.

CHAPTER FOUR

Noah's gait was heavy, lopsided, as he made his way across the squad room. As hard as he tried, he couldn't avoid a limp, but at least he didn't have to emphasize it with a cane any longer.

Two days and they were no closer to solving the Gwinn case than the day she died.

He'd spent the weekend catching up on chores: grocery shopping, laundry, paying bills. He'd skipped the belated neighborhood Fourth of July party. Too many memories of last year's celebration. If anyone mentioned Betsy and her cherry cobbler, he'd lose it.

Sunday afternoon, he'd taken Emma and Iris to an animated, 3-D movie with a theme song he couldn't get out of his head, then to James Coney Island for hot dogs.

Their vegan mother didn't approve of his dinner choice, but she was smiling about her alone time with her husband. Something Noah didn't want to think about too deeply.

But always, in the back of his mind, was the Gwinn case. Why did that one case dog him so?

He'd dealt with husbands killing wives, and vice versa, since his rookie days. Although, he was willing to admit those cases were harder to face now. Abuse cases were worse, and this didn't seem to fall into that category.

Losing Conner for six weeks of family leave bothered him, but not as much as the idea of losing him to another department. After the baby came, his partner might decide he wanted to work in an area with a lower stress level, fewer late-night calls, and less chance of a bad guy showing up at your door. Or outside your pregnant wife's window. The pangs of jealousy he felt for Conner and Jeannie and the new life that awaited them were just that— pangs. Deep in his soul, he was overjoyed at his partner's good fortune.

Money. Now there was a mixed bag. He'd seen those poor as the proverbial church mouse share their last meal while another stole his shoes. He'd seen the rich give of their time and energy and money to help the needy while others stomped on the fingers of those trying to pull themselves up.

Maybe he'd seen too much, but it wasn't the money that worried him. It was the power and influence that came with an excess of money. The power to sweep secrets under the rug. The power to buy justice. The power to have the mayor call in an attempt to shut down an investigation.

But not the power to stop him. No amount of power could influence him when he was on a case.

Noah eased himself into his seat, dropping the final two inches and causing the chair to let out a groan. Conner glanced up from his computer. How did the guy always get in before him?

"Good morning, Twinkle Toes. Glad to see you're improving."

Noah snarled at his partner's early-morning cheerfulness. "I'd be better if we had some answers on the Gwinn case. Have you learned anything?"

"Since quitting time Friday afternoon?"

"Let's stir things up. Call Wade Gwinn in here for a conversation."

Conner rubbed his chin and Noah could see his brain working, weighing, considering every angle. "Might be best to wait until we have the results of the autopsy."

"And when will that be?" The usual refrain: hurry up and wait. Noah was sick of waiting while Gwinn laughed at them behind their backs.

Conner tapped the screen of his computer and his face took on an expression somewhere between wonder and excitement. "Eleven o'clock this morning. Meanwhile, the boutique hotel down the street sent over their security tapes *without demanding a warrant.* Don't expect much the way their cameras were positioned, but it does restore your faith in humanity."

Noah didn't have anything against humanity. It was people he didn't trust. At any rate, with two new avenues to pursue, this day wouldn't be a waste after all.

The air in the interrogation room was stifling and smelled of too many sweating suspects, but it was the only spot Noah and Conner could find where they wouldn't be disturbed. They sat side-by-side, their shoulders not more than an inch apart, as they studied each frame of the grainy video. For the last thirty minutes, the only sound was the *whirr* of the recorder.

Noah leaned back and massaged his neck. "I hate to complain about the quality of the tape—after all, they had one and the fancy-schmancy security firm across the street didn't—but this is from an exclusive hotel. You'd think they could afford better equipment."

"The camera is good quality. But they'd used the tape too many times. That's what happens when you get complacent."

"What worries me is the patrons look around and see all the cameras and security and feel safe. Then *they* get complacent, not realizing the guys watching out for them are little better than a blind watchdog. Don't notice anything unless it's waved under their noses. Chaps my ass. If you have a job, do it. Otherwise, go home."

"Can't say I disagree with you on that one, but we've got what we've got. Back it up a few frames. I thought I saw a shadow."

Noah fiddled with the knob, rewinding and replaying the video several times.

Conner leaned forward, his face inches from the screen. "I don't know what that is, and I don't like it when I'm in the dark."

"In the dark is right. That's a minute speck one millimeter darker than the rest. A spot of ebony against a background of charcoal."

"Yeah, but it's there. And it moves. Why?"

"A cat. A tree branch. A cloud crossing the moon. One flicker among others in a crappy video. It's nothing. Definitely not big enough to be a person."

Conner leaned back. "Depends on where the person was standing. If we can't identify it, that leaves a big question mark. Defense attorneys love an open question."

Noah hated it when Conner was right. If they didn't pursue

this, they weren't any better than the overpriced security guards who found a quiet place to nap while on duty. The one's he'd just complained about. "You contact the techno geeks. See if there's any way to clean up this video. I'll look in on Madlyn Gwinn's autopsy. Maybe luck will shine on us and her death will be ruled an accident."

Miracles did happen, but usually not to him.

Lola roared to life and Noah eased out of the parking garage. A couple of hours out of the office was exactly what he needed to get his head on straight. Even if it did mean spending time at the morgue.

Traffic was light. The morning rush was over and the lunch rush hadn't started. Noah made his way through downtown and onto OST—Old Spanish Trail—toward the morgue. An afternoon thunderstorm threatened but was several hours away. If it came at all. Odds were good it would blow on past without a drop of rain to cool the parched city.

The building's exterior was as cold and uninviting as ever when he turned into the parking lot. The lobby smelled more like an office—air conditioning, floor wax, window polish—than what it truly was. It wasn't until he reached the heart of the building that the atmosphere began to change.

At first, wisps of cleaner, solvents, antiseptics filled the air. As he neared the autopsy room, another odor grew stronger.

Noah braced himself and pushed through the double doors. Even prepared, the stench of death slapped him in the face. How did these guys spend all day surrounded by the stink?

Hunched over the table, a white-coated figure wearing a

cap, surgical mask, and gloves, along with a generous dusting of blood, glanced up. His face might be hidden, but there was no disguising those bushy white eyebrows or deep blue eyes.

"Ah, Detective. I wondered when you'd arrive. You remember the late Mrs. Gwinn?"

Noah looked up and down and everywhere except the table. Madlyn Gwinn hadn't been at her best the last time he'd seen her. The M.E.'s work hadn't improved her one iota. Pale, bloated flesh puddled in unrecognizable shapes. Much of her insides were missing and lumps of what he could only think of as meat set in plastic containers.

The stainless steel table and harsh overhead lights removed any last degree of dignity. Noah hoped all this desecration resulted in information useful in catching her killer.

"What you got for me, doc?"

"Less than you might wish. There was no skin or evidence under her fingernails except a minute piece of cotton, blue. It could have come from what she wore that day, or someone else she may have touched, or the towel she used, or her napkin at dinner. If you can find a piece of material, the lab can test it for a match."

Had Wade Gwinn been wearing a blue shirt the morning her body was discovered? He couldn't remember, but Conner would. He always did.

The doc nodded toward a clear plastic jug of murky fluid. "The victim definitely asphyxiated due to water in the lungs. The same water contained in the hot tub where she was found."

"She was murdered."

The M.E. ignored him and continued with his recitation. "Due to the condition of the body—water temperature, etc.—I estimate time of death somewhere between ten p.m. and three a.m. This is dependent upon Mr. Gwinn's memory of what time she entered the hot tub. Also, I estimated she died approximately three to three and a half hours after she last ate, which was eight thirty according to Mr. Gwinn."

"So she died between eleven thirty and twelve?"

"Perhaps. If Mr. Gwinn has given us the correct times. And if the lady ate at an average pace, neither shoveling down her dinner in ten minutes nor lingering over it for an hour. Or digging in for seconds while she put away the leftovers."

"What about—"

"Drugs? Toxicology will take a few more days but her husband claims she often took several Xanax at a time and there was an open bottle on her dresser. I'm assuming you sent the wine glass to the lab to be tested for drugs?"

Noah nodded. No telling how long that would take.

"Blood tests showed an alcohol level of one point seven six. Twice the legal limit. Of course she wasn't driving but still not recommended while using a hot tub."

"Are you saying it was an accident?" He would have placed money on that skeezy husband.

The doc straightened to his full six-foot-four height and glared down on Noah with scorn. "Did I say that? Look at these marks." He motioned Noah closer and he had no choice but to comply.

"This is one reason you shouldn't rush an autopsy. The body is a wondrous thing. Sometimes contusions received at the moment of death may not be immediately obvious to the naked eye. Though in excellent health, Mrs. Gwinn was not a thin woman and had subcutaneous fat on her shoulders. Her skin is quite tan, a disgustingly dangerous habit. At any rate, these are factors that make slight extravasation of blood difficult to determine on skin that has been submerged in water for a substantial length of time. Each shoulder now exhibits a row of three round hematomas on the front and another on the back. Finger marks if you will."

A grin split Noah's face. "The little prick held her under the water until she drowned."

"A decent attorney might make an argument that the bruising was post-mortem. Made when the lady was pulled from the water and placed on the gurney. Yes, that is possible despite the lack of blood flow."

"Be a little tough to lift her with your fingers in the front and thumb behind. Taking into consideration all the booze and pills she'd ingested, did she know what was happening?"

The doc raised one of Madlyn Gwinn's arms. His face was hidden behind a pale blue surgical mask, but his eyes had turned to ice. "Both wrists show slight bruising where she flailed about. Probably how the wine bottle and glass got knocked over. The back of her left heel is also bruised as if she thrashed against the opposite seat. She knew. She was aware of every terrifying second."

If Noah had his way, Wade Gwinn would be every bit as aware when the State of Texas inserted an IV into his arm and sent a fatal drug cocktail coursing through his veins.

CHAPTER FIVE

CONNER STARED ACROSS the table at Wade Gwinn, waiting for a reaction.

Gwinn stared back, his face a blank mask. Exhaustion, grief, or something practiced?

The interrogation room—concrete floor and walls, cracked-plastic chairs, table bolted to the floor, odor of cleaning fluids trying but failing to override the stench of sweat and urine—was nothing like the opulent luxury of his home, but there sat Wade. Not at ease, not comfortable, but not nervous either. No sign of guilt in the set of his shoulders. No twitching of his pale, almost feminine hands.

Sitting beside him, Noah gave his patented glare, known to send drug lords crying for their momma.

Gwinn didn't blink.

Conner kicked his partner under the table and he seemed to remember it was his turn to play Good Cop. "Can I get you something while we wait for your lawyer, Mr. Gwinn? Water?

Soda? Cup of lousy coffee?"

"No, thank you. I'm fine." Gwinn shifted in the hard-backed chair. He crossed his legs at the knee and brushed an invisible piece of lint from his linen slacks. Six inches of bare skin, tan and glowing with good health, showed above navy deck shoes. His silk Tommy Bahama print shirt the only spot of color in the room.

Nothing like a collage of red and orange plumeria flowers to brighten up gray walls. *I guess wearing black to denote mourning is passé.*

Gwinn lifted a hand to cover his mouth as he yawned. Conner caught a glimpse of teal paint ringing his manicured thumbnail and had his opening to start a conversation.

"I understand you're an artist, Mr. Gwinn."

"I'm not supposed to talk to you without my lawyer present."

"Of course not. Not about the case at least. I was just wondering if I had seen any of your paintings." *And trying to get a feel for you as a person.*

"You've been in my house. You've seen my work."

Those scribbles hanging on the walls? Conner was surprised anyone would claim them. He certainly wasn't an art connoisseur, but Jeannie was. In college, she'd started out majoring in art history, only switching to elementary education when she realized she preferred eating to starving.

She'd fallen in love with teaching and swore she didn't regret her decision, but they spent many weekends at museums while she taught him about lighting and focal points and brush strokes.

He might prefer to have a Mary Cassatt or a Monet hanging on his walls than a Picasso or a Jackson Pollock or a Matisse, but that didn't mean he wasn't able to recognize quality when he saw it.

And Wade Gwinn didn't fall into that category.

Gwinn apparently didn't agree. "Last year I won the Blaffer prize for Best New Artist. I'm also exhibited in several local galleries."

Exhibited, maybe, but seldom purchased if his research was correct. Maybe Gwinn's wife was tired of supporting him.

Before Conner could comment, the interrogation room door opened and Lieutenant Jansen stepped inside. "Mr. Gwinn's lawyer is here."

A thick head of snow-white hair appeared from behind the Lieu's shoulder, followed by an Armani suit and Ferragamo loafers.

What the hell? Conner gaped in surprise. What was his own lawyer doing here?

Last he'd heard, his case was going well. Internal affairs had agreed the death of Aldo Rodgers was a righteous shooting despite the fact that Conner had shot him in the back. Of course, the guy had abducted a well-known singer as she left the stage, knocked Earl Sparks unconscious, shot a rookie who luckily was wearing his vest, and was drawing down on a defenseless Noah at the time.

The only thing left was for Tom Meyers to convince Aldo's worthless family to fade into the woodwork. Considering how much he was paying the high-powered attorney, that better happen soon.

Meyers nodded his direction. "Detective Daugherty, Detective Crawford. You haven't been interviewing my client without my permission, have you?"

Conner's head buzzed. Meyers was here as *Gwinn's* lawyer?

With all the attorneys in Houston, what were the odds?

Noah stood. "Certainly not. You're welcome to view the tapes if you want."

"Don't worry. I intend to. For now, I'd like all recording equipment turned off and for you both to leave the room. I need time to consult with my client."

Conner didn't budge until Noah took his arm and pointed him toward the door. The sight of that man had thrown Conner off his game.

The memories he brought up were still unnerving.

Was it Gustav Flaubert who wrote that with each death, something inside of you died also? If that was true—and he didn't doubt it—he knew exactly what had died the day he shot Aldo Rodgers.

Crazy as it was to realize he had any left, but after thirty-seven years on earth, ten of them on the force and four in homicide, when he pulled that trigger, he lost the last of his innocence.

And innocence, like honor, could never be reclaimed.

Noah paced the hallway while Conner went to the breakroom for coffee. One look at his partner's ashen face told him the sight of Tom Meyers brought recollections of that awful night crashing down.

Hell, the entire incident was due to Noah's incompetence. No way would he allow Conner to play Bad Cop against the man he was depending on to save his own ass.

No reason for them to play any role. Meyers wouldn't fall for it.

Conner rounded the corner, a cup of coffee in each hand

and a file folder tucked under his arm. Noah accepted the offered coffee, but before he could let his partner in on his change of plans, the interview room door opened.

"Gentlemen." Tom Meyers glanced from one detective to the other. "My client is ready to speak to you now."

Fuck. All he'd needed was two minutes with Conner, but his partner was sharp—sharper than he was—he'd figure it out.

The men trooped back into the dingy room and resumed their places. All except Conner who placed his coffee on the scarred table but remained standing.

"A few ground rules, if you please." Meyers proceeded as if Conner's standing was of no concern to him. "This is a voluntary interview and I expect it to be conducted in a civil manner. My client will answer questions when and if I say he can. At the first hint of intimidation, we will leave. Is that understood?"

Noah glanced at Conner. What the hell was his partner up to? He couldn't pull on the man's arm to get him to sit down and he couldn't kick his shin to remind him not to overplay his role. He'd have to act as if this was normal. "I understand. We're simply trying to establish a timeline for the evening of Mrs. Gwinn's death. What time did she come in from work?"

"I gave all this information to you that morning. Do we have to go over it again?"

"If you don't mind. It's been several days and you were understandably upset at the time. You might have remembered some pertinent piece of information or I could have neglected to write it down correctly. That interview wasn't taped."

Meyers gave an almost imperceptible nod.

"Okay. Okay. Madlyn came in a little after eight, maybe eight thirty. Not unusual for her. She kicked off her shoes and poured a glass of wine while I took dinner from the warming oven and set it on the table."

Noah tried to ignore Conner—standing like an obelisk, silent, his back straight, unmoving—and return to the questioning. "What was her mood when she came home?"

Gwinn blinked a couple of times, surprised. "No different than usual. She was pissed at someone at work. She needed to vent a little, to—"

"Did she mention who she was angry with or what it was about?" He didn't for a minute believe one of her office staff climbed an eight-foot fence, sneaked across the yard, and drowned her while she wasn't looking. But he had to cover every possible scenario.

"She never went into detail. Just that everyone but her was stupid. She handed them money on a silver platter and what did they do in return? Bitch. I didn't pay much attention. It became part of her evening routine. The griping, the wine, the hot tub. It was how she unwound every night."

"And what about you, Mr. Gwinn?" Conner's voice was pure ice. Noah whipped his head around in time to see his partner slam the folder on the table with a *slap* that echoed around the tiny room. "Were you one of those who got money handed to him on a silver platter?"

Gwinn had blinked twice before, now his eyelids beat the air like a hummingbird's wings. "I… I…"

"That's enough, Detective Crawford. Decorum please. Or I'll have to take my client and leave." If Conner's voice had been cold, Meyers's tone held a glacial edge, like a knife coated with frost.

The chair scraped against concrete as Conner yanked it

back and sat. He jammed one finger on the folder. "The only two paintings you've sold in the last year were to vendors of your wife's company. And that prize you're so proud of? A shill charity your wife set up."

Conner tapped the folder again. "According to the security gate computer, you picked up dinner at six and were back at six twenty. Your wife came home at eight forty-seven. How did that make you feel, keeping dinner warm for two and a half hours and who was the ungrateful person she was angry with? You?"

"I never knew when she'd be home," Gwinn wailed. "Sometimes she came in at five. Other times it was midnight. Whenever it was, she wanted her meal right then. Or maybe she breezed in and right back out again for a dinner meeting she hadn't told me about."

Meyers patted Gwinn's hand. "That's enough."

Gwinn didn't hear him, or didn't care, or couldn't stop himself. "She wasn't an easy woman to live with, okay? Some people are type A. She was an A plus. That didn't mean I didn't love her. We were good for each other. I brought her back to earth, and she encouraged me when I got down on myself."

Noah watched in awe as Conner closed in. "Then why did you live on the fourth floor while she lived on the third?"

"That's it. Wade, we need to leave." Meyers tugged at Gwinn's sleeve. Gwinn was too wound up to notice.

"Her bedroom has an office attached. She's an insomniac and stays up all hours working then sleeps till ten or later. My room has a studio with a skylight. The best natural light is in the early morning. I get up and start painting when the sun comes up. When the work's going well, I don't stop for coffee or breakfast or anything until the first shadow hits my easel."

"What happens when the work isn't going well? Do you get

frustrated? Are you allowed to vent? How do you unwind?"

Meyers shoved his chair back and yanked on Gwinn's arm. "We are leaving. Now."

Who was this person questioning Gwinn? Noah had always been the one who jumped to conclusions, not Conner. What happened to his calm, levelheaded partner? He'd never seen the guy take his role so seriously. His role. *Shit!* He was supposed to be playing Good Cop and all he'd been doing was sitting with his thumb up his ass.

"Calm down, everybody. Detective Crawford got a little carried away. Let's all take a deep breath and get back to the reason you're here. The timeline. If Mrs. Gwinn passed through the gate at eight forty-seven, do you think you sat down to dinner at nine?"

"There's a maid's room off the kitchen. She uses it as a dressing area. She spent about ten or fifteen minutes berating life in general, then took her glass of wine in there, washed her face, put on this caftan thing she likes to wear and some slippers. It would have been at least nine thirty before we ate."

He'd claimed eight thirty before. Discrepancy number one.

"And then?"

Meyers sat on the edge of his chair. Ready to spring at the first question he didn't like.

"Madlyn drank another glass of wine with dinner and another while we watched the news. I went up to bed after that. I never saw her alive again." He hiccupped with the last few words.

Meyers leaned closer. "Are you alright, Wade? Do you need to finish this another time?"

Noah held his breath, but Gwinn shook his head.

"No. I want to finish today. I want this over with."

"Do you have any idea what time she went out to the hot

tub?"

"No, I didn't hear her. Odds are, she took the wine upstairs while she worked in her office for a couple of hours. Later, she would have opened another bottle, grabbed a towel, and headed out back. She wouldn't have bothered with a suit. No one can see over the fence."

She certainly hadn't bothered with a suit. A sight Noah wished he could unsee. But he did notice she was as waxed and clean as a newborn babe. Was that for Wade or someone else? He'd find out.

Conner leaned forward, the calm in his voice unsettling after his earlier outburst. "Didn't you worry about her alone in the hot tub after drinking so much?"

"What was I supposed to do? She wouldn't listen to me and resented it if I *hovered*." He made quotation marks with his fingers.

Noah considered air quotes the mark of an intellectual poser, but he was today's Good Cop. That meant he tried to keep his expression neutral. "So you went upstairs to bed and left her alone, knowing her habits?"

"I did the only thing I could. I turned the water temperature down. She didn't like it, but she appreciated that I tried to take care of her, you know what I mean?"

Yeah, he did. Whenever he insisted on checking that Betsy had gas, or that she text him when she got home if he worked late, or waited up for her the few times she went for a girls night out, she fussed at him. But, she had a smile in her eyes while complaining.

Did that mean even though Wade and Madlyn Gwinn had an unconventional marriage, they still cared about each other? Did he suddenly think Wade was innocent while Conner thought he was guilty?

No, Conner had done a damn fine job of it, but he was only playing a role. Bad cop to his good cop.

Meyers drilled Noah with eyes that could shoot laser beams through a steel door. "I heard a rumor that Madlyn's autopsy was scheduled for today. Does that have anything to do with this sudden interest in my client's activities on the day of her death? You wouldn't have an official manner of death you've neglected to tell us about, would you? Mr. Gwinn is anxious to have his wife's body returned so he can follow her wishes and have her buried next to her parents in their family plot."

Conner lifted the manila folder and tapped one corner on the table. "As a matter of fact, I received this fax while waiting for you to speak with your client. The M.E. has ruled Mrs. Gwinn's death a homicide by drowning. He's waiting for toxicology results, so it may be a while before he releases her body for burial."

Gwinn dropped his face into his hand. A low, keening sound slipped between his fingers. "She got drunk and fell asleep, I tell you. She did every night. When will this nightmare be over? How much more do I have to endure?"

Any sympathy Noah harbored for Wade Gwinn evaporated. The jerk was more worried about his own skin than his wife's death.

Meyers hustled Gwinn out of the room before he could say anything incriminating, but stopped just inside the door. He swung around to face the detectives. "Before you convict my client in your minds, think about this. Mrs. Gwinn had a half million dollar life insurance policy. But she made substantially more than that a year plus a sizable year-end bonus. You've heard of cutting off your nose to spite your face? Mrs. Gwinn was worth much, much more alive than dead."

Noah glared at Meyers's back as the door closed. Texas might have community property, but it didn't have alimony. He could ask the judge for spousal support, but at best he'd get a pittance for five years, maximum.

If the Gwinn's were upside-down on their house note, it wouldn't matter how much money Madlyn made in a year, Wade was shit-out-of-luck in a divorce.

Conner gripped the file folder so hard, his knuckles turned white. "That prick is going down. We should have arrested him today."

Noah cut his eyes toward his partner. Had the entire world turned upside down? If he was left to be the only levelheaded one, they were in trouble. He could hardly function in a world where everyone stuck to their designated positions. He was supposed to jump to conclusions while Conner stayed calm. If their roles were reversed, it might make a hole in the space-time continuum and all of humanity would fly away.

There had to be an explanation. "You just don't like the idea of your lawyer representing a real criminal."

"I don't like the idea of that creep murdering his wife and getting away with it because he has money while my wife may have to go back to work in the fall to pay off my legal bills and I. Didn't. Do. Anything. Wrong."

Now it made sense.

He'd already talked Tom Meyers into cutting his partner's bill in half and raised enough from other members of the squad to cut it in half again. But he couldn't tell any of that to Conner.

The remaining amount would still be painful. Especially

with a baby on the way.

"What about our union? Won't they help?"

"If I use their lawyer instead of Meyers, but Jeannie won't hear of it. She insisted I have the best, and I've got to admit, this isn't something I'm comfortable skimping on. The idea of sitting in jail because I couldn't come up with the cash, while Gwinn goes free to enjoy his ill-gotten inheritance, chaps me big time."

"Cool your jets. Money's not going to get him off, but sloppy police work might. We have him on record establishing a timeline. The rest is grunt work. Tomorrow morning we start at Beneficial Products and question anyone who ever crossed paths with Madlyn Gwinn. Find out what they can tell us about our victim."

He'd keep his mind open, but the gap was closing quickly. Wade was the only one home with Madlyn when she died and he was angry that she came in late while he kept dinner warming. Had she threatened to cut off funding for his painting?

If she'd confided that decision to anyone, he'd find out. Once that happened, Wade could sure as hell start packing his brushes because that money he coveted wouldn't buy his freedom, but it might get him a cell with all the natural light he could handle.

CHAPTER
SIX

NOAH GAZED AT the closed blinds of Lieutenant Jansen's office. A sure sign their boss was in a sour mood. He leaned over his desk and whispered to his partner. "What say we hit the road before the Lieu corrals us with questions we aren't ready to answer?"

One glance over his shoulder and Conner grabbed his weapon, clipped on a radio, and pushed back from his desk.

Once outside, steamy air slapped Noah in the face. "It's going to be another scorcher. Let's skip the pool car and take Lola. Her air conditioning works better." Besides, Conner drove like an old woman.

What was the point of having a badge if you were afraid to use it?

He left the Travis Street headquarters behind and made his way toward midtown. With each block away from the concrete canyons and looming skyscrapers, the air quality improved. Not only the heat, but the exhaust, the traffic, the noise. The ability to see the sky without craning your neck at a forty-five degree angle.

Keeping Lola between I-45 and Studemont, he meandered past the last vestiges of creeping gentrification, through pot-holed streets lined with weeded lots and sagging chain-link fences. When he reached Taylor, he doubled back. Always good to get the lay of the land, the feel of an area, before approaching an occupant.

Perhaps more necessary for a residence than a factory, but you never knew.

Conner was used to his methods and didn't say a word. He kept busy pulling up information on his iPad and jotting it in his memo book. He glanced around as Noah turned into a drive not much different than half a dozen they'd passed. Only this one had a scattering of cars instead of weeds in the parking lot and steam coming from the factory portion.

Noah stopped to study the bedraggled building. "Doesn't look like the kind of successful business that could afford to pay Madlyn Gwinn the big bucks it would take to support the lifestyle she enjoyed. Wade claims she was worth more alive than dead, but not if the company craters. Maybe Wade's not a gambler. Could be he prefers a sure thing like life insurance to an iffy paycheck from a firm teetering on the brink."

Conner tapped his iPad. "They've only lived in that monstrosity of a house for eight months. Before that, they were out in suburbia. A nice enough neighborhood, better than yours and mine put together, but nothing compared to what they have now."

"Any chance of taking a peek at their tax returns for the last few years? I'd love to know if somebody died and left one of them a shitload of money."

"Not anytime soon unless your pal Wade hands them over voluntarily. How likely do you think that is?"

"Not fucking likely if Meyers has any say in the matter. Still, we know she was bringing in half a mill a year plus a bonus. That's not chopped liver. That's not even foie gras with a side of Chateaubriand."

"Only if Meyers was up-front with us. Are you willing to believe everything he said?"

Conner didn't wait for an answer, flipping to another screen on his tablet. "Stock in this company has climbed steadily for the last year and a half. If we'd invested one paycheck eighteen months ago, we could each pay off our house *and* buy a new sports car. Maybe she was worth that much money after all."

Noah took another look at the grime-encrusted windows. "I'm willing to bet that fictitious sports car you and I wouldn't have been invited in on that windfall. Only the select few jumped on that bandwagon."

"A little insider trading?" The gleam in Conner's eye was unnerving. "Maybe we can bring down the whole bunch of them."

This sarcasm wasn't like Conner and the recent change in his partner worried Noah.

To hell with this. He shoved open Lola's door. The damn thing hung ever since he'd been run off the road by a certified psycho. "Come on. We're not going to solve this case sitting out here gossiping like a couple of neighborhood biddies."

The heat bounced off the pavement, causing the bottom of his shoes to *shuup* with every step. Conner gathered his iPad and followed him to a gray door carved into a windowless expanse of galvanized metal. A faded *Entrance* sign was stenciled in blue above the access. Half the *E* had flaked off, leaving three unconnected dashes.

Inside, the carpet had seen better days and so had the receptionist. Her coal black hair showed an inch-wide stripe of silver at the part. Her mouth gave new meaning to the term *lipstick red.* Half glasses perched on the end of her nose. "May I help you gentlemen?"

Pictures of smiling babies, fat and healthy, lined the walls. Apparently, Beneficial Products formula guaranteed rosy cheeks and a good nature along with organic vitamins, high protein, and beautiful parents. The gleaming photos looked out of place on the dingy walls.

Noah looked away. How was he going to handle things when Conner expected him to *oooh* and *aaah* over his new baby? He'd worry about that another day. But he was running out of other days. "I'm Detective Dougherty, this is my partner Detective Crawford. We're investigating the death of Madlyn Gwinn. We'd like to ask you a few questions."

"I've been instructed to refer all inquiries to our new CEO, but he's out of the office at the moment. I don't expect him back before the end of the day. I'll be happy to schedule an appointment for say…" She checked her computer. "How does Wednesday at three o'clock sound?"

It sounded like a brush-off to Noah. He glanced at the nameplate on the battered desk. "I'm not sure you understand, Mrs. Dennis. My partner and I are homicide detectives. When we say, *we'd like to*, what we mean is we're going to. We'll begin by having a look around her office—"

"You can't do that. There are important papers in there.

You'll need a warrant." The receptionist's face turned a shade of red to rival her lips. Her hands fluttered around her sunken chest. Her heavy perfume formed a protective barrier, keeping him back several feet.

Conner withdrew the warrant from his suit pocket, placed it on her desk and stepped away into the zone of breathable air.

"And then we'll begin the interviews. We'll start with those who worked closest with her and spread out from there. Any we miss today, we'll catch first thing tomorrow. That includes your new CEO. Please make sure he's here by eight in the morning." He and Conner wouldn't be in that early, but she didn't need to know that. "Meanwhile, you can email his information to my office so that we can check him out." He laid his card on the corner of her desk.

How many times had he dealt with people like Mrs. Dennis? The gatekeepers. No real power of their own so they made themselves important by obstructing others.

"Now, do you want to point us in the direction of Mrs. Gwinn's office or shall we wander around until we find the right spot?"

Madlyn Gwinn's office could have been lifted directly from an ad in *Office Beautiful* and dropped into the rundown corridors of Beneficial Products, Inc.

Noah's feet sank into a carpet of rich cream with hints of gold. Her mahogany desk was polished to a shine which reflected walls covered in accolades and awards and trophies interspersed with souvenirs of her travels and examples of her husband's art.

Heavy drapes hid the fields of weeds outside her floor-to-ceiling windows while accentuating the gold tones of the floor and walls. The entire room seemed to be covered in a fine layer of gold leaf.

The gaudy décor made Noah want to gag, but didn't surprise him after seeing her home. It was the juxtaposition of her ostentatious office to the shabby condition of the rest of the building that caused him to stop short.

What did this tell him about their victim? That she was a self-centered narcissist? Probably. Did it change his opinion of her killer? No. But perhaps he needed to keep his mind open a little longer.

Not a sheet of paper cluttered the desk of the supposed workaholic. Of course, he only had Wade's word on that. The one thing out of place was an industrial sized bottle of hand sanitizer. Could she have been a germaphobe? Only one way to find out.

Time to start learning other people's opinions of the late Mrs. Gwinn.

He and Conner took the overstuffed sofa and let a succession of nervous employees sit in the straight-backed chair in front of them, like kids called into the principal's office.

They started with Mrs. Dennis, the receptionist. She remained tight-lipped at first, divulging very little, yet her dislike for her boss managed to creep into every word she uttered. Once the dam broke, she admitted there had been sweeping changes since Madlyn took over.

"Not many of us left from before. New management came in and did a lot of belt-tightening. Good for the company I suppose, but hard on employees. People who had been here thirty years were let go without a day's notice. Not only here in the office, but on the factory floor also. *Here's your pink slip. Pack up your things and go.* I had to escort friends out to their cars. Do you have any idea what that's like?"

Conner took notes on his memo pad but used the recording app on his phone as backup. Noah nodded, encouraging her to keep going.

"I guess it worked, though. The place seems to be making money now. Or at least not losing it anymore. I'm hanging on here with my fingernails. I only have a year to go before I'm eligible to retire. If the new CEO fires me, I don't know what I'll do. He's off today meeting with the bankers and investors, trying to hold this company together."

For her sake, and the other employees, Noah hoped the man was a miracle worker.

Next on their list was Sandy Ivins, Madlyn's secretary. She'd only worked for the company six months, replacing the secretary who had replaced the secretary who had worked for the last CEO.

She confirmed Wade's account of his wife's working hours. "I'd come to work in the morning and find half a dozen emails sent out after midnight. Then she'd breeze in at ten expecting everything to be taken care of, along with all my regular work. She was a real witch of a boss, but I make more than I did selling shoes and all I have to do is bow and scrape and let her insults roll off me like water off a rain slicker. I didn't want her gone. I was planning to use my year-end bonus to buy stock in the company."

"What about her husband? Did she ever talk about their relationship?"

"She had me make her hair appointments, her nail appointments, and take her clothes to the cleaners, but she never mentioned anything personal. I think she was a robot in disguise."

Was there a reason she didn't share personal information with her secretary? "Did she ever slip out without telling you where she was going, have you lie to anyone about where she was or when she'd be back?"

"She had meetings. She didn't tell me the details, just what to do before she came back and to call her cell in case of an emergency. I never suspected anything but business if that's what you're thinking. Near as I could tell, she had a one-track mind. And that track was making money."

Conner glanced up from his note-taking. "Her desk is certainly clean for a workaholic. Where are all her papers, folders, notes?"

"All filed and put away. She believes an uncluttered desk equates to a clean and organized mind. She doesn't...didn't approve of any mess or grime."

Was that the explanation for her squeaky clean body and not an unknown lover? Much as he'd like to hang this on Wade and be done with it, he and Conner hadn't come up with any convincing motive. Yet.

The rest of the day wasn't much different. They talked to the accounts receivable clerk, the accounts payable clerk, the filing clerk, mail clerk, and every other clerk, guard, operator, messenger, or executive they could find.

Every person they interviewed tried to hide the fact that they disliked Madlyn Gwinn personally, but the truth came through in subtle ways. So far, no one seemed to have any reason to wish her gone.

They had skipped lunch and Noah was starving. One glance

at Conner, and his partner switched off his recorder, stood, and started for the door.

Noah took a moment for one last survey of Madlyn's personal domain. Next time, they'd use an empty office, the break room, an alcove. Anything but this pretentious palace of vulgarity.

Conner yawned. The leather seat fit his back and shoulders, the air conditioning was cool but not cold, and the setting sun glared on his face causing him to close his eyes.

If he was this tired now, how would he manage fatherhood? As it was, his eyes popped open every time Jeannie stirred. And she stirred plenty.

She went to the bathroom three or four times a night. She tossed from one side to the other. She rearranged pillows. She stuck first one leg then the other in the air, twisting her ankle and flexing her foot. Leg cramps?

Then when he got up for work in the morning, she was sound asleep.

He sat up straighter. If he fell asleep now, Noah would never let him hear the end of it.

"Feeling better?" Noah's eyes remained on the road, but a smile played around the corners of his mouth. "Nothing like an afternoon nap to recharge the batteries."

Darn it. He was in for a ribbing now. "I didn't get much sleep last night."

"If you're having trouble already, what are you going to do when the baby gets here? Supposedly, you won't get a full night's sleep for the next eighteen years."

Yeah, about that. It might be time to fill his partner in on the latest details.

Noah broke in before he had a chance to put his thoughts into words. "What do you think about our interviews today? Not much doubt she was a bitch to work for, but apparently she saved the company. Not sure why anyone there would want to kill her."

"Maybe, but we have a few people left to talk to. I want to get down on the factory floor and see what's going on with the real workers, but Wade and anyone she's let go in the last few months are looking better and better."

Much as he'd like to slap the cuffs on Wade and call this case closed, he'd have to wait another day.

CHAPTER SEVEN

Sweet Pea bounded out of her zebra-striped bed and rushed to Noah as he opened the back door. The sight of her jumping and quivering with excitement at his arrival made coming home to a silent house almost bearable. Almost.

"Hello, girl. Did you have a good day? Any burglars or mailmen try to get in while I was at work? I thought I saw that calico cat from down the street scoot over the fence as I turned in the drive. You know my rule about no company when I'm not home."

Noah scooped up the ball of fur as he set his take-out dinner on the table. At his touch, she showed her appreciation by wiggling from head to toe. When he scratched behind her ears, her rear end practically hummed, almost like she was twerking.

"How about we eat dinner together and then play tug with Mr. Squeaky Man? I don't have time to take you for a walk tonight." There'd been a time, less than a year ago, when he resented having to take her out as soon as he got home from work instead of settling in front of the TV and kicking off his shoes. Now he looked forward to their walks more than she did.

He fixed Pea's bowl with a scoop of expensive dog food. The meal was already soft, but he chopped it into minute pieces so she could manage with her limited number of teeth.

The aroma of his own Szechuan chicken filled the kitchen and made his stomach growl in anticipation, but he didn't start eating until his dog had wagged her approval.

Thirty minutes later, he had done the dishes—thrown his cardboard carton in the trash along with the plastic chopsticks— changed into jeans, sat on the floor to play with Sweet Pea, and grabbed his guitar.

He used the thirty-minute drive to Earl Sparks's rustic ranch-style home to transition from cop to entertainer. Not always an easy switch.

The gray-haired, velvet-voiced detective lived on two acres at the end of a cul-de-sac. With no close neighbors to complain about the noise, his garage made the perfect spot to rehearse. Noah, Earl, and Danielle Hopkins from Missing Persons made up the trio they had jokingly called The Death Squad until Ian Langston retired a month ago and Danielle had taken his place.

She could play the fiddle like Johnny B. Goode but they were used to Ian's bass and the change required some adjustments.

Seven o'clock and still hot enough to melt butter. Add in ninety percent humidity and the air felt like a steam bath. Noah fanned-out his t-shirt and downed half a bottle of water. Good thing it was light enough to see without using the flood lamps. They would have added another five degrees and attracted even more mosquitoes.

He applied a second layer of spray, effectively drowning out the smell of pine needles and night blooming jasmine.

They practiced for an hour before Danielle's phone chirped with a text and she put down her bow.

"I've got to head home. My husband forgot to turn on the dryer and the baby's blankie is wet and he can't get her to sleep without it. Men." She rolled her eyes.

Noah didn't argue. He'd once misplaced Emma's favorite stuffed animal while babysitting and thought he would have to page his sister at the movies. Instead, he'd put both kids in the car and driven them around until they fell asleep. He never mentioned the incident to Rachelle.

After Danielle left, Earl broke out two beers. They sat on plastic lawn chairs and watched as a bank of clouds covered the moon.

"Where are you with the Gwinn case?" Earl unfolded legs as skinny as a grasshopper.

Noah used a thumbnail to peel the label from his bottle. "Not wrapped up yet, but getting close. No one we've interviewed so far seems to have a motive except her husband. She's made a lot of money for the company so the employees are happy. Except for the ones she let go. We'll check on them tomorrow, and if nothing jumps out at us, I'll be asking you to prepare an arrest warrant for hubby."

"So how'd she make the money?"

"What?" Noah's heart gave a little hiccup. Had he missed something?

"You said she made money for the company. At whose expense? Cutting costs by shrinking the work force can stem the outflow, but doesn't do much for the income. Did she step on any toes? Steal any accounts? Laid-off workers are more likely to carry a grudge, but you can't afford to ignore other possibilities, Hoss. You know as well as I do any defense attorney worth his salt would jump all over that omission."

Shit. Had he been so determined to close this case before Conner took family leave that he'd done a sloppy investigation?

He glanced at Earl, his skin pale in the moonlight. When had his face become skeletal? Almost as emaciated as the cancer-ridden children they sang for at the hospital.

This man was a wealth of practical information. The department couldn't afford to lose his experience. Yet he was wasting away before Noah's eyes.

He didn't have so many friends he could afford to lose one. That damned black dog of despair nipped at his heels. His world seemed to shrink a little more every day.

Craig Spencer closed the garage door behind him as hard as he could manage without being accused of slamming it. He wanted to kick something. Anything. But odds were he'd break a toe then have to face Evie and ask for a ride to the hospital.

Didn't she understand he did it all for her and the kids? First she bitched because they didn't have enough money. Then she bitched because he worked too many hours. She couldn't have it both ways. Time or money, take your pick. *Tell me which you want then let it be.*

He flicked on the overhead light. The fluorescent bulbs hissed and buzzed as they flickered, finally settling into a steady hum. The harsh glow illuminated more equipment than most small gyms.

Mistake number one. Or was it two, or three, or four? He'd

lost count.

Evie had complained that he spent all his free time at the health club, so he'd built a workout room here, in the garage.

Was that good enough for her? *Nooo.*

First it was the money he'd spent—if she knew he'd secretly kept his health club membership, she'd blow a gasket—then it was the noise. Hell, he'd soundproofed the whole place.

More money.

Then she was back to her original gripe. The time. But all the complaints were smokescreens for what truly bothered her. The nitty-gritty. The one thing she never admitted. Even to herself.

After three kids and twenty-five years, Evie was unrecognizable as the woman he married, while he looked better than ever.

He lifted his T-shirt and posed in front of the mirror, turning right, then left. How many fifty-year-old men had a ripped six-pack and buns of steel?

Look at those guns. He flexed his arm and watched the cotton fabric stretch tight over his bicep.

Even the young hotshots envied him when he went to the gym. Back when Evie *let* him go to the gym.

She had accused him of cheating on her. That wasn't the problem. He still loved her, respected her. She was a great mom and helpmate. He'd lost interest in her physically, that's all. Didn't that happen to most couples after so many years of marriage?

Maybe if she took a little time, fixed herself up, it would be a different story. Instead she chose to blame the time he spent working out. If she ever found out about the pills he scored off the internet…

He didn't take that many and only before competition. It

wasn't like he'd grown breasts or his balls had shrunk. He just needed help for that little bit of an edge. He hadn't taken any in weeks—he was totally out—but he'd need more soon to have any chance of winning his next match. And hiding that type of purchase from Evie was getting harder and harder.

The rage he had to fight so much of the time these days threatened to boil over and he fought it the only way he knew how. With sweat therapy.

He'd done everything he was supposed to in life: got an education, stood up like a man and married the girl he got pregnant, supported his family. And what had he gotten in return? A nag of a wife. Two kids who'd moved away from their parents, and one who never would.

And now this job. Sure, the money was good, but he didn't want it. Wouldn't have taken it if anyone else was available. So long to his safe, quiet world of numbers. From tomorrow forward, he'd have to deal with people. He'd already had to face a room full of bankers.

Assholes that had the key to the funds, but not the brains to recognize a good deal when it was sitting in front of them.

He flexed once more and the man staring back at him from the mirror smiled.

Instructors loved to preach: *Start slow. Stretch out. Warm up.* Bullshit. He was already plenty warm. He could feel the heat working from the inside out. Starting in his core and traveling out through every vein and tendon. Down his arms and legs. To the tips of his fingers.

He reached for the chalk and covered his hands before sliding into position on the padded bench. The weights were where he'd left them an hour ago when Evie demanded he come inside and help her get Joey to sleep.

Yeah. Nine-year-old Joey who couldn't—or wouldn't—go to bed on his own. Who refused to take his medicine until Mommy and Daddy had checked under the bed and in the closet and that the windows were locked and what was that shadow moving on the wall? And God forbid he didn't take his medicine because then no one in the house got any sleep.

Maybe they should have quit after two kids like he wanted to.

He longed for good old-fashioned business trips like other men complained about but secretly cherished the peace and quiet they offered. Instead, he got an hour in his own garage. If he was lucky.

He gripped the bar and heaved up with a grunt that echoed through the makeshift gym. Then down with a groan. Then up again. And down. Five more times. He was almost in the zone.

His eye caught a reflection to his left in a spot that should have been a square of black nothingness.

The florescent lights reflected on the glass of the side window.

A window that should have been shut but was angled out, halfway open.

What the fuck? That's why he'd installed air conditioning. So the window could remain closed, keeping out bugs and moths and other flying things that bit and fluttered around his face, distracting him.

Should he stop and fasten it? Hell no. He'd had enough interruptions tonight.

Another grunt came from deep in his chest and the weights lifted. He locked his arms above his head. That's right. This was what he needed. The endorphin rush was better than sex. Better than making money. Better than a gold-painted plastic trophy with his name engraved on it.

Better than the undisguised envy in the eyes of those not willing to spend the necessary hours working out.

Something flickered by the window. Something shiny, white. Long and thin. A snake? He hesitated, trying to make sense of what he saw.

It crept closer until it rested, cold and metallic, against the inner surface of his elbow. The moon caught on a pair of eyes, just outside the window, as a quick thrust collapsed his arm.

Expensive soundproofing muffled the crash of two-hundred pounds falling across his throat. Air wheezed out of his lungs, but the crushing weight prevented him from drawing more in. A red haze swam before his eyes.

He choked out a strangled gurgle as the gleam of a smile slowly revealed itself in the darkness, like the Cheshire cat in reverse.

CHAPTER EIGHT

Noah's attempt to slip out without talking to his boss for the second morning in a row failed miserably. Lieutenant Jansen stood in the door to his office with his hands on his hips. Those bushy eyebrows knitted together until they almost touched, making a fuzzy line like a piece of yarn a cat had been playing with.

"Going somewhere, Daugherty?"

"No, sir. Just looking for Conner before we reported our progress on the Gwinn case."

"He's in my office, waiting for you to join us."

He felt like an old time movie villain: *curses, foiled again* or some such shit.

Noah followed Jansen into his office. When the Lieu turned to close his door, Conner gave a slight shrug indicating he'd been cornered also.

"Isn't this pleasant. I so seldom see you two in the office anymore."

Jansen's sarcasm fell short. Noah wasn't in the mood. He and Conner hadn't been goofing around. They'd been working their tails off. Though maybe he should have tried harder to keep his boss in the loop.

"We've got another couple day's work on the Gwinn case. We hope to be able to wrap it up before the week is over. We have to search out and interview some disgruntled former employees and follow the money trail." He hadn't even had a chance to tell Conner about Earl's suggestion.

"I don't give a flying fuck about the Gwinn case. If the mayor doesn't like it, he can kiss my hairy butt. He's not going to be reelected, anyway."

If this wasn't about the Gwinn case, what was it about? Noah tried to think of anything he'd done lately to cause trouble, but he kept looking at Jansen's bushy eyebrows and wondering how hairy his butt was. An image he could do without.

"Junior Redden is suing the city, this department, and you personally."

Noah struggled to bring his mind back around to Junior Redden. "The fat, beer-breathed idiot who cut a six-inch gash in my leg? A gash that aches every time I take a step? That I have to wrap a plastic bag around to shower because I'm not supposed to get the stitches wet? Stitches that keep me awake at night with their incessant itching? And, by the way, I'll need to take off half a day next week to get those stitches out."

"He claims you didn't identify yourself as a police officer."

"Forget I've interviewed him three times and he knew who I was. Forget he stopped at his trailer and Kelly Manus told him I was there. Forget my badge was plainly visible. He attacked me! I was on my back on the ground when he started wailing on me.

I should be suing him."

This was too much. The roar in his head threatened to drown out Conner's corroboration.

"We were there three weeks ago. The first thing he did when he opened the door was call us by name. He added some choice profanity but there was no doubt he knew us by sight." Conner half rose in his chair, his face flushed with anger.

The sight of his partner jumping to his defense lowered Noah's blood pressure. This lawsuit was a joke, nuisance litigation. Yeah, but it was his nuisance. His time, his money to deal with it.

Jansen shrugged scrawny shoulders. "I don't doubt you for a second and I'll vouch for you when the time comes. That doesn't change a thing. You're due at legal in fifteen minutes."

He didn't have time for this nonsense, not right now. He had a case to solve. "We have an appointment with the new CEO of Beneficial Products first thing this morning." And he'd gotten up in a good mood today, ready to face Madlyn Gwinn's replacement as long as he didn't have to do it in that gilded office.

"Conner will have to go alone. When the brass issues an order, we object at our own risk. And you have enough risk on your plate for one day."

Conner shook his head. "Why don't we let Mr. Beneficial Big Wig stew in his own juices for now? You go see what legal has to say. I've got at least an hour of paperwork to place all the files and reports in the murder book, plus run down addresses of ex-employees. We can head over there when you finish."

Noah nodded, unwilling to speak. The day might be shit, but the people he worked with were golden.

Every nerve in Noah's body ached to slam the door. The people in that room weren't his enemies, just not his friends. They wanted to make this thing go away. He did, too.

But not at the price they were willing to pay.

The idiots had already tried throwing money at Junior Redden, but surprise, surprise. Even Junior was smart enough to figure out money wouldn't do him any good in jail.

When they decided to offer Junior a reduced sentence, Noah had left. He couldn't stay closeted with that bunch of numb-nuts one second longer. Next, they'd be offering Junior a get-out-of-jail-free card. On a double murder. Of his parents.

The fools.

Putting aside the horrendous nature of the crime, giving in to threats would encourage every criminal with half a brain to try something similar. Soon the courts would be overflowing with nuisance cases.

The two go-getters assigned to his case didn't look old enough to drive, much less buy beer. The guy tried to make up for his youth by growing a scraggly beard while the woman wore a severe navy power suit and three-inch hooker heels.

They'd learn. Or they wouldn't, and they'd soon be looking for another job. Either way, the DA would never approve reducing the charges against Junior which would leave them back at square one.

With all the shit falling directly on Noah.

He needed to talk to Junior's girlfriend. The one thing he'd been warned against.

Kelly Manus had originally told the Sheriff's deputies Junior burst into their trailer demanding to know whose truck was parked out front. When she told him, he nearly ripped the door off the hinges in his rush to stop Noah from looking in the dumpster.

What had changed her story? Threats or bribery?

Didn't she understand? The minute Junior stepped out of jail, her life wasn't worth a pile of dog crap. The only difference between her and Junior's parents was that her body would never be found. Then, even if the DA didn't reduce the first degree murder charges, Junior could afford a lawyer like Tom Meyers, which amounted to the same thing.

Noah couldn't let that happen. Not any of it. Not letting Junior loose on an unsuspecting world. Not what would happen to Kelly. Not what would happen to him if Kelly disappeared.

He was already stumbling under the weight of the guilt he carried every day.

Kelly's death would be the final blow.

A jolt of adrenalin surged through Noah's body. Junior didn't have to be released for Kelly to be in danger. If the fat slob didn't know people on the outside willing to snap that slender neck for a few bucks, he could find someone on the inside who had the right connections.

Madlyn Gwinn was already dead. Her case could wait.

Conner made one last note on his computer and ran his finger down the list of phone numbers Sandy Ivins had sent him.

One hundred and twenty-three employees had left Beneficial Products since Madlyn Gwinn had been hired, eighteen months ago. Several obviously saw which way the wind was blowing and left for new jobs within the first few months. Two more moved out of state. Another died in an auto accident and one was in jail on unrelated charges. A part-time employee returned to school. Three had taken early retirement.

Those names had to be checked out, but they were at the bottom of the list of possible suspects. Earl could make those calls.

That left him ninety-seven calls to make. Impossible. He'd have to let Earl start with the first to leave while he called the most recent to get the axe. Noah could work from the middle out.

It was the distribution he didn't understand. Other than the usual shuffling of top tier employees you'd expect when a new CEO took over, few of the laid-off employees were upper or middle management. That went against what little he knew about business practices.

Coups were avoided and money saved by getting rid of those who made the big bucks while keeping the little guys who did all the actual work. But Madlyn Gwinn had done the opposite.

On the other hand, she was the one who attended Wharton School of Business. Not him.

He folded the list in thirds and was about to tear it when Noah stomped into the room and threw himself into his chair. "Fucking idiots."

"Meeting went well, did it, and the department attorneys were helpful?"

"Their daddies wasted a shit load of money sending those two lightweights to law school. They're so scared of a lawsuit, they'll hand Junior everything he wants and beg him to take more."

"They're going to pay him off?" Noah was obviously

exaggerating.

"Worse. They're going to *let* him off."

Surely he heard wrong. "They actually said that?"

"No, but they were working up to it. Right now, they're at *reduce the charges*. Junior, mental giant that he is, will figure out in about two seconds to hold out for a better deal."

"The DA will never go for that." Would he? It depended on how his week had gone and what the latest poll numbers said.

Noah's face was flushed and his eyes became twin dots of blackness. "Doesn't matter. Junior will be out on bail before the DA reads their report which will probably be written in crayon. I have to get to Kelly before Junior does."

"Why? What'd she do?" His voice caught in his throat and came out a squeak. This couldn't be good.

"Recanted her story. Said that's what happened *last* time we came to the trailer to question him. She didn't see him this time, so she doesn't know what he thought."

Conner took a deep breath and forced himself to sound calm, authoritative. "You can't go anywhere near Kelly Manus. That's witness tampering. You could end up in jail, not just fired."

Noah lowered his voice to a whisper. "And what do you think happens to her if Junior gets there before I do?"

Noah would do whatever Noah decided to do and he covered for him at his own risk, but the guy was his partner, so... "The Lieu can't know what you have in mind. For now, Junior is safely locked away. Let's head over to Beneficial Products and see if the new CEO has anything to tell us. After we finish there, if Kelly's home, we might decide to stop by and make sure she's all right."

Conner's chair squealed as he passed the list of phone numbers across the aisle to Earl Sparks. "I hate to dump this on you, but can you start calling to see if any of these people hold a grudge about being fired by Madlyn Gwinn? Maybe you can get Lefty Bob to help."

"Lefty Bob caught a new case early this morning, on top of the ones he already had. Looks like an accident, but he still needs to check out the guy's office. He should be back in a couple of hours. You want me to start at the top or the bottom?"

What the hell. Earl was better at this than he was any day of the week. "Start at the bottom. You never know. Somebody might slip up and admit pushing her under the water."

And if they didn't, that left the way clear to charge Wade Gwinn.

With any luck, they could close the book on two cases in one day, leaving Noah a manageable work load if Jeannie went into labor early.

CHAPTER NINE

THE BABIES ON the wall were still smiling, but Mrs. Dennis, the receptionist wasn't. Her nose and eyes were red and she'd chewed off most of her lipstick. She glanced up from blowing her nose as Noah and Conner entered the run-down lobby of Beneficial Products.

"You two again? The other officer is already here." She motioned with the tissue in her hand. "You might as well go on back. I give up. I can't handle this anymore."

Noah scooted down the hall before she had time to wave any more germs his direction. Summer colds were the worst and he didn't plan to catch hers. The new officer better be here and ready to see them. He didn't want to waste any more time than necessary.

"Nothing like a warm welcome," Conner muttered two steps behind him.

"If the new guy has started redecorating, I hope he hasn't thrown out the bottle of hand sanitizer."

The hall was adorned with faded portraits of long dead or dishonored CEOs of the past. A hint of industrial chemicals from the plant hung in the air. His shoes slapped against worn linoleum like he hadn't seen since his grandmother died. If Madlyn Gwinn was a germaphobe, she'd have done better to spend half as much money gold-plating her office, and the rest on new flooring and a coat of paint. No wonder Mrs. Dennis was sick.

Remnants of every cold, flu, virus, or infectious disease any employee in the last twenty years came across probably clung to the dingy walls and outdated light fixtures. Working here would make him sick, too.

"Let's cut this interview as short as possible. I'm anxious to get out to Lost Pines Trailer Park." There was something he never thought he'd say again in his lifetime. The mere mention of that place caused his leg to throb like a kettle drum.

"I agree, but we've got to question this guy. Find out if he knows anything about Madlyn Gwinn or this place that would shed any light on her murder."

For a moment, he was back at Lost Pines. The stench of the rotten dumpster, the taste of grit in his mouth, the feel of dirt under his fingernails as he clawed his way across the hard-packed ground, and, for fifteen disgusting minutes until the Sheriff's deputies arrived, the sight of Junior's flaccid johnson peeking out the leg hole of skid-marked skivvies. A sliver of ice raced down his spine as he relived how close he'd come to death.

He was a trained police officer. With a gun. What chance did Kelly Manus have if Junior reached her first? "Half an hour. If this new officer can't give us anything helpful in that length of time, he doesn't know or won't tell, and pumping him any longer won't change a thing."

"I agree. We'll check out the new guy. See if he can give us any insight into who would hold a grudge against Madlyn Gwinn—either point us in a new direction, or leave us to focus on her husband—then we hunt down Junior's flighty fiancée and have a *Come to Jesus* talk with her. We can always come back later to interview the plant workers and check out the factory floor. I'd like to finish here and get home as early as possible tonight. Jeannie's been having trouble with Braxton-Hicks the last few nights."

"Who's that? Is some neighbor giving her a hard time? Want me to come by and put the fear of God into him?"

"False labor pains. It's the body's way of gearing up for the real thing."

"Shit. Practice labor? Isn't going through it once bad enough?" Sometimes it amazed him, all the things he didn't know.

"They aren't too strong, at least not so far, but enough to make her nervous."

"Doesn't she have about three more weeks?"

"Originally, but after that last test, the doctor warned us to be ready at any time. It seems she's—"

"Jeannie always was ahead of her time." Noah tried to make a joke, either to calm Conner or himself, he wasn't sure which. "This won't take long. With any luck, you can beat the traffic home."

They rounded the corner to see gold-tinted light spilling out of the CEO's office. Noah's knock on the doorframe competed with the slamming of a file drawer. A large, heavy-set man swung around to face them.

What the fuck was Lefty Bob Hernandez doing in the new CEO's office?

Conner was still trying to wrap his head around the fact that Mrs. Dennis had sent them in to see a police officer when they were expecting to find the Chief Executive Officer. Two dead CEOs in one week in a company this size defied all mathematical probability.

"You want it, you can have it. I've got cases coming out my wazoo." Lefty Bob tossed his memo pad to Conner. "Here's my notes, although there's not much there. I was five minutes away from calling Craig Spencer's death an accident. Still not sure it wasn't."

Conner flipped open the small spiral notebook. How was he supposed to decipher Lefty Bob's left-handed chicken scratching? He'd have to start over from the beginning. Better that way anyhow. Lefty was a good cop, but this was his case now, and his responsibility.

He drummed his fingers on the ornate desk—was it Madlyn Gwinn's or Craig Spencer's? Didn't matter. Neither of those two had any need for it now. "We weren't much behind you in closing ours. The husband had means, motive, and opportunity. But you know how I feel about coincidences. They pick at me like a kid with a scab."

Noah glared at his cell phone and didn't look up. "I hate them too, but sometime a cigar is a cigar or some stupid adage like that."

"You don't actually believe that, do you?" Conner groaned inwardly. He couldn't do this without his partner's help.

"No, I'm just pissed. I thought we had the case all but solved."

Conner did too, but that didn't mean he planned to write off a suspicious death because it was inconvenient.

Noah jammed his phone into his pocket. "We've been here a good part of the morning and I can't reach Kelly Manus. There's no phone in the trailer, she's not answering her cell or Junior's, her boss says she cancelled her shift at the last minute, and the trailer park manager says her car is gone."

"What'd we know about Junior's whereabouts?"

"The itty-bitty-baby lawyer lady says he's behind bars."

That should help. "Do you trust her?"

"I trust her to say what she believes is true. I don't trust her to know what *is* true. I have Earl working on the case. He'll get to the bottom of it."

Which meant Earl wasn't working on the Gwinn case. Damn. Still, it had to be done.

Lefty Bob hitched his pants over a substantial belly. "If you two have this under control, I'll head back to the station and get to work on my other half dozen cases. I owe you one for taking this lemon off my hands. Call me if you have an emergency. Just make sure it is one."

He paused at the door and looked back at Conner and Noah. "Coincidence or not, I say this was an accident. The wife…well, you'll meet her, but she's got no motive. She needs him too much, plus I don't believe she's capable. And there's no sign of anyone else on the premises except the son. Mom wouldn't hesitate to cover for him, but he'd blurt it out if he was there."

From the interview Lefty Bob described, he agreed. At forty-seven, Lefty had ten years on him, but that didn't make Conner a novice. He was closing in on fifteen years experience that told him to keep investigating. He stuck with an early morning jog these days, but he'd lifted weights plenty in the past and he'd never seen or heard of weights crushing someone's throat.

Thirty minutes later, Noah slammed the bottom drawer of the single file cabinet. "Not a single scrap of paper worth a second look."

Conner swiveled the heavy leather chair to face him. "Anything of interest on this computer is password protected. If she wrote down the code, I can't find it. Her secretary doesn't know or won't tell, and his secretary claims he never had a chance to come in this office to change anything. We'll have to take this thing in and let the techies have a go at it."

They'd brought a big box of Madlyn's things into the station, had her purse been one of them? The passcode might be in her wallet, or one of those zipper compartments women seemed to be so fond of. The ones Jeannie put things in for safekeeping, never to be found again.

Maybe Wade could give them the code, especially since he'd dropped down on the suspect list to second place, right below SODDI—*some other dude did it.*

Noah's phone chimed with a text. One glance and his face brightened. "Earl's contact at the jail says Junior is in his cell, yelling about injustice, the lack of privacy, the ethnicity of his fellow cohabitants, and the quality of the food. Should make him popular with the other inmates."

Good. They could concentrate on the case at hand. The one where somebody was actively murdering people. "Let's carry this stuff out to Lola and swing by Craig Spencer's house. Lefty Bob was somewhat cryptic about the widow and son. I'd like to see what he was talking about."

"Sorry, there's been a death in the family. My sister's not receiving visitors today." Evie Spencer's brother stood behind a front door open a full five inches. The eye and half a face visible looked soft, doughy.

Noah tried one of those cleansing breaths Betsy used to suggest. The jerk-wad was attempting to help his family. A family laboring under the illusion their loved one's death was an accident.

An illusion he was likely to crush at any minute. Was an accident easier to accept than murder? Probably. He'd lived through it and didn't know the answer. In fact, he still wasn't sure what to call Betsy's death. Was it simply a traffic accident because she was hit by an eighteen-wheeler? Or murder because the driver had literally been asleep at his job? He knew which one he called it. But any name left her ripped from his life just as their dreams were within reach.

He opened his jacket far enough to show his badge but not his gun. "Detectives Daugherty and Crawford. We're looking into Mr. Spencer's death."

The door opened an additional five inches. "What happened to the other man? Detective Hernandez."

"We've taken the case over from him as we have more time to devote to it."

"But it was an accident. What's to investigate?"

Conner leaned closer to the man who blocked the partially open door with his girth. "We're required to investigate any death that doesn't happen under a doctor's care. You wouldn't want any less for your loved ones, would you, Mr...."

"Palmer. Brice Palmer. I just want what's best for Evie and the kids." The man stepped back to allow them room to enter. His small head rested almost directly on sloping shoulders without benefit of a neck. He filled the narrow entry hall, leaving Noah and Conner barely room to squeeze past.

The buttons on Palmer's shirt strained against a substantial belly. His left hand gripped a sandwich containing several layers of ham on a Kaiser roll as he motioned with unnaturally short arms toward the back of the house.

Noah followed the sound of voices to a living area filled with adults and children whose size and shape marked them as members of the Palmer family. The whole bunch looked like a set of Russian nesting dolls.

The room fell silent except for the background noise of a TV game show as a dozen pair of eyes followed their every move.

"Evie's gone back to catch a few winks. She didn't get much sleep last night. Woke up around two and realized Craig never came to bed. When she went to check on him she found… Well, you know what she found. Hey, can I get you fellas something to eat or drink?"

A long table groaned under the weight of ham, casseroles, congealed salads, and desserts. Either the neighbors had stopped by with food offerings, or the family brought their own supplies, but Noah had been to buffets with smaller selections.

Despite the abundance of food, the house gave off a musty smell. The furniture—what Noah could see of it—looked shabby and worn. The carpet had been flattened with use, the pattern showing only near the wall.

"Why don't we let Mrs. Spencer rest a few more minutes while my partner and I check out the scene of the accident?"

Palmer tried to nod, but his double chin restricted the movement of his head. "Right this way. Craig had his garage turned into some kind of exercise area." His voice took on a disapproving tone. "Spent all his spare time in there. Left Evie to deal with Joey on her own."

Noah reached the door and came to a complete halt. He tried to keep in shape—went to the gym occasionally, even had a couple of pieces of equipment in his spare bedroom—but he'd never seen a better equipped workout room in his life. There were machines he had no idea how to use.

He stepped aside to allow Conner to enter and reached for the door, blocking Brice Palmer. "Is everything just the way your brother-in-law left it?"

"I think Evie tried to move the weight off Craig before she called 911. She was screaming, sort of hysterical like, when she called me. That other detective and another fella walked all around looking at things and taking pictures. Not sure if they moved anything or not."

Palmer glanced around and pointed to a bench in the corner. "I'll wait over here, out of your way."

Not good. He and Conner needed to be able to discuss what they found and any theories they came up with privately. A family member watching over their shoulders might become upset, especially if suspicion turned to the wife.

Conner patted Palmer on the shoulder while maneuvering him back toward the living room. "I'm sure your sister would appreciate it if you saw to it everyone was taken care of while we check around here. This might take us awhile."

Palmer left without ever realizing he'd been manipulated. Noah bit back a laugh. Damn, Conner had the touch. Did he ever pull that shit on him or was he immune to his partner's ways?

Noah's grin faded by the time Conner returned and pulled the door shut behind him. The sound of voices, utensils, and a TV game show dropped off immediately. This place was better insulated than his house.

Conner turned in a circle, checking the room. "This house is okay, but nothing compared to the Gwinn's place, however, the amount he spent on this room and the equipment in it would have gone a long way toward upgrading their standard of living."

"I'll bet real money not one person in that room was related to Spencer by blood. Did Lefty Bob mention any family problems?"

Conner flipped through the memo book he'd been given. "Parents deceased. An older sister in Waco. That's all he says. Or at least all I can decipher. There's three kids, Joey nine, Heath eighteen, and Candace twenty-one. The two older kids are off at college and supposedly making arrangements to get home. One's at some Ivy League school up north and the other's doing her junior year abroad. France, I think. Guess we can write them off the list."

"What about the youngest one, Joey?"

"I don't know. Lefty didn't make any notes about talking to him, but the last time the wife saw Spencer was when she needed his help getting the kid to bed."

"Nine years old and it takes two people to make him go to bed? We definitely need to interview him."

CHAPTER
TEN

THE GARAGE/WORKOUT ROOM was hot, but not nearly as sweltering as it should have been at noon in July. Noah took off his jacket and hung it on the doorknob. Sweat formed at the back of his neck and trickled down between his shoulder blades.

They weren't supposed to touch anything, but the air conditioning unit set into the wall seemed to dare him to switch it on.

Craig Spencer's weights had already been dusted for prints. If the universe was smiling on him, the results would be on his desk by morning. If not, there was nothing he could do to rush them. Forensic prima donna nerds.

To his left, Conner stood immobile, staring at the floor.

"Watcha' see, partner?"

"Cricket."

"And?" A cricket in Houston in summer wasn't worth a second look, much less a prolonged stare.

"Wondering how it got in here. This place is sealed up like an isolation lab."

"Think the M.E. took the body out through the garage door?"

"Naw, it's been cover over with drywall."

Damn if his partner wasn't right. A new wall replaced the old, metal, electric door. What about the window? Noah stepped over the barbell to get closer. The caulking looked tight all the way around. No critter slipped in that way. "Do you think someone could jimmy this lock with a credit card or something?"

"We can get crime scene back out here to check for prints, but it doesn't look like enough space to me."

"While they're at it, have them check outside for footprints. See this scuff mark here?" He pointed to an almost invisible line on the window sill.

Conner took out his cell phone and snapped pictures from every angle. When he finished, Noah used his gloved hand to unlock the clasp. The glass pivoted open from the middle, cutting the window in half. "Don't give me that look. You know prints wouldn't adhere to this rough surface." Conner didn't argue with him. Why would he? He knew it was true.

The outside sill didn't have a corresponding line, but the dirt was smeared.

Again, Conner took photos from several angles, but shook his head as he put his phone away. "We're grasping at straws here. No one could get through that window, not even a child. Whatever happened, if anything, came through that door." He nodded toward the closed door leading back into the house. "The wife, the kid, a stranger, or nobody. Just an accident. I suppose they happen sometimes."

"Do you believe in a coincidence like that?"

"No."

Good, because if he had to be the logical one and Conner the impulsive one, they were in deep trouble. "The cricket? How did it get in?"

"That's the question, isn't it?"

Noah took a step forward when his foot hit something that skittered across the cement floor. He picked up a piece of dull metal about two inches long, an inch to an inch and a half tall, and no more than a sixteenth of an inch thick. It wasn't solid, but carved into a design almost, but not exactly, like a butterfly. He ran his thumb over the edges. Smooth.

"What the hell is this?" He held the object up for Conner's inspection.

"Something to hold the weights in place? Could it have broken off and caused the weights to slip?"

Wouldn't it be great if it were that simple? They could close the case and get back to real work.

Fifteen minutes later, Noah had tried to fit the object on every piece of equipment in the room. His knees were screaming from crawling around on the cement floor. He flipped the piece of metal to Conner who caught it in the air. "No telling. Bag it and tag it. If anything ever comes up, we'll have it. Now, let's go talk to the widow."

By the time Noah and Conner returned to the living room, the smell of garlic bread and the brisket Brice Palmer was carving had overpowered the room's original aroma of old furniture and stinky feet.

Even Brice's offer of bar-b-que wasn't enough to tempt Noah, despite the fact he and Conner skipped lunch in an effort to get moving on this new case.

"I hate to bother Mrs. Spencer at this time, but we need to talk to her. Could you wake her for us?"

"I knocked on her door five minutes ago. She's up and expecting you. Could you take her some lunch when you go back? I know she'll be hungry by now." Brice held out a plate overflowing with two kinds of meat, baked beans, mashed potatoes, corn on the cob, and hunks of bread.

Noah was six foot two and dangerously close to two hundred pounds, but the dish he carried down the hall contained more food than he could eat in a day.

He let Conner knock on the bedroom door while he balanced the plate in one hand and napkin, utensils, and a glass of orange soda in the other.

"Come in." The voice was almost a whisper.

The room was deep in shadow. The only light came from a muted TV and what little sunshine escaped closed drapes. Noah stopped to let his eyes adjust to the darkness.

Evie Spencer sat in an oversized armchair. She wore some type of loose, flowy garment that might have been what Betsy used to call a caftan. The straps of her flip-flops were obscured by bulging flesh. She held out her hand and motioned him forward. He thought she wanted him to sit beside her, but she was only reaching for the food.

"I've smelled this for the last hour. I thought Buddy would never finish it."

"Buddy?" Was there someone here he hadn't met?

"Brice. My little brother. I suppose you want to ask me more questions." She used child-sized teeth to tear at a fried chicken breast. Noah's stomach rolled in rebellion.

He placed the drink and utensils on the table beside her, but she wasn't interested in anything but the food. "Yes, ma'am. Did your brother explain that we had taken over your husband's case from Detective Hernandez?"

"Ummhhp."

He'd take that as a *yes*. "I know you went over this with Detective Hernandez, but we need you to start at the beginning and tell us what happened. Did you go out yesterday?"

Amazingly, half the food on her plate had disappeared. "Joey's monthly appointment with Dr. Graham was at three o'clock. The doc wanted to do some blood tests, which put us running late. We didn't get out of there until after five. Any change in routine, especially involving needles, upsets Joey so I went and stopped at a drive-thru and got him some chicken nuggets. That usually calms him down, but it didn't last night."

Evie attacked the corn like a starving hyena and Conner flipped the page on his memo book. "Was Mr. Spencer home when you got here?"

"No. He worked late. Came in about seven."

Noah glanced at Conner with a half-smile. Good question. That meant no one was home for at least two hours. "Did you lock up before you left for the doctor's, set the alarm?"

"Getting Joey into the car is tough if he don't want to go. Once he's settled, I don't dare leave him and come back to take care of those things, but we use the back door and it's inside the fence. Nobody's ever bothered us."

Empty house, unlocked door behind a privacy fence. Why not put up a sign saying *come on in*? "When Mr. Spencer got home, was he tired, frustrated? Did he say anything about the company or Madlyn Gwinn's death?"

"He never talked much about work. He didn't like Madlyn, nobody did, but her death shook him up, being so sudden-like. You know, if it happened to her—here one minute and gone the next—it could happen to anybody." Her head drooped. "And I guess it did."

Yeah, and wasn't that the pits? Noah's heart gave a little hiccup but he pushed it aside. "Was he excited about his promotion?"

"He enjoyed working with numbers, so running the company wasn't a job he was looking forward to, but the extra money would be helpful, what with Joey and the kids in school."

"What did you talk about when he got here? Was he in a good mood?"

"Joey and I drove to the park and ate in the car and watched people walk their dogs. Joey loves that so we didn't hurry. Craig got in about twenty minutes later. He turned fifty last month and was gearing up for his first seniors' body building tournament. He changed his clothes, made himself a protein shake, and went to work out. I put Joey in his pajamas, but when he saw the Band-Aid from his blood test, he got upset all over again. He started crying and throwing stuff. I had to use the intercom to call Craig to come help. He doesn't like to be interrupted once he's started his routine."

Now they were getting somewhere. Craig was angry. The kid was angry. And Evie's tight-lipped face said she was angry. A house full of angry people and one of them ended up dead.

"Took us more than an hour to get him to sleep. Craig and I took turns reading to him and patting his hand. I can't read out loud too long or my asthma kicks in. Once Joey was asleep,

Craig went back to the garage and I went to bed. The TV was on, but it's set to switch off after an hour. I woke up around four and realized Craig never came to bed. I went looking for him and…"

If tensions from a new job he didn't want, longer hours away from home, and stress of an upcoming competition caused Craig Spencer's death—either because he was careless with the weights or someone in the house was angry—did that take this case out of the realm of coincidence?

Maybe.

It was up to the M.E. to declare manner of death. All he could do was gather the facts. And that included talking to a troubled nine-year-old with unresolved anger issues.

Evie Spencer stood between Conner and her son's bedroom with her arms crossed, using her substantial body as a barrier. "Joey don't talk that much." Her pupils narrowed to pinpricks. "And he don't like strangers."

Conner lowered his voice, smoothed the edges of his words. He resisted the urge to hurry simply because he was worried about Jeannie and wanted to get home. "Joey's a minor, so we can't talk to him without you in the room. If he gets upset, say the word. We'll break it off."

Evie's breath came out in a heavy *wheeze* as she shuffled around to face the closed door. A window the size of a sheet of paper was set in at about the five foot mark. "This here's one way glass. That way we can check on him. Don't keep the door shut except at night or when strangers are over. I've got a baby monitor so I can hear if he calls."

Inside, a boy with a twisted body sat on the floor playing

with action figures. A hospital bed with guard rails lined one wall with an intricate motorized wheelchair parked behind it.

Evie placed one hand against the glass, as if touching her son. "I'd appreciate it if you didn't try to talk to him. He wouldn't be able to answer you and it would upset him. Took me most of the morning to calm him down what with all the police and ambulance people here. Poor thing. He wasn't but a couple of ounces over two pounds when he was born. Doctors kept telling me he wasn't going to live, but he did. Then he wouldn't make it to five, but here he is."

Conner's throat closed. He couldn't swallow. Couldn't get more than the shallowest breath. Couldn't make his heart behave. Is this what happened to babies who came too early?

He gripped his pen so hard his fingers turned white. Dark spots floated in front of his eyes, like black snow. He struggled to gain control of his trembling hands.

"It's called Spastic Quadriplegia. Rare to this extent even in cerebral palsy patients. Aren't we the lucky ones?" Sarcasm coated her words.

Heavenly air worked its way into Conner's starved lungs and the spots before his eyes cleared.

Evie let her hand drop and swiveled toward Noah. "I shouldn't have said that. We are lucky. I thank God every day Joey is with us. It's just that change is hard on him and he's had so much of it lately. First his sister and now his brother have gone off to school. Then his dad took the job with Beneficial Products with its extra hours at the same time he started that stupid weightlifting hobby. And with Madlyn's death he would have been working even more."

She glanced from Noah to Conner and back. "I used to call

my neighbor to help me get Joey into the car for doctor visits, but then she got sick and my fibromyalgia and asthma started acting up and he grew bigger so Craig would have to take off work to help me. The extra money when he started working at Beneficial Products paid for that wheelchair and a van to put it in, but Joey misses the time with his daddy."

Conner glanced her direction, expecting to see tears. Instead he saw exhaustion, bewilderment, despair. His voice caught. "Will you be able to handle this on your own?"

"I called my sister an hour ago. She used to be a nurse. She lives up north now and hates the ice and snow. Wants to come back home but hasn't been able to afford a place of her own. I might be able to talk her into moving in with me. If I sell all Craig's workout equipment, I ought to be able to afford to turn the garage into a spare bedroom."

Noah cleared his throat. "Speaking of Mr. Spencer's workout room, I have a couple of questions, then we'll let you go back to your family. Have you ever seen this before?" He held out the baggie containing the metal piece he'd found on the floor.

"No. Could it be a broken piece of the weight I pushed off Craig's throat? It made a pretty big crash."

"What about the window or the air conditioner, did you touch them?"

A flush spread over her pale face. "I closed the window and turned off the AC. I know I shouldn't have, but I kept picturing dollar bills pouring through the opening like green smoke."

Why would the guy have the AC on *and* the window open? Did it have something to do with his training routine? AC to keep the room cool but window open for the fresh air? Conner had never heard of that system. He made a note on his spiral to check online. Anything was possible.

Noah had finished his questions and waited, giving Conner a turn, but he didn't have anything else to ask. They left Mrs. Spencer watching her son through the one-way glass.

Conner offered his condolences to everyone as he and Noah made their way back to Lola. The only sound was the *click* of their seatbelts as they sat motionless and stared down the empty street.

Noah switched on the engine, but didn't put Lola in gear. "I think we're back at square one. The kid didn't do it. He couldn't have made it into that room on his own. The wife's kind of like Wade Gwinn. Not one hundred percent out of the picture, but highly unlikely. She couldn't have surprised him, not with that heavy tread and wheezing with asthma."

"I don't know what kind of insurance the guy had, but putting aside the fact she needed him— physically, emotionally, monetarily—I don't think she'd have done that to her son. Which leaves us with problems at Beneficial Products."

After a moment of silence in which Conner couldn't get the image of Joey Spencer out of his mind, Noah shifted into *drive,* and Lola roared to life.

"I know watching that kid unnerved you. Hell, it shook me up. But Jeannie's much healthier than Evie Spencer ever was plus she's already a couple of months further along. She's only got what, two weeks left?"

"Twenty-three days, if she lasts that long, which is doubtful."

"You'll make yourself sick, worrying. Relax. She's past the danger point."

Not exactly. You don't know half of it, literally. He wasn't being fair. Noah was his best friend. Logic told him he'd feel better if he unburdened himself to his partner, but reading what could happen to preemies and seeing it for himself had left him tied in knots. Talking would only make his nightmares seem real.

Noah flipped on Lola's blinker. "Let's skip returning to the office. We can check in with Earl over the phone and see if he had any luck with the ex-employees."

"What do you have in mind instead?"

"My gut says Evie Spencer didn't murder her husband, but there was definitely some anger there. We only have her word for the seriousness of her physical condition, for what time she got home from the doctor's office, and whether Craig was already there or not. For that matter, we're taking her word for what Joey can and can't do. We only saw him playing on the floor."

"Wouldn't hurt to talk to that doctor. See what time she left his office. Ask his opinion on what Joey's capable of. Maybe get his take on Evie."

"Check in with Earl before we decide what to do next. Could be he's already solved the case for us."

"Yeah, wouldn't that be nice?" Conner hit Earl's number and listened as a voice so mellow even the speaker phone couldn't distort it filled the truck cab.

"Don't be dropping all your work on me then calling to nag me about it."

"We thought you might have convinced someone to confess."

"I'm good all right, but not that good. Everyone admits the lady was a bitch with a capital B. No strong opinions on the man either way, just that he was odd, standoffish, preoccupied. Some folks had found jobs, some hadn't. All admitted the company was about to fold and leaving with a bit severance pay, no matter how small, was better than being on the street without any."

Traffic started to pick up as they neared downtown. Nothing about this case—make that two cases—was easy. He'd never wrap it up before Jeannie went into labor. That would leave Noah with twice as much work to do. "Nobody worthy of a second look?"

"You might try one guy, Hunter Lassen. He was the shop foreman. For some reason, he was allowed to retire at fifty-five. Took his pension in a lump sum payment. Everyone else left with pennies on the dollar."

At last. An actual lead. "Now we're getting somewhere. I've got one more favor to ask. Could you ask Craig Spencer's secretary what time he left last night?"

"How long have I worked here, Hoss? You think I'm wet behind the ears?"

Nothing would stick behind those ears. What had Conner's father always called some big-eared singer? *Like a taxi with both doors open.*

"That was the first thing I asked. Secretary doesn't know for sure, but he was in his office when she left at five-fifteen."

Conner waited a beat, knowing better than to hurry Earl.

"Security guard says his car was in the lot when he made his rounds at six o'clock but gone at seven."

That jived with his wife's statement. "Thanks, buddy. I owe you one. Can you text me the contact information on the foreman guy?"

Noah pulled into the headquarters parking garage and stopped behind Conner's car. "Why don't I see if I can track down Kelly Manus then check on that financially fortunate foreman while you see what that doctor has to say about the Spencer family? We never had any lunch so the Lieu shouldn't object if we leave early. Tomorrow, we'll dig into that box of paperwork

Madlyn Gwinn's secretary sent over. The secret has to be in there somewhere."

That suited Conner just fine. The sooner he got home and put his arms around Jeannie, the sooner that softball-sized lump in his stomach might ease.

CHAPTER
ELEVEN

A CANARY-YELLOW *SOLD* BANNER was splashed diagonally across the tilting *For Sale* sign in Hunter Lassen's yard. Two muscular workers carried a leather sofa onto a moving van.

Noah parked Lola across the driveway. *Good thing I didn't wait until tomorrow.*

He picked his way around furniture waiting to be loaded and waltzed in through the open front door. "Hello?" His voice echoed in the nearly empty room.

"Back here," a gravelly voice called out.

He followed the sound into a kitchen/breakfast room area filled with enough bric-a-brac to supply a quaint antique store. A middle-aged woman in shorts and an Elvis for President T-shirt stood at a counter wrapping dishes in old newspaper.

"Is Hunter Lassen home?" he asked.

The woman's hands stopped in mid-air, a red, white, and blue ceramic chicken half wrapped. She stared at him, unblinking, for several seconds.

Noah was good at the waiting game. He'd outlasted professional con men, but this woman didn't give in. He'd planned to size up Mr. Lassen before he identified himself, but he might have to wait all afternoon for that to happen and he still had another stop to make.

"I'm Detective Noah Daugherty. I've been assigned to investigate the deaths of Madlyn Gwinn and Craig Spencer. I'd like to ask Mr. Lassen a few questions."

She finished covering the knickknack, set it on the counter, stepped into the breakfast area, and reached for a pack of cigarettes. "Good luck with that, unless you have really good long distance. I hadn't heard about Mr. Spencer, but I doubt anyone shed any tears for Mrs. Gwinn. I know I didn't."

Most people didn't express such open dislike for a murder victim, but Noah suspected she didn't care what he thought.

She pulled a chair up to the kitchen table. "Have a seat Mr.…. Detective—"

"Daugherty. Noah will be fine."

"Sarah Lassen." She tapped the ash off her cigarette into a chipped saucer already overflowing with crushed butts. "Hunter begged me for years to quit. I finally manage and he goes and dies on me. What the hell, my eyes are shot anyway. I've got macular degeneration, the wet kind, and my sight is going fast."

Shit. Another dead end.

"I'm moving to Port Aransas to live in my daughter's garage apartment until that's more than I can manage." She glanced around the room as if seeing it for the first time. Packing boxes, tape, tissue, and newspapers cluttered the little empty space. "What am I supposed to do with all this *stuff*? It all means something to me. I can tell you where everything came from."

She held up a jug that looked like it was made by a two-year-old. "Hunter and I bought this on our first trip to Branson fifteen years ago." She crossed the room and dropped it into a stainless steel trash can. The resulting *claanngg* echoed through the room. "The kids don't care. It's only clutter to them. Wish I had all that money back now, I'm going to need it."

For a moment, Noah couldn't speak. The agonizing pain he'd felt when his sister demanded he clean out Betsy's closet returned and took his breath. *Snap out of it. You're at work here.*

"Can't you sell it? This stuff must be worth something to the right person." He didn't know who that person was, but it took all kinds.

"I took the good pieces to a resale shop, but they'll keep fifty percent of the sale price. Guess I'll take the rest to Goodwill, or maybe leave it here for the new owners to worry about."

Time to get this interview back on track and she'd given him an opening with her comment about money. "I understand your husband was able to leave Beneficial Products at fifty-five and still receive his retirement package. Was that due to his health?"

"No, more likely mine. We were going to travel, see the world while I could. What a joke. Now I get to live in a one-room apartment and impose on my daughter and son-in-law. Doesn't that sound like fun?" She turned her head in a phlegmy cough and stubbed out her half–smoked cigarette. "I'm trying to finish off this pack before my daughter gets here this afternoon. She's insisted I can't smoke at her house. Afraid I won't be able to see what I'm doing and set the place on fire."

She leaned a hip against the kitchen counter. "I'm going to have a cup of coffee. Join me?"

"Sure. If you have enough. Black is fine." Now what? Should he offer his condolences, and for what, the loss of her husband or the loss of her eyesight? One glance said she wasn't in the mood to accept either.

She fussed around for several minutes making coffee and setting the table with matching plates while Noah tried his best not to fidget. He wouldn't have time to check on Kelly if she didn't hurry.

Finally, she sat and pushed a plate of chocolate chip cookies his direction. "My neighbor sent these over as a whatever the opposite of a housewarming gift is."

While accepting a cup of coffee was a ploy he often used to keep a subject talking, he usually avoided taking any type of food. He didn't want anyone saying he was too friendly with a possible suspect or witness. But those cookies smelled *good*.

The English muffin he'd eaten at seven o'clock had long since been forgotten. He took one cookie. It was soft and warm from the oven and the little bits of chocolate were creamy.

Damn. His neighbor, Mrs. Powell, never baked him anything. In fact, he gave her goodies as a *thank you* for watching Sweet Pea if he went out of town or worked late.

He needed better neighbors. Or maybe he needed to actually talk to the neighbors he did have. The only one he knew by name was Ryan Howell and that son-of-a-bitch tried to kill him.

No, he had Rachelle, Emma and Iris, Conner and Jeannie and soon their baby, Earl, Lefty Bob. Why risk opening himself to anyone else who could be snatched away at any moment.

His life was fine the way it was.

Sarah Lassen lit another cigarette and raised her coffee cup to her lips, nearly burning her hair with the glowing ember.

"Hunter's retirement package was severely discounted due to his age and I'm going to need every penny of it if I don't want to be a burden to my kids, but he couldn't work another day under that witch."

"Mrs. Gwinn was that unpleasant an employer?" Finally, someone who was willing to tell the truth.

"I don't know. Hunter never told me. But I do know she did something he couldn't live with. It was eating him up inside so I encouraged him to go up to the front office. Talk to her. And that's what killed him."

Whoa. Did he have another murder on his hands?

"This is what I've pieced together, without him ever saying it directly. That woman gave him three choices. Keep your mouth shut and hold onto your job. Keep your mouth shut and leave with your retirement intact. Or open your mouth and lose everything. He chose retirement, but in the end, he couldn't handle the guilt. He sat in that recliner." She pointed to a ratty faux leather chair with duct tape on the arm rest, "And drank beer and lost interest in life until one day he gave up and died."

Not exactly a murder, but the first person to admit something was wrong with Beneficial Products.

"I begged him to blow the whistle on that company when I saw what it was doing to him, but he'd signed a non-disclosure agreement and was afraid she'd come after everything we had. I thought about hiding the money in an off-shore account, but wasn't sure how to go about that."

He was used to death, saw it every day. But this case was like a cancer itself, eating away at the lives of everyone it touched. "What did Mrs. Gwinn do that he couldn't live with?"

"I couldn't get it out of him no matter how many times I

asked. But you know… babies. I like to think I would have told him, *Fuck your retirement. Speak up.* But who knows when your livelihood is at stake?"

Noah reached for another cookie, but hesitated when he saw a folder with a photo of a white sand beach and palm trees on the cover. Sarah squirmed as he flipped open the packet. Inside were tickets for a cruise leaving Galveston in four days and stopping in the Cayman Islands.

She pushed back and carried her cup into the kitchen for more coffee. "I'm taking my kids and grandkids on a last trip, while I'm able to see them enjoy it."

"Good. The Cayman Islands are beautiful. You should try the snorkeling, if you're up to it. What you shouldn't do is anything stupid. Whatever's happening at Beneficial Products won't stay secret for long. I give you my word."

Conner parked in front of a two-story frame house that had been converted into a professional building. Accented with lavender gingerbread trim, the turquoise and mauve structure reminded him of the painted ladies he and Jeannie had seen in San Francisco on their honeymoon. Had that been four years ago already?

The building was divided into quarters, with two offices upstairs and two down. Dr. Graham's office was on the first floor, across from an acupuncturist. A sign at the foot of the stairs indicated a lawyer and a CPA were located on the second floor.

Conner opened the door to a cheerful, sunshine yellow office. One corner held a mini-playroom with children's books and toys. Only one mother and child waited, seated on primary-colored chairs. Probably the doctor's last patients of the day.

The child curled in the woman's lap didn't look right. Almost unhealthy. Well, sure. He was in a doctor's office. What did he expect?

But this was different. Not a cold or flu. The kid's hair was dull and limp. His skin had a gray pallor. Listless eyes stared at him from a skull that seemed too big for such a malnourished body

The mom didn't look much better.

Maybe he should have taken the plant foreman and let Noah interview the doctor. Obviously he'd turned into some kind of wuss when it came to sick children.

A receptionist in scrubs covered with pictures of playful puppies smiled from behind a window. "Hi there. May I help you?" Her words bubbled across the room.

Conner lowered his voice. No sense scaring an already stressed-out mother. "I don't have an appointment, but I was hoping for a few words with Dr. Graham."

"He only sees pharmacy reps in the morning, before office hours." Her tone cooled, but she remained pleasant.

"I'm Detective Crawford. I want to ask him about Joey Spencer."

Her smiling facade dropped and protective dragon lady came out. "We couldn't discuss a patient's condition without a warrant, maybe not even then."

We? He hadn't asked her a thing. "Why don't we let Dr. Graham decide what he's legally able to tell me?"

"You'll have to wait until he's finished. Patients always come first." She closed the window hard enough that the frosted glass rattled.

Fine with him. Not only was he stubborn enough that he'd outlast the guy if it took all night, but he didn't want the sick kid to have to wait any longer than necessary. Or did he just not want to look into those empty eyes?

Thirty minutes passed before the receptionist, still in dragon mode, called him back.

Dr. Graham's private office bore no resemblance to his outer one. What little Conner could see of his desk under notes, and folders, and reference books was battered and scarred. File cabinets bulged. Medical journals were piled on every surface.

The walls were covered with photos of children, but not smiling babies like in the waiting room. These were candid snapshots of sick kids in hospital rooms, in wheelchairs, with oxygen masks or IVs. Too many were on a black-rimmed bulletin board.

The man himself looked tired. Not end-of-the-day tired, but end-of-life exhausted. His skin sagged and drooped like a bloodhound, but his eyes weren't soulful. They were ice cold.

"I believe Miss Henson informed you that I'm not able or willing to discuss a patient's medical history."

"I'm not looking for confidential information. If I ask you anything you are uncomfortable answering, let me know and I'll move on. Were you aware that Joey Spencer's father passed away late last night or early this morning?"

"Yes, Evie contacted me at home around six-thirty this morning. I called in something to help calm him down while the house was full of strangers."

How many parents had their doctor's personal phone number? Was that unusual?

"Mr. Spencer was in their garage, lifting weights, when the

bar holding the weights fell across his throat, killing him. I was wondering if you thought Joey was capable of making his way to the garage by himself, possibly startling his father and causing him to lose his concentration."

The doctor's eyes may have been cold before but they turned laser hot in an instant. "So you're trying to figure out a way to blame Joey for his father's death? I'd throw you out on your ear if the question wasn't so ludicrous. Hell no. The child is incapable of mobility without help."

"What can you tell me about Mrs. Spencer?"

"Nothing. She's not my patient. Joey is."

"Will she be capable of taking care of Joey by herself?"

"Evie's health, much like Joey's, deteriorates when under stress. In my opinion, she would not have killed her husband. She needs him too much. Do you have any other questions?"

Did he? He'd better think of them now. Dragon lady would never let him back inside. "What's your specialty, doctor?"

"Children. I'm a pediatrician."

"Your patients seem…sicker than most."

"It wasn't intentional. Little by little, I acquired a reputation as someone who would take the time necessary to diagnose and treat rare conditions. Most of these new doctors won't bother. There's no money in it. You can spend half the day with one patient."

Conner leaned back and studied the room. What was it? The man's attitude seemed off. Framed certificates lined a shelf behind the doctor's desk. Some were yellowed with age. The gold leaf still sparkled on others.

A pink and blue cardboard carton with a smiling baby marked *Beneficial Products 100% Organic, High Protein Baby*

Formula caught his eye.

No. Too much of a coincidence. "Is that a product you recommend to your patients?"

A flash of fear crossed the doctor's face before he had time to rearrange his wrinkles. "Occasionally. Not always. Every case, every child is different. If I do, we monitor the patient carefully. If there's no improvement, we move on to something else."

The product was for fragile children. Dr. Graham specialized in at-risk patients. Maybe there was no coincidence.

And maybe the moon was made of green cheese.

Lost Pines Trailer Park hadn't improved any since the last time Noah visited. The paint identifying lot numbers was still faded. Awnings sagged with age. Flies buzzed in the summer air. Not a living soul ventured outside in the heat.

No one answered his knock at Junior Redden's door. Junior's truck was parked where he left it when the Harris County Sheriff's deputies arrested him.

Kelly's multi-colored, duct tape wearing Honda was nowhere to be seen.

A door slammed and the trailer park manager speed-walked across the crushed-shell street. Dewey Lynch hadn't been any help when Junior was trying to kill him and he didn't look in a helpful mood now. An angry red flush covered his face as beads of sweat popped out on his forehead.

"Get away from there. Haven't you caused enough trouble already? Nobody's home and you're not getting in there this time without a warrant. I gave Junior my word I'd keep an eye on things until he gets back."

"I don't need Junior. I'm looking for Kelly."

"Do ya see her car? I threw the bitch out like Junior asked me to."

What the fuck? Did he have the right to do that if she lived there?

The asshole must have read his mind. "The lease is in Junior's name. She don't have no rights that I know of. And neither do you."

Noah tried calling her number one more time, just in case. Inside the trailer, a phone played a pop song he didn't recognize. He swung toward the door and beat on it with his fist. "Kelly, Kelly. Are you okay? It's Noah Daugherty. Answer me."

"Get the fuck away from there." Dewey reached for Noah's arm, but jumped back when he saw his face. "I told you. She's not there. I saw her pack up and drive away myself."

"Her phone's ringing."

"It's not her phone. It's on Junior's plan. He told her to leave it."

What a prick. How did a good-looking woman like Kelly ever stoop to living with a middle-aged loser like Junior?

"Did she leave a forwarding number?"

"Not with me."

Noah studied the old man. A scraggly three-day growth of beard. Twelve gray hairs pointing in different directions and about the same number of teeth. T-shirt containing evidence of every meal for the last week. Shorts hanging loose on his skinny frame. A bulbous nose that looked as if some kid had drawn on it with a red pen.

Yeah. He wouldn't want the guy knowing where he was either.

One more place to try before heading home.

The aroma of spilled beer and stale peanuts assaulted Noah as he waited for his eyes to adjust to the dim lighting. A country song with too much fiddle and too little bass blared through the room. Ten pairs of unfriendly eyes watched as he made his way between stained tables.

He lowered his voice so it wouldn't carry across the room and placed his badge on the counter. "I'm looking for Kelly Manus."

The manager of Cooter's wasn't as disgusting as Dewey Lynch, but only slightly more helpful. "I don't care who you are, I don't give out personal information on my employees to anyone."

He'd tried to do it the easy way, but maybe the guy was nearsighted. Noah shoved his badge under his nose. "I'm not just anybody. I'm a police detective."

"So, get a warrant."

He couldn't get a warrant. He wasn't supposed to be in contact with her. Time to try another track. "I'm worried about her safety if Junior gets out of jail."

"Then I won't tell him, either."

"Junior's not one to take *no* for an answer."

"Let him try."

Junior had nearly killed him. This old guy didn't have a chance.

Noah eyed the manager. He was in good shape for his age, but his age wasn't anything to write home about. Gray hair in a crew cut. Tattoos on both arms—one of which read *USMC*—eyes that could hold a stare without blinking. Somehow, a baseball bat appeared from under the counter. The notches carved in the handle gave Noah pause.

Okay, maybe the guy could take care of himself, but that didn't help in finding Kelly.

The bat made a *pop* as he slapped it against his palm. "I'm holding Kelly's last paycheck. When she contacts me, I'll tell her you want to talk to her. What she does with that information is up to her."

Fair enough. That was all he could ask for.

Of all the people he'd talked to today, Cooter, if that was the guy's name, was the only one up front and honest with him. What did that say about his ability to conduct an investigation?

Hell, even his own partner was keeping secrets from him.

CHAPTER TWELVE

JUNIOR WAS STILL incarcerated and Kelly still AWOL when Noah drove home. The back of his neck got hot every time he thought of those two. Junior might be on his shit list, but at least he understood the guy.

Kelly was another story altogether.

How could she be so foolish? He alternated between anger that she betrayed him and fear for her safety. Once Junior had what he needed, her life wasn't worth a counterfeit nickel. He'd done his best to explain that to her.

Instead, she'd turned on him. Swore she hadn't told Junior who he was or given permission for him to search the trailer or the dumpster.

Most of the charges he could beat. How would he have known where to search and what for if she hadn't told him? He wasn't psychic.

Even if he squashed every accusation, made the whole hot mess disappear, there'd be meetings with lawyers, depositions taken, time and money wasted. That's what infuriated him.

Lola's brakes squealed as he pulled into his driveway, reminding him to put a lid on his personal problems. He had a busy evening and he couldn't face what he needed to do if he was already angry at the world.

Heavy cloud cover kept the heat from dissipating as he piled into Lola forty-five minutes later and headed for the children's hospital. He'd fed Sweet Pea and given her a twenty-minute walk plus five minutes worth of tug-o-war with Mr. Squeaky Man. The one thing he hadn't bothered with was eating something himself.

The smell of antiseptic and the sight of sick children and worried parents would make anything he ate turn sour. And that was *before* he met Joey Spencer and his mom.

Earl was waiting inside the hospital lobby when he arrived, and Danielle scooted in right behind him.

"The air is thick enough to swim in," she said, trying to smooth hair that had expanded to twice its normal volume.

Betsy had hated humid weather. He never understood why. He'd loved her curls.

They checked in and headed up to the rec room where a crowd of kids wearing IV poles, bandages, and pint-sized hospital gowns greeted them. A scattering of adults—some parents, some hospital personnel—ringed the back of the room.

They played every kid's song they could think of for the next hour, ending with a stroll through rooms with patients too sick to join in the fun.

Near the end of the hall, a girl around fourteen or fifteen with a bald head and dangling earrings ignored them as they stood in the doorway. Too good to mix with the little kiddies?

The name on her door read *Madison.* First name or last? He

didn't know.

"Got any requests?" If they could give up one night a week, she could at least pretend to appreciate their efforts.

"I've got to study to have any chance of graduating on time, but if you wanted to do my algebra homework I wouldn't complain." She held up a textbook he hadn't noticed.

"I'd like to act all holy and say you have to do it yourself if you want to learn, but the truth is, I probably don't know how. Are you sure there's nothing we can play for you?" He waited, holding his breath. Truth was, they had only practiced songs geared to young children. Some of the patients in this hospital were older, teenagers. No wonder she wasn't excited about their visit. They needed to expand their repertoire.

"That's okay, but thank you. I know how much this means to some of the kids. They get so scared, anything helps."

Fuck. Sometimes he could be an asshole. "How about this one? We haven't practiced it, but I think we can wing it."

Noah strummed a few cords on his guitar. He hadn't played the song in three months. Not since he sang it in the Chief's office in front of the composer.

The girl leaned back against the bed, a slow smile transforming her features, as she closed her school book.

"When the wind reaches out to grab my hand,
And the stars light the way to Heaven,
I'll think of you lost in that distant land,
I'll dream of you searching for me."

He knew Earl had at least heard the song when Paige Reimer sang it in concert, the night her stalker conked him on the head and nearly killed him. He had no idea what type of music Danielle listened to in her spare time, but they both joined in after the first chorus.

When they finished, the girl clapped, a grin stretching across her face. "Wow. That was great. I love that song."

"Earl and I worked security for the Shadow of Spring concert last April. We got to hear Paige sing it. She's a real nice lady. Someone you'd be proud to know."

Was he? Proud to know her? Yes, although she might not feel the same way about him. He'd treated her shabbily. Sleeping with her one night, then breaking up with her the next time they saw each other.

The secrets she'd kept about her stalker had endangered him, caused Earl and another officer to be injured, and led to Conner having to shoot the bastard and live with the consequences. Consequences he knew all too well ate a hole in your soul.

But Paige'd had no idea how things would spiral out of control.

It wasn't like he'd lived a perfect life. The mistakes he'd made and the secrets he kept even all these years later were ten times worse. Not to mention the final plans he was still considering. He owed Paige an apology, if she'd accept it.

She wasn't a bad person. Just not the person for him. Betsy would never have done those things to promote her career. Would Laurel Bledsoe, the only other woman he'd noticed in the last eleven months?

He didn't think so—the last time he'd seen her she was helping her murdered friend's drug addicted brother get into rehab—but he'd love to find out what she was doing now. Had her divorce come through? Should he call and ask?

No, leave her alone. She deserved better than him. He didn't have anything to offer her.

Wow. Where did that come from? The thought shocked him with such force he took a step back and bumped into Danielle.

Earl spoke from somewhere behind him. "Time to call it a night. Thanks, miss, for letting us play for you."

"My pleasure. I'd say I look forward to hearing you again next week, but I hope to be out of here by then."

Noah saluted her with his guitar. "Then I'll say I hope we never see you again."

He turned off the radio on the drive home. He had some serious thinking to do. Last spring he'd been too hard on Paige Reimer. This week he'd done the same thing with Kelly Manus, Wade Gwinn, and Evie Spencer. Just because his life was shit was no reason to take it out on other people.

It wasn't good for him personally and it wasn't good detective work. He needed to learn to keep an open mind until he knew all the facts. Wade Gwinn had means, motive, and opportunity, but he loved his wife. Same for Evie Spencer. Her husband might be a jerk, but he was her jerk and she loved him.

He didn't know about Kelly Manus, but he'd give her the benefit of the doubt until he located her and asked.

Junior Redden didn't deserve any consideration. That son-of-a-bitch was going down.

"Back here," Jeannie called.

Something smelled delicious and Conner followed his nose to the kitchen. "What are you doing in here? You're supposed to have your feet up, resting. I said I'd cook supper." Every time he saw her on her feet, he had an irrational fear her water would break and she'd go into premature labor. After seeing Joey

Spencer today, maybe the fear wasn't so irrational.

"I couldn't stay on that sofa watching game shows for one more minute. I put a roast on to cook this morning along with carrots and potatoes. I was checking to see if it was ready. It is and you're up."

"Let me take over from here. I'll do everything, including the dishes, if you'll promise to *sit down*. I thought you were going to spend the day reading."

She replaced the lid on the crock pot and waddled to the nearest chair, letting out an *ooof* as she sat. "Finished my book an hour ago. Why is it when you have loads to do, you wish you could put your feet up and read, but when all you're allowed to do is read, you're dying to get up and move around? And, I've got to tell you, this dreary weather hasn't done my mood any good. How was your day?"

He certainly didn't intend to tell her about meeting Joey Spencer. No reason to upset her. She was a stronger person than he was, though. Always had been. "Nothing particularly interesting. It's looking like neither Madlyn Gwinn's husband nor Craig Spencer's wife killed their spouse. Tomorrow we dig deep into Beneficial Products' records. Try to figure out who has a grudge against the management."

"Come on. Take pity on me. I'm bored out of my skull. What about Noah's lawsuit, anything happening there? How's he taking it?"

"The guy suing him is locked up, but the witness who could clear him is missing. I suspect he needs to hire Tom Meyers, but the mood he's in, he'd bite my head off if I suggested it."

"I thought he was doing better these days."

"He was for a while. I hate to say this, it makes me sound like a romance novel, but I believe he needs to find a woman."

Jeannie shot him that secret smile that sent waves of warmth surging through his body. "Of course he does. That's not a romance novel, that's real life."

"He improved, briefly, when he met Laurel Bledsoe. I'm fairly certain nothing happened there, except he realized being happy wouldn't dishonor Betsy's memory. Then last spring, no matter how much he denies it, he had a fling with Paige Reimer. Whatever it was, it didn't last long. I'm not sure why. I thought they were a good match."

"Rebound woman. She wasn't what he wants, but she was what he needed at the time. Anyway, a woman isn't his problem right now, unless that woman is me."

What the hell was she talking about? Noah didn't have any feeling for Jeannie except friendship. He'd bet his pension on that.

"He's worried about me, and you, and the baby, and what's going to happen when you take off on family leave. You know he texts to check on me almost every day?"

No, he hadn't known that, but he wasn't surprised. A warmth, different than the kind Jeannie inspired, settled in his heart.

Jeannie shifted her considerable girth in search of a more comfortable position and Conner's heart froze until she settled down. What he wouldn't give to be able to carry some of that weight for her. Hold it so she could sleep, sit or stand, walk across the room with her old fluid grace.

"Noah's worried after you take your leave, you won't want to come back to Homicide. That you'll ask for a transfer to a less demanding department."

What? He'd never said a word to make his partner think

that. He'd kept it buried in the back of his mind. "Did he say that to you?"

Her Mona Lisa smile returned. "He didn't have to. It's exactly what you'd have been thinking if your positions were reversed."

Conner busied himself making gravy while the succulent aroma of Jeannie's roast filled the room. Who was he kidding, claiming he was helping her? He'd have been making the gravy anyway. Jeannie had many, many talents, but gravy wasn't one of them. And fussing around the kitchen while she rested helped him more than her. He was the one who had become a nervous wreck.

He grabbed a spoon from the drawer for a taste. Personally, he'd like a bit more salt, but if Jeannie couldn't have any, neither could he. Other than that, perfect. Worrying hadn't made him lose his touch.

Jeannie took a sip from the glass of water he set in front of her. "Have you talked to Noah?"

"No. Every time I try, the phone rings or the Lieu calls us into his office." *Or I see Joey Spencer and chicken out.*

"Don't wait too long. He's your best friend. Talk to him."

"About which development?"

"Both of them."

CHAPTER
THIRTEEN

THE SKY HAD been a uniform gray all day. Like the entire world was wrapped in a flannel blanket.

That worked.

Sunshine would have been an invitation to go outside. Take a walk. Plan a trip to the beach. Picnic in the park. Things that were never going to happen.

Gray was a stay inside day. Make a list day. Plan the next step day.

Even so, concentration was a problem. The yellow legal pad lay on the coffee table, still blank. The felt-tipped pen sat beside it, silent, as the gray sky threatened to turn black. Another day wasted. Time to make a decision and act on it.

Where to start? At the bottom and work up, or at the top and work down?

So far, the police had no idea, not a clue, not an inkling. What idiots. How many more bodies before they caught on? Did that mean it was best to start at the bottom, with someone they would never suspect was involved, or go straight to the top—the most evil among them—while there was time?

Ah, time. Sweet time. Marching steadily on and on with no way to slow it down. What was the old saying, *Time is wasted on the young*?

To a kid with the whole of life stretching down the road, a week, a day lasted forever. Time meant nothing. Morning slipped into evening and they laughed and played as another day they could never get back bit the dust.

The only ones more oblivious were teenagers. For them, time was a thing to waste. Daydreaming, texting, and of course, all that social media crap: Twitter, Snapchat, Instagram. They didn't comprehend the joy of being truly *with* someone: feeling their touch, smelling their hair, watching their eyes, tasting their sweetness with a soft kiss. What did they know? They thought they were infallible. Ha. They'd learn all too soon.

Learn that one day you awoke and time had passed you by. An hour lasted an instant. A day was a glimpse through a bullet train window. *Time and tide wait for no man.* And who the hell cared about the tide? Ships had engines now. They could leave when they wanted, not be stuck inside, waiting, waiting, waiting.

A list was pointless. There might be time for only one more, and that person had to count.

There was one. Too evil to rank near the bottom but separate enough not to be suspected of involvement. And old enough to pass for natural causes.

That way, if the fates allowed, there was the possibility of squeezing in an additional one or more before the end.

If time was kind and allowed the *pause* button to be pressed. If only this once.

And if the rain held off for another hour so the old devil could follow his usual routine.

So many ifs.

But for now, a plan had been made and action was the best antidote.

Rodney Graham took a sip of single malt scotch and puckered his lips. Damn. Getting old was hell. Nothing on his body worked right anymore and now his taste buds were going. He might as well buy the blended stuff. He couldn't tell the difference.

The plastic cushions on the patio chair had soaked in the heat from the summer day and soothed his aching back. He set the glass on the wrought iron table and gazed around him at the expanse of perfectly manicured lawn rolling down to Braes Bayou. If he squinted his eyes just right, he could almost see his kids playing tag or chasing lightening bugs with the dog at their heels and Marcie laughing and running with them.

He'd always been too busy to join in. There were professional journals to read and articles to write and connections to make. They never understood he did it all for them.

The kids were grown and busy with their own lives now. Rodney Junior a partner in that fancy law firm, Harold in New York doing something he didn't understand with stock—*please, please, please, let it be something legal*—and Robin with her face plastered all over the side of busses hawking real estate. Even the grandkids thought they were too grown-up to come over and play or keep an old man company.

If he wanted laughter, he'd have to wait for great-grandkids.

But a guy could die waiting for that to happen.

So why did he keep this big old house? For the memories? With Marcie gone two years, the memories were fading, and the walls gave off a chill that went straight to his bones.

All the memories weren't good ones.

He'd pulled every string he could find, twisted every arm, to get her into new and improved clinical trials. Each one made her sicker instead of better until finally she begged him to let her go. He could never deny her anything. Why hadn't he picked that decision to fight her on?

For the first time, he was glad he hadn't. She wouldn't have to see what he'd done. The pain he'd caused. All for nothing. She'd died anyway.

He lifted the heavy, cut crystal glass, inhaling deeply before taking a sip. The scent of scotch warmed him more than the actual drink.

Now what? Go public and stop this madness or keep his peace and let nature take its course? So far, the only ones harmed had deserved everything they got. Was his legacy, his good name, worth saying nothing?

He tried to take another sip, but the glass was an enormous weight in his hand. His arm dropped and the glass settled in his lap before it tipped, spilling the last few precious drops.

Footsteps sounded behind him, but he didn't have the energy to turn his head. The gray day had faded into a dull evening. Somewhere behind the clouds, the sun was setting without ever having made an appearance. He would have liked to watch the stars as he drifted away, but no light could escape the blanket of darkness above him.

A shadowy form took shape in front of him. He studied the

figure through half-closed lids. "I've been expecting you."

"Then why didn't you unseal a new bottle of scotch?"

"*Que sera,sera.* If you came, you came, and I didn't have to make a decision. Is this it? Are you satisfied?"

"I'll never be satisfied."

He struggled to lift his drooping head. "You realize you won't get away with this. The police will figure it out."

A harsh laugh blew warm breath across his face. "You better hope not. If they do, all your good work will have been for nothing. Your name will be dirt. But you don't need to worry. Your reputation is safe. You're an old man with trembling hands and a heart condition. Dead wife, indifferent kids, forced out of your job. Who wouldn't believe you committed suicide?"

Was that right? Was he that obvious? Worse, would anyone care he was gone? His kids would put on a show, crying in public, rubbing their hands over their anticipated inheritance in private. Wait until they discovered how little was actually left.

His eyes closed. Sleep crept nearer. A disembodied voice whispered in his ear. "I have only one regret. That I couldn't arrange for you to suffer. To spend days crying until your throat was raw. Your stomach cramping. Your breath ragged. You're getting off much too easy."

That was true. He welcomed death. If only he could see Marcie one more time before God decided which direction to send him.

CHAPTER
FOURTEEN

NOAH GLANCED UP when Conner set an extra-large coffee from the shop across the street on his desk. Damn. He'd kiss the guy if he was better looking. The brown sludge from the vending machine hardly smelled like coffee, much less tasted like it. Yet he continued to buy it every morning in the unfounded hope it would improve.

His only worry was that Conner had something up his sleeve. And about time, too. He was tired of waiting for the guy to come out with whatever he'd been bottling up the last week.

"Thanks." He reached into his pocket. "How much I owe ya?"

"Don't worry. I've got it."

Shit. This can't be good.

Conner took the plastic lid off his coffee and blew gently to cool it down. Steam billowed up, making him blink. "Learn anything last night?"

Two can play this game, old partner. I'll go along until you're willing to admit what's bothering you.

"That Junior Redden is an even bigger prick than I thought. He kicked Kelly out and took her phone. No one seems to know where she's gone, but her boss promised to let her know I'm looking for her if she ever comes in to pick up her paycheck."

"As long as Junior doesn't know where she is either, she should be safe."

Maybe, but Junior was closer to her than anyone. He might have an idea where she'd go. "I couldn't find any record of her family, but I asked Earl to check. He's better at it than I am."

Conner must have decided his coffee was the right temperature because he took a sip. "I'm worried about you going around asking for her when you've been warned to stay away and not influence her testimony. Maybe I should be the one looking for her."

And put Conner's career in jeopardy when Jeannie was so close to giving birth? No way. "You're not supposed to talk to her, either. Let's wait. See if she contacts me. If we learn Junior's getting out, then we'll worry. And speaking of worry, what I found out about Hunter Lassen is of more immediate importance."

"Who's Hunter Lassen?"

Conner was really off his game if he'd forgotten that. "The lucky foreman who left with his pension intact while everyone else got a smile and a kick out the door."

"Right. What'd he have to say?"

"Pension was contingent on signing a non-disclosure agreement."

"So what's he not supposed to disclose?"

"Don't know. His wife says it was eating him up, but he died before he told her what was going on other than he couldn't work there any longer."

"Not another murder."

"No, heart attack. What about your guy, the doctor? Did he have anything to add?"

"Joey Spencer could not have made it into the garage on his own and his mother's health is such that she needs her husband to help take care of him. I didn't like the guy, he seemed too nervous, but answering questions about patients is something that causes all doctors a moral dilemma. The thing that bothered me most was the package of Beneficial Products baby formula sitting in his office."

Damn. Another complication. "I don't like it, but he *is* a baby doctor."

"I know. I chewed on that all night. First thing this morning I called Earl and asked him to run a background check on the good doctor."

"Damn. What are we going to do without Earl? We might have to learn to look this stuff up ourselves." He'd say Earl was worth his weight in gold, but skinny as the guy was, that wasn't enough.

"It seems the doc is famous. Around here, at least. Past president of every pediatric society in the county. Beloved by rich and poor alike. Miracle worker with high-risk kids. Which leads me to another subject we need to discuss."

Slap

Conner jumped as a manila folder slammed onto his desk. His coffee flew out of his cup like a Yellowstone geyser, landing on his desk, his shirt, and his pants.

Lefty Bob's voice was a low growl, like a dog that had spotted the mailman coming up the walk. "I'm getting tired of this shit."

Noah reached over to grab the file as Conner wiped spilled coffee off his desk. Judging by the weight, the folder only held a couple of pages and no name appeared on the front. "What shit is that?"

"You two lightweights stealing all my easy cases."

"Would you consider Dr. Graham depressed?"

Dragon Lady had lost her fire and slumped in her chair, refusing to look Conner in the face.

"I guess that's what you'd call it. He had Parkinson's. His hands shook. So far, he'd been able to control it with medication, but the tremors were getting worse. A couple of times last week he spilled his coffee. He used to talk about retiring and how he and his wife would travel, but after she died, he buried himself in his work."

Conner stole a sideways glance at his partner. If anyone knew about using work to mask pain, Noah did, but the big guy didn't react.

Taking over Dr. Graham's suicide from Lefty Bob gave them additional work just when they were trying to clear their case load, but it also gave them extra time to solve Madlyn Gwinn and Craig Spencer's deaths. If they could figure out why the doctor chose last night to kill himself, it might set them on the right track.

With Jeannie's due date so close, Conner's frustration tolerance was at an all-time low. Bumbling around in the dark on any case set him on edge. When the crime involved multiple murders, it drove him mad.

They'd decided on the way over he should take the lead since he was more familiar with the doctor and his staff. "What about money? That fancy house on the bayou must take a lot of upkeep. Could he handle that if he stopped working?"

"That would be his personal business and I wouldn't have any idea about that. Although…" She dropped her head even lower. "There was a time, when his wife was sick, that funds were tight. None of the office staff got a raise for a couple of years. I know he was sending her for all kinds of experimental treatments. Scams, if you ask me. Anyway, he was a real grouch and she didn't get any better."

She was surprised the man was grouchy when his wife was dying? Noah's wife had been gone for eleven months and he was still hell to be around on a bad day. And for someone who didn't know about the doctor's personal business, she sure was well informed. Might as well see what else he could find out.

"What about his family, were they close?"

"They weren't what you'd call *estranged* or anything but they were all busy. They didn't see much of each other."

Yep, she knew it all. Probably could have told him how much the guy had in the bank. He'd softened her up with the low-ball questions, now for the kicker.

"I noticed a carton of Beneficial Products baby formula when I was talking to the doctor yesterday. Was that something he recommended? My wife and I are about to have a baby, so I wondered."

"Doc loved that stuff. You can get it in the store, but he kept a large supply of it here and sold it at a discount. I don't know what I'm supposed to do with it."

Her face lit up and Conner knew he'd hit on something. "Would you like to buy some? You could be all ready when your baby comes. We have it in all concentrations for infants to older kids who have trouble digesting regular food. You were asking about Joey Spencer? He used to take it as a supplement until the last year or so. I should call Mrs. Spencer. She might want to stock up before the office closes. In case he has a bad spell."

Why did he suspect any money would go straight into her pocket instead of the office coffers? "You know, why don't I take one? My wife's planning to nurse the baby, but it never hurts to have a backup for an emergency."

Dragon Lady scurried off to find a carton before he changed his mind.

"There's one born every minute," Noah whispered under his breath.

"Hey, I want to see what all the fuss is about."

Dragon Lady returned, but she was no longer a fire-breather. Now she was the smiling Pollyanna that greeted him the first time.

"That'll be $68. I'll give you a break and not charge you tax." She stopped short when it dawned on her she was talking to two police officers. "I mean, the doc already paid the tax."

Conner almost choked on his tongue. $68? The container was smaller than a carton of oatmeal. He'd never priced any formula, and it might be expensive, but $68?

Behind him, Noah made an unnatural sound that he tried to pass off as a cough.

He was trapped now. He couldn't refuse. He'd never convince the Lieu to reimburse him. And Noah would hold it over his head for the rest of his life.

Plus there wasn't any sales tax on baby formula. If she'd tried to charge him, he'd have arrested her on the spot.

Noah wrinkled his nose. The house smelled stale, like unwashed clothes or old shoes. The doctor had only been dead a day and his home had the feel of an abandoned museum. The inside had a worn, tired look that contrasted with the outside.

Putting on a front for the neighbors? The world?

The walls needed a fresh coat of paint. The sofa sagged. The recliner—surrounded by an old man's detritus of TV remotes, reading glasses, and pill bottles—was threadbare. The kitchen appliances were outmoded and chipped.

Nothing had been updated in years. Was this lack of funds or lack of interest?

The house was definitely old money as opposed to new like Madlyn's neighborhood. But it was big money, nevertheless. More money than most hardworking citizens saw in a lifetime.

And that fact chapped at Noah. Why did one old man who worked long hours need this much space? Even his thoughts would echo in rooms the size of a basketball court.

Another case of obscene greed.

A red light on the TV caught Noah's eye. He picked up the remote to see what the old man was recording.

A WWII documentary about the Battle of the Bulge came on, the footage in black and white. Noah went to *scheduled recordings*. The guy must have been a history buff. Different programs on varied aspects of war were set to record over the next week.

Some were series where one click set a recording for every episode, but others were individual showings and had to be specifically programmed.

Noah turned off the TV and set down the remote. When he did, an appointment book fell off the table. An entry for noon on Saturday said: Lunch with Robin and Dannie. Here. Order seafood salad from Brennan's. Call cleaning service.

Why would a guy bother to record programs a week or more in advance if he was set on killing himself? And why would he do it two days before his daughter and granddaughter were due to come over? A man like Graham would know exactly the condition his body would be in after that long in the Texas sun.

He'd seen corpses left to rot and he wouldn't wish it on his worst enemy. Did Graham hate his family that much or did this suicide stink like garbage left under the sink too long?

Conner came in the French doors, blotting his face with the handkerchief he always carried in his back pocket. "He had a glass of scotch and an empty bottle of hydrocodone on the table beside his chair. I called his doctor. The prescription was old, from last winter when his back went out. Supposedly, Graham never took but one pill because it upset his stomach."

Noah had tried hydrocodone for a toothache once. It made his head spin like a seven day drunk. He never finished the bottle, but he didn't throw it away, either. Had Graham been planning ahead?

And was that what *he'd* been doing when he saved his bottle?

He shook the thought from his head. "I've been listening to the M.E. bitch. Seems the sprinklers went off while he was examining the body. The Prima Donna. He thinks the scene should be in picture perfect condition for him to work."

"Yeah, Crime Scene isn't too happy either. They can't tell one set of footprints from another. I keep thinking about this morning. My favorite receptionist sure was in a rush to convince us Graham killed himself. Did that bother you?"

"It didn't at the time. It's starting to now. But then you resent her because she took you for $68." He tried never to laugh at crime scenes, but sometimes he couldn't help it.

Conner ignored the dig. "We don't even have the autopsy for Spencer yet and now we have Graham. The bodies are stacking up in the morgue faster than firewood before a Montana winter."

"Spencer is scheduled for first thing in the morning. I'll call the Lieu and see if he can get the M.E.'s office to at least start a tox screen on this guy. Maybe that will tell us something."

"Why don't you go back to the office, see what Earl dug up on the doctor and put a bug in the Lieu's ear about the M.E. and, while you're at it, see if he'll light a fire under the lab to tell us what's in this stuff." Conner handed him the carton of baby formula. "I wouldn't feed this overpriced slop to a starving rat."

The black cloud that had descended on him when he stepped inside lifted a millimeter at the thought of leaving. "I would like to get moving on this. Who knows? Earl could have solved this turkey while we're standing around talking. What about you?"

"I'll stay until the scene is cleared, then get one of the guys to drop me back at headquarters. On the way home I want to stop at the grocery store and see what formula is supposed to cost." Conner pulled out his cell phone. "Think I'll call the pediatrician Jeannie has lined up and ask for an opinion on Beneficial Products."

"He might not know about special needs kids."

"She. And yes, she does. The problem's going to be getting hold of her. She's always busy. Hard to get in to see."

"Okay. We'll touch base in the morning. See where we stand." Noah swung around and bolted for the door. He couldn't get out of this dreary place fast enough. Maybe the old guy did kill himself. He'd want to if he lived here.

They'd been on this case a week and didn't have a viable suspect, but they were getting close. Something was about to break. He could feel it in his bones.

Noah turned the corner in Lola when he spotted a faded pink Sentra coming the opposite direction. Behind the wheel, a head of gray, Don King hair. R.J. Perry from the *Chronicle*. He'd have to text Conner to be careful when leaving.

The vultures were closing in.

CHAPTER
FIFTEEN

NOAH'S PLASTIC CHAIR let out a *whoosh* as he plopped down. The stack of papers and reports on his desk, waiting for his attention, almost made him wish he were back at Dr. Graham's.

Earl swiveled to face him. "You still interested in former employees of Beneficial Products?"

Hell, so much had gone on the last couple of days, he'd almost forgotten. "Hit me with it." Anything was better than filling out reports.

"The nicest thing anyone called Madlyn Gwinn was a bitch. And believe me, I heard some other colorful names. I even learned a couple of new ones. I put the list on your desk, giving each pissed off employee a number on the anger scale from one to five. The only thing is, there were no fives."

"I thought you said they were mad."

"They were. They cussed and vented and told me tails that made *me* mad. But I didn't find anyone who exhibited that final degree of animosity, a fury that led me to believe they would do anything about it."

Well, shit. So they were back at the starting line? Nobody, nothing, no clues, no trail to follow?

Earl rubbed his hand over a face so thin it looked like a skull covered in parchment paper. A chill ran over Noah, the kind his mother used to describe as someone walking across her grave. He'd lost so much in his life. He couldn't afford to lose a friend.

"I did the best I could, but I'll be the first to admit, phone interviews can only go so far. I didn't look them in the eye, see that little hesitation before answering. Couldn't watch them squirm."

Yep. He'd never had much faith in phone interviews. If he didn't get a break soon, he might have to drive all over the state re-interviewing these people. Fun times. "What about Kelly Manus?"

"I can't find anything about her."

"You mean she's using a fake identity?" Was she in hiding? If so, from him or from Junior?

"I didn't say that. I said *I* couldn't find her. I can track down someone who's out there, on the internet. Posting on Facebook, Snapchatting, Instagramming, whatever. Anything more difficult than that, I'm lost. The guys in Computer Crimes could probably find her in five minutes."

Then he was shit-out-of-luck. He couldn't search for her using official channels. And he couldn't ask Dewy or Junior. That left hoping she contacted Cooter.

"Did you learn anything about Dr. Graham?" The doctor certainly wouldn't be posting selfies for his patients' entertainment. The thought of that old man posing in his undies, making a duckface gave Noah the willies.

"Now *he* is a different story. Conner called me twenty minutes ago with the guy's password. Seems he had it taped to his computer. I'd laugh, but I do the same thing. Going back a few years, his bank records paint an interesting story." Earl came to an abrupt halt. "This is all, what'd they call it? *Off the record.* Background information only. I definitely didn't hack into his bank account. And I certainly didn't tell you anything that would require a warrant."

"Tell me anything? I'm not even here. I haven't seen you all day."

"The old guy was making a decent living. Not obscene money, but more than you or I'll ever see. Probably more than the mayor or Chief. His practice was thriving, he sat on a few boards, gave the occasional speech. He paid all his bills on time and socked away a healthy chunk for retirement. His house was only a couple of years from being paid off. Then the wife got sick and things changed."

Yeah, that would do it. Maybe the doctor did commit suicide. Hell, the thoughts he'd had—still did have—he didn't have any right to point fingers. "So the guy was broke?"

Earl gave his best steely glare, but since his accident, he couldn't hold it long. "You want to hear the story or just jump to conclusions yourself?"

He wanted the abbreviated version, but if he had any hope of Earl helping him again, he'd have to sit through every long, boring detail.

"I'm guessing he cut back on his hours, because his practice fell off to barely covering rent and salaries. He resigned from all boards and didn't accept speaking engagements. This lasted for more than a year. Then his expenses started going up. First he hired a day nurse, then twenty-four hour care. He started dipping into his savings a little at a time. Nothing drastic."

Noah bit back a sigh. If he stopped Earl now, he'd never get to whatever pot of gold he was holding for last.

"About eight months before she died, money started flowing out like he'd turned on a tap. That's when he refinanced his house. When that ran out, he got behind on bills. He didn't pay his mortgage for three months in a row. The finance company was dunning him daily."

"What was he doing with the money?"

"He was paying every, sham, fake, fraudulent scam artist, imposter posing as his wife's savior with a newly discovered medical miracle that could be his for only x amount of money. He even had her flown to Costa Rica in a private jet for a ten-day stem cell treatment."

So the guy was broke, and depressed, and about to lose his house. And probably suicidal. Even the bitter brew the vending machine passed off as coffee wouldn't keep him awake if Earl didn't get to the point.

"That's when the tide turned."

Noah's eyes shot open. A yawn died in his throat. Now the story got interesting? After listening to Earl yammer on for five minutes?

"In one day, he paid off his credit card bills, including the one covering his trip to Costa Rica. He took care of the overdue electric and water bills—for his home and office—and caught up on his mortgage."

A bolt of energy surged through Noah. The heaviness he'd felt since entering Dr. Graham's house vanished along with the sound of computers, printers, and phone conversations that made up the background hum of a busy office. "Where'd he get the money?"

"Don't know. Maybe the computer whizzes can follow the money trail. Backed up as they are, you'd probably have to wait a month or more to get your ass in the door."

Shit. Nothing helpful. "Can you tell me anything I can use?"

"I can tell you this. All those so-called friends dropped him when he no longer contributed to their fancy causes. Only one person still loved him. Madlyn Gwinn. She called him every day for two weeks before his windfall. She sent him take-out dinners from expensive restaurants. Arranged for a cleaning service. And, best of all, sent him a bucket load of Beneficial Products inventory which he's been singing the praise of to anyone who'd listen for the last year and a half. Something he'd never done before he and Madlyn Gwinn got all buddy-buddy. As past president of every pediatric origination in the county, he influenced a lot of baby doctors."

That didn't even count the stock he'd kept for himself, to sell to unsuspecting patients. If the guy hadn't killed himself, he might dig him up and kill him again.

Noah drummed his fingers on Lola's steering wheel. Right now, he had only one clear-cut case of murder. Madlyn Gwinn. Not a pleasant woman. She made enemies wherever she went. Everyone who crossed paths with the woman wanted her to eat shit and die.

Only no one wanted to do the job themselves.

Logic told him to wait for tomorrow. Until then, he didn't

know for sure anything untoward *had* happened to Craig Spencer or Rodney Graham.

But logic never had been his strong point.

Rachelle had invited him for supper, but if he arrived too early, he'd have to talk to Frank. It wasn't that he disliked his brother-in-law, just that they didn't seem to have anything in common. He tried, really he did, but he could never find a topic of conversation other than fishing. Something he didn't find exciting.

Maybe he did dislike the guy a little. Hopefully, not simply because no one was good enough to marry his sister.

Craig Spencer's home wasn't exactly *on the way* to Rachelle's, but it wasn't *out of the way* either. He could swing by his Carrelton Street address and ask Evie Spencer's opinion on Dr. Graham. Maybe get a better feel for the guy. Find out his relationship with Beneficial Products.

Then get to Rachelle's in time to play with Emma and Iris before supper. He'd have to hurry if he wanted to stop at the *golden arches* for a hamburger first. Rachelle hadn't said what she was serving. If it was another tofu casserole, he didn't want to arrive hungry.

He pulled into the Spencer's driveway as the man next door made the turn with his lawnmower. The man was tall and skinny and winter pale despite the July sun. His dishwater-blond hair dripped sweat.

Noah nodded as he stepped out of Lola and the man switched off his mower.

"Looking for Evie?"

Was the guy being helpful or protective? Either way, no reason to be secretive. He opened his coat far enough to show his badge, but not his weapon. "Yeah, Detective Noah Daugherty. I hate to disturb her, but I had a couple of quick questions I wanted to ask."

The man wiped his palm on the leg of his shorts and shook Noah's hand. "Brandt Kittrell. Sorry, you just missed her. I helped her load Joey into the car not ten minutes ago. Lucky thing I was home. Don't know how she'd have managed otherwise."

"That's right. She said her neighbor often helped her with Joey." Now what, head over to Rachelle's?

"She was probably talking about my wife. Chelsea used to help Evie all the time before she got too sick."

More sick people. Had there always been this many out there and he never noticed? "What about Evie's sister? I thought she was going to move down and help her."

"Didn't work out. She told me her sister has to work another year or two before she's eligible for retirement and full benefits. She's planning to hire someone, but she's worried about a stranger living in her home. And now she's on the search for a new doctor."

"That's kind of why I'm here. I wanted to know what she could tell me about Dr. Graham."

"Yeah, I heard about that. Poor old man. Nothing left to live for if he couldn't work."

Maybe, but the neighbor didn't look that torn up about it. "Did you know the doctor?"

The lawnmower suddenly became a thing of interest as Brandt knelt down and fiddled with the gas cap. "We used him for a while. Evie recommended him when our son... When Aaron..."

Now the height adjustment on the mower needed attention

as Brandt kept his back to Noah.

This wasn't going to be easy. Best to come right out and ask the guy. "What can you tell me about Dr. Graham and any relationship he might have had to Beneficial Products and Craig Spencer?"

"Not sure we ever met the caring, compassionate physician Evie raved about for Joey. The man I met, and I realize I didn't go to every appointment because I was working, was cold and standoffish. Chelsea stopped her chemotherapy when she discovered she was pregnant, but it wasn't soon enough. Aaron was born at six months and he wasn't fully developed."

Brandt threw down the greasy rag he was holding and sat on the grass. Noah squatted beside him. The day smelled of oil and gasoline and new-mown lawn with a hint of ozone that held the promise of rain. The sun reflected off the cement driveway in waves. Sweat coated Noah's forehead, but he didn't mop it off.

"He was such a tiny thing. No bigger than a can of soup. He looked perfect on the outside, but he couldn't digest food. He did all right the first two weeks—not great, but adequate— while Chelsea nursed him, but her doctor insisted she go back on chemo. Said Aaron was going to need his mamma."

Sobs broke out as Brandt lowered his face into his hands. Noah kept his mouth shut and let him talk. "Dr. Graham really pushed that Beneficial Products formula. It's organic which means no chemicals to upset sensitive stomachs and it has a higher percentage of protein which was supposed to help Aaron since he could manage only a little at a time. I didn't like the guy personally, but there's no doubt he saved Joey's life several times and he did his best for Aaron. The little fella just wasn't strong enough."

"Does Joey take the stuff?"

"Not any time recently, at least. He's older and has a different type of problem. The formula is ridiculously expensive. I asked Craig if he could get me some for free or at a discount. Hell, maybe there were some cartons that had the label printed upside down or something, but no, he couldn't. Or wouldn't. He advised me to use a different brand. Said there wasn't that much difference."

"And did you?"

"Chelsea wouldn't hear of it. The great and wonderful Dr. Graham said it was the best so there you have it. I went into debt, Aaron died, and Chelsea's cancer came back with a vengeance. None of it anybody's fault. Just…bad luck, I guess. Who knows? I must have done something evil in a previous life 'cause I know for sure it couldn't have been Chelsea."

Noah couldn't speak for a moment. The idea of losing both a wife and a baby hit too close to home. His football knee gave a loud *crack* as he pushed off the cement, anxious to change the subject. "Do you think I could talk to Chelsea? You said you didn't know the man that well."

"You can try. She gave up on the chemo and started taking some new experimental drug. It leaves her with good days and bad. Today's a bad one."

Without another word, the man pivoted and strode across the lawn. Noah followed him into the darkened house.

Good thing he didn't believe in ghosts or he'd have turned and run. Chelsea's skin was as washed out as the white face-paint clowns used, broken only by a bright red scarf wound turban-like around her head.

She sat propped, her back against the arm of the sofa, with a blanket over her knees, staring at a TV with the sound off. What little Noah could see of her body was cadaverously thin.

"Honey." Brandt took her hand. "This is Noah. He's a detective. He wants to ask you a few questions. Are you up to talking to him?"

She gave something that might pass as a smile. "I'm much better now. That peppermint tea you fixed me did the trick. Thanks."

"Then I'll head back outside and finish my mowing before the rain starts." He put a hand on Noah's shoulder and whispered "Don't tire her out."

Chelsea's voice was velvet soft. "What can I do for you, Detective? Seldom as I leave this house, I doubt I know anything that would interest you."

"I only wanted your opinion on a couple of things. What can you tell me about Dr. Rodney Graham?"

A tiny spark might have lit her eyes for an instant, but was gone before he could be sure.

"The world famous physician? Beloved by patients and colleagues alike? What is it Detective, do you need a recommendation for a pediatrician?"

"No. I'm checking into his death."

"Brandt told me about that a little while ago. What can I say that you don't already know? Sort of like the Great and Powerful Oz, don't look too close or you'll see the man behind the curtain."

"What makes you say that?"

"Oh, how the mighty have fallen. His hands shook, his voice was weak, his eyes were going. He wouldn't be able to work much longer. But he was nearly broke. Nothing to leave those spoiled, ungrateful kids of his. He'd spent every dime he had on dubious cures for his wife. Something I'm trying to avoid with Brandt."

Noah's eyes adjusted to the gloomy room. A family portrait hung over the mantel. Brandt, an infant he assumed was Aaron, and Chelsea, her hair long and glossy. They stood in front of an azalea bush in full bloom. On another wall, a shadow-box displayed a photo of Chelsea wearing the colors of the USA with a gymnastics gold medal mounted below.

Which would be worse? To never know a day of good health, like Joey, or to have a life filled with physical accomplishments like Chelsea or professional achievements like Dr. Graham only to have it snatched away?

Noah mentally shook his head and focused on Chelsea. "Your husband said you were trying a new treatment."

"So new it's considered experimental. And the experiments haven't gone well. All this is costing me is an uber cab ride to the Medical Center and back once a week. I'm doing this for Brandt. So he'll feel he's done everything possible to save me. Because we couldn't save Aaron. He wanted to drive me but, if he lost his job, bye-bye insurance. Then we'd be up shit creek."

She took a sip from a mug on the table beside her, made a face and set it down again. "My first treatment didn't really bother me. The second left me queasy for a couple of hours, but nothing I couldn't ignore. Today was my third and I threw up in the cab on the way home, in the front yard, and in the kitchen sink. Don't stand too close because it could happen again any minute. When you came in, I was sitting here trying to decide if there'd be a fourth. Say this stuff works and buys me a month, even two. At what cost if I spend the time on this sofa or hunched over the toilet? When I quit chemo, I felt good for the first time in ages. Tired, not a lot of stamina, but if I sat for a minute I was fine. What do you think I should do?"

Damned if he knew. He'd have given anything to have Betsy for another month, another day. But what if she were in pain and wanted to be released? Could he let her go?

"Was there anything else you wanted to ask me, Detective?"

"Craig Spencer. Did you know him well?"

"Well enough not to like him. I didn't realize how little he did to help Evie until I saw Brandt with me and with Aaron. My husband even changed to the night shift at work so he'd be home to help me in the afternoons. Now, I'm at my worst in the mornings when he's sleeping and he can't switch back for another three months. Craig would never do that for Evie. He managed with the older two kids—however, they were brilliant and never caused a minute of trouble, so who wouldn't?—but he didn't know how to handle Joey. Oh, he'd help Evie get him in and out of the car and read to him occasionally, but he resented every minute it took from his workouts."

"Do you know how he got along with the people at work?"

"I can hazard a guess. You know the stereotype of engineers and accountants? It was written for him. He was the most brilliant stupid guy you would ever meet. Give him a calculator or computer, and he could rule the world. Put him in front of a live human, and he'd say the wrong thing every time. And then have no idea why they were offended. Then again, he might have just been a selfish, narcissistic jerk."

So, neither Craig nor Madlyn were well liked at work. Where did that leave him? Should he focus on office politics instead of company policies?

She leaned against her pillow and turned her face toward the window. Her voice dropped to a near whisper. "Evie's life will be easier with her sister helping."

"Her sister's not coming. She has to work another year to be eligible for her retirement and insurance."

He watched Chelsea for a moment, wondering if she'd fallen asleep. If so, was that a tear in the corner of her eye or the reflection of the setting sun?

Now what? He had confirmation Dr. Graham's personality had changed over the last two years and that the man was likely depressed due to his health. Although the question of money bothered the shit out of him, he still wouldn't know if the man had committed suicide until the M.E. finished with the body.

This had been a waste of time. He should have headed straight over to Rachelle's and spent the hour playing with Emma and Iris.

CHAPTER
SIXTEEN

"THERE YOU ARE, Noah. We were getting worried about you." Frank's grip was soft, damp.

"My witness interview ran a little long." The house smelled of garlic and something else. Something…good.

Noah would have felt guilty about being late if he hadn't seen Frank three cars ahead of him at the McDonald's drive-thru. Knowing Rachelle's husband slipped out for an occasional hamburger without telling his wife almost made Noah like the guy.

The only hint Frank ever gave that Rachelle's tofu casserole wasn't his favorite dish in the world was his heavy-handed use of the pepper shaker. If his brother-in-law kept it a secret in order to make his wife feel better, Noah certainly wasn't going to carry tales.

And if avoiding red meat and germs made his sister feel she was protecting her family from the injustice of fate after losing their father, mother, and Betsy, he would go along.

Although, in his opinion, backing off the gas pedal while driving would do more good.

Noah kissed his sister before hunting for his nieces. He spent half an hour on the floor playing Chutes and Ladders with the girls—the best part of his day—before Rachelle called them to dinner.

"What's this?" He watched as she scooped something cheesy onto his plate.

"Vegetable lasagna."

Things kept looking better and better. If he got home and Sweet Pea forgave him for being late, the day would be one for the plus column, despite anywhere from one to three murders plus a missing witness and pending lawsuit.

He took a tentative bite. Then another. Had his cooking-challenged sister finally made something not just good, but delicious?

"How are Conner and Jeannie?" Rachelle asked way too casually.

"Fine," he answered around a mouth full of garlic bread, every cell in his body on high alert. "Why? Did you hear something?"

"She seemed tired when I talked to her the other day. I called to offer her some of the girls' hand-me-downs. She thanked me, but suggested I let you give them to Conner instead of inviting me over like I expected her to."

He tried for a deep breath but only managed a shallow sip of air. "Isn't that normal? I mean, aren't most women tired this close to their due date?"

"Oh, sure. I was dragging around like I had a bowling ball attached to each ankle. Of course she's tired. I didn't mean anything by it."

Sweet air filled his lungs. He had to stop being paranoid. Little Aaron Kittrell, Joey Spencer, and all the photos of sick kids on Rodney Graham's wall were getting to him. Rachelle had two babies and he hadn't worried this much.

But he knew more about life and death now.

He drove home with the first fat splatters of rain hitting Lola's windshield. Hopefully, Brandt Kittrell had finished mowing in time.

Sweet Pea wouldn't get her evening walk, but he'd play tug with her, spend forty minutes on the treadmill in the extra bedroom and hit the sack.

Tomorrow he'd start fresh. Time to figure out how many murders he was investigating.

Last night's storm was over, but gray clouds, pregnant with rain, hinted at more to come. Flags and banners hung limp and wet, unmoving in the slight breeze. Water ran down the curbs and into drains. Impatient drivers ignored slippery streets and rushed to work, throwing mud in every direction, coating cars and pedestrians alike.

What was their frigging hurry?

It wasn't that Noah hated Fridays, exactly. There'd been a time when he looked forward to the weekend like everybody else. Even now, a dreary winter weekend with football on every channel was bearable.

In summer, he didn't watch much baseball except for the Little League World Series, but there was always something to do outside—mow the lawn, barbecue, take the girls to the park. Golf wasn't worth thinking about unless he wanted a Sunday afternoon nap.

But a rainy summer weekend with nothing to do could drag on indefinitely. Other than sports, he avoided TV, unless Netflix had an old classic movie he hadn't seen recently. Last night he'd stayed up too late watching *L.A. Confidential*. One of his all-time favorites.

He should have saved it for the weekend if it was going to be this gloomy.

He flipped on Lola's blinker and turned into the Headquarters parking garage. Was that what he was worried about, or was he concerned about wrapping up this case before Conner took off for Family Leave?

Working Homicide seldom meant dealing with paragons of virtue, but he'd always managed to give it his best, be it prostitute or priest, dealer or drunkard, crook or crackpot. Maybe he was tired of spending his days with the scum-of-the-earth.

Maybe he needed the time off as much as Conner.

He strongly suspected Madlyn Gwinn, Craig Spencer, and Rodney Graham deserved everything they got, but he couldn't allow a vigilante to go around doing God's work for him.

He knew exactly how big a mistake that was.

Conner had reached the office before him and glanced up, surprised, when he parked a hip on his desk. He pushed an extra coffee in Noah's direction. "With Junior Redden in jail and Doc Mackie promising a cause-of-death report on our only other open case by five o'clock, I want to solve this case today and be done with it. That way we can end the week with a clean slate."

That made two of them. "I like your plan. Want to tell me exactly how you expect to achieve this?"

"You head to the morgue for Craig Spencer's autopsy and

Rodney Graham's tox screen. Then we'll know how many murders we're investigating. Meanwhile, I'll go to Beneficial Products and walk around the factory floor. Somebody over there knows what the hell's going on in that company and the person who had the least to do with any decision making will be the most likely to talk. Let's meet back here after lunch and put our heads together. See if we can figure out who did what to whom and why before somebody else bites the dust."

"I'm all for that, although I'm not sure our victims didn't deserve everything they got."

"Their loved ones didn't."

Shit. Leave it to Conner to bring him back to Earth. He glanced away, embarrassed to have sounded like an ass in front of his partner.

Conner didn't seem to notice. "Before we start, I have to discuss something with you."

In the corner of his eye, Noah noticed their boss push back from his desk and stand. "It'll have to wait. We need to get out of here before the Lieu asks us for a progress report we don't have."

He grabbed his coffee and sprinted for the door, Conner two steps behind him.

The rain had started again and the wind picked up, causing overhead street signs to swing back and forth like a kid at a playground. Noah cut off the CD he'd been listening to and searched for a weather forecast. Maybe he should have listened to the news last night.

The radio dial gave him nothing but static before he caught the tail end of a weather report. "...inches of rain. Expect flooding of local streets and underpasses."

Nothing new there. Houston flooded every time a hard rain hit. No need to worry yet, he could still see patches of blue sky off to the west.

He sat in Lola long enough to finish his coffee before dashing into the morgue during a respite in the rain, stepping in a puddle and getting his feet wet but not his head. He'd just as soon have had it the other way around.

Dr. Mackie was doing the post and had already started. "There you are, Detective. I knew a little rain wouldn't keep you away. Not like my staff. The bunch of wimps. They want to get home before the storm hits."

Noah took a moment to adjust to the smell. It was something he would never get used to. Good thing he'd finished his coffee first. "I don't need to watch every moment, Doc. Just hit me with the high spots. Was this a freak accident or was the guy murdered?"

"Always in a hurry. Rushing here. Rushing there. What happened? Who did it? What's the time of death? The murder weapon? Cause of death? If you don't learn to enjoy life, I'll have you here on my table before your time. Is that what you want?"

He'd enjoy life a lot more if he could get out of this place with its bright lights, cold air, and disgusting sights. And Doc M. wasn't the one who'd decide when his time was up. He had that date picked out himself.

When he didn't answer, the M.E. held up one of Craig Spencer's pale arms. "Do you remember our talk about bruising during Madlyn Gwinn's autopsy?"

Noah nodded, trying not to breathe any more than necessary.

"There's a slight bruise on the inside of the victim's elbow."

He pointed to a spot Noah couldn't see. "While the answer isn't definitive, the discoloration seems to match, in size and shape, the piece of metal you sent with the body."

The M.E. reached behind him and retrieved a plastic evidence bag containing the object Noah had found on the floor of the Spencer's garage.

"What is it?" Noah asked.

"My assistant has been scouring data bases and proclaims it to be part of a bridge for a pool cue."

"What?" He'd played pool once or twice as a teenager but he'd been more interested in the girl he was with than the game. The term didn't mean anything to him. The only bridges he knew about crossed rivers or belonged in music.

"This little gizmo attaches to a long stick and when your shot is especially difficult, you rest your cue on it to steady your aim."

Sounded like cheating to him. Had the Spencers ever had a pool table in their garage? If so, there might be an innocent explanation. If not….

"What about the time of death? Have you nailed that down?"

"I'm listing it at as between eleven forty-five and twelve thirty. That's if Mrs. Spencer is correct about the time of his last meal. I hate to depend on hearsay, but other factors indicate this to be correct."

"Thanks, Doc." If he hurried, he had time to run by Evie Spencer's before he met Conner.

"Are you forgetting something, Detective?"

He swung around to face the doctor, confused.

"The tox screen you insisted I run immediately on your second victim."

Third victim, but who was counting? "Oh, yeah. What'd you

find out?"

"Indications are the gentleman had a bad heart in addition to his other ailments."

"So he died of natural causes?" One less murder to investigate.

"*Au contraire.* He definitely died of a barbiturate overdose, but he passed away faster than someone had planned. His blood contained traces of Rohypnol."

"Someone gave him a date-rape drug?"

"Yep. He was *roofied*. In any case, he was most likely conscious but unable to call for help when he realized what was happening."

Holy shit. He hadn't really believed it until now, but someone had actually murdered three people, making each one look like an accident or suicide. That was bad, but something else worried him more.

If they searched further, would they find cases they'd missed?

Noah managed a full-out run through the rain despite an inch of standing water on the sidewalk. Three murders. Did that constitute a serial killer?

Probably not. True serial killers picked their victims for random reasons—hair color, height, body type, availability.

Did it really matter?

Not to him, but it would to the Chief. The mayor. They wouldn't want a serial killer roaming the streets of Houston. A psycho vigilante was fine. Just not a serial killer.

Still, he better have someone in custody before the media caught wind of this. He glanced over his shoulder, half expecting to see R.J. Perry waiting to ambush him.

He had to talk to Conner. Now. Not an hour from now when they met at the office.

Noah slid onto Lola's front seat and switched on the engine, all while digging in his pocket for his cell phone. *Damn.* He'd turned it all the way off while talking to Dr. Mackie. The doctor would have thrown him out if it had rung during an autopsy.

He fumbled to enter his passcode as he backed out of his parking spot. Nothing happened. *Calm down. Calm down.* That was his home alarm code.

He'd pulled out onto Old Spanish Trail by the time he entered the correct number. Nanoseconds lasted hours as he waited for the phone to boot up. When it did, it exploded in missed calls and texts.

What the fuck had Conner found?

No. Wait. It was Jeannie. Oh crap. This couldn't be good.

He didn't bother listening to voicemail, just drove with one hand and thumbed *return call* with the other.

She answered after the first ring. "Noah? Where are you?"

"On OST. What's up? Is Conner hurt?"

"No. It's me."

"You're hurt?"

"No, idiot. I'm in labor and I can't find Conner. He doesn't answer his phone." Her voice turned into a wail. "Why would he turn his phone off? He knows how dangerous this is. He's supposed to be available at all times."

Dangerous? "He's at Beneficial Products. On the factory floor. The signal probably can't get through. I'll send a message to him right away. Hang on."

"I can't hang on. Things are happening fast. Get your ass over here now if you don't want me to give birth in a cab."

The wailing, the cursing, the palatable fear. None of this was like Jeannie. She'd pulled a shotgun on a stalker three months ago and hadn't batted an eye.

"I'm on my way. Don't worry. I'll take care of everything. Do that deep breathing thing and be ready to go the minute I get there."

He disconnected, but the phone rang again before he had time to call the office.

Earl.

"Hey, Hoss. I had five minutes where nobody was ordering me around so I looked into that other death."

"I need you to get hold of Conner. Fast. He's at Beneficial Products, but he's on the floor. Cell signals won't go through. You'll have to call the main office and tell them to find him. Use the loudspeaker, send a warm body, whatever. Go yourself if you have to. Find him. Have him meet me at the hospital. Jeannie's in labor and she needs him. Now."

"Got it. I'm dialing as we speak."

"Earl?"

"Yeah?"

"What other death?"

"The car crash. The guy was head of R&D. Drove race cars for a hobby. Until the brakes went out on one of them."

Oh, shit.

The rain turned into a downpour. Sheets of water hit Lola's windshield with gale force winds. The wipers couldn't keep up, even on high.

Noah didn't bother with the flashing bubble light. He'd have had to stop and roll down the window to place it on the roof and who knew if it would stick in this weather? Attaching it to the dashboard would only distract him.

He did flip on the siren but so little traffic was on the road it wasn't necessary. Besides, with water standing in the streets, he couldn't drive more than twenty miles an hour without the danger of fishtailing.

What the hell was going on? His all-news station was all-static and he couldn't take his hands off the wheel to search for a new one.

He approached an underpass with caution. This is where the runoff gathered during storms and it was almost impossible to determine if the water was three inches deep or three feet. He slowed and let an idiot in a maroon Toyota speed past him.

Water spewed up like a rooster tail on both sides of the red car, but the fool made it through. Lola was much higher and shouldn't have any problem. He followed, keeping his speed steady. Not too fast. Not too slow.

He backed into Conner's driveway, leaving the passenger-side door closest to the front porch.

Jeannie waddled out immediately, gripping the railing in one hand and an umbrella in the other.

As a kid, Noah had begged his parents for a cute little Great Dane puppy he'd seen in a shop window. His mother caved when the puppy licked her face, but insisted it sleep in the laundry room until it was housebroken.

Each morning when he let the puppy out, it had grown an inch or more. Its first few steps were awkward, like a newborn colt or a teenager with a growth spurt. Like it had to relearn the skill of walking on such long legs.

That was how Jeannie moved.

It had been ten days since he'd seen her and she had grown exponentially. Her baby bump had morphed into something the size of an ottoman.

The wind blew her hair around like Medusa. A gust caught her umbrella and turned it inside out. She stared at it for two seconds before throwing it on the ground.

He rushed around to open the truck door for her and gave her a hand up. "Don't you have a bag or something?"

Her eyes bore through him like lasers. "Fuck the bag. Get me to the hospital."

He wanted to tell her to buckle up but was afraid the belt wouldn't reach around her.

The water level in the street had risen an inch in the time it took her to get into the truck. No other cars were visible so he drove down the middle of the road, where the street was highest.

"How far apart are the pains?" That should be a safe subject.

"Two minutes, last I checked."

Fuck. "Shouldn't you have called sooner?" One glance her direction and he knew he'd made a mistake.

"I tried! Neither of you answered. Shoot me. I wanted my husband with me today."

"I thought you weren't due for another two and a half weeks." What would have happened if she'd gone another eighteen days? Would the baby come out sitting in its own car seat?

"I've done everything I could. I haven't moved off the bed or sofa in days. I think Charlotte's arrival started things happening."

"Charlotte?" Was that the baby's name? He could barely hear her over the roar of wind and rain.

Jeannie twisted to face him, as well as she could. "Charlotte, the storm?" She pointed out the window. "You do know we're in the middle of a hurricane."

Was that what everyone had been buzzing about this morning? Last he'd heard, they were due heavy rain, but not anything with a name.

A gust of wind hit the side of the truck and rocked it from side to side as Jeannie grabbed her stomach and whimpered.

He had to get her someplace safe. Fast.

Ahead, the neon lights to the hospital glowed like a welcome beacon, barely visible through the blowing rain. Two more minutes if the wind didn't push them off the pavement first.

"Did Conner talk to you this morning?"

What? They talked every day. He couldn't drive and think in this weather. "We were kind of busy. We planned to meet up at lunch. Why?"

She did that funny breathing, like she was trying to blow out candles but didn't have enough breath. "I'll let him take care of that. Just get me inside."

He turned into the Emergency entrance and leaned on the horn. A man in a white coat came out with a wheelchair. The coat was plastered to his skin before he reached the truck.

"Are you Mrs. Crawford?"

"Yes." The wind snatched her words away.

The man turned toward Noah. "I'll take your wife upstairs and get her settled while you park."

Noah didn't bother to correct the man as he took Jeannie's hand and helped her into the wheelchair. "Dr. Owens is waiting for you in Labor and Delivery and Dr. Jankowski is in the NICU."

"Who's he?" Noah knew Dr. Owens. He and Betsy had seen him when they were trying to get pregnant, but he'd never heard of Jankowski.

"She. The neonatologist. Specialist for the baby. Find Conner and get him here. Now." With that, she was gone. Whisked away through the automatic doors of the hospital.

CHAPTER
SEVENTEEN

CONNER TAPPED HIS pen on his notebook. He'd talked to everyone in the factory and that was the problem.

He'd talked to them, but they hadn't talked to him.

Not one person could explain to him how a factory that used to employ seventy-something workers could run with less than a dozen. Or why some machines didn't seem to be in operation. Or what made their product so expensive. Or what had changed over the last two years.

They all did one thing alike though. They glanced surreptitiously at the upstairs window to the foreman's office. And they all acted nervous to be seen talking to him. Every one of them repeated the same phrase, *I just work here.*

He glanced at his phone for the twentieth time. So far, so good. No message yet. With this storm coming in and the change in barometric pressure, Jeannie would never last through the weekend. He had to get back to the office and talk to Noah. She'd shoot him if he didn't get it done today.

The factory floor smelled like yeast and something else he couldn't identify, but the miniscule break room smelled more like cheese puffs and old bologna. He was hungry, but the unpleasant aroma put him off.

Should he give up and return to Headquarters?

He completed his notes as an overhead speaker came to life.

Conner Crawford, report to the main office. Detective Conner Crawford, report to the office immediately.

They'd finally figured out he was here. Probably from that foreman in the upper window. Now what?

The metal chair scraped against the cement floor as he leaned back. He couldn't face Noah without some type of evidence. And he couldn't go home to Jeannie with this case unsolved.

He wasn't leaving empty-handed. They'd have to drag him out bodily.

A workman he hadn't seen before came in and counted out coins for the vending machine. "You the cop everybody warned me about?"

"Guess so. Conner Crawford. And you are?"

"Billy Bowman. Doubt I can help you. I don't know anything about these machines."

"Let me guess. You just work here."

"No, I work for the delivery company. I pick up stuff at the airport and bring it here."

Conner eyed the truck driver. This was no casual conversation. The guy had information begging to come out. That's why he came into the break room. All he needed was a little push. "What kind of stuff?"

"How would I know? The writing's in Chinese. Fifty pound bags of some kind of powdery stuff they pour into that vat in the corner. Then they add two or three smaller bags and mix it up. Sometimes the bags are from Taiwan instead of China. Once it looked like Russian writing."

"And you don't know what's in the bags?"

"Nope, but I'd bet my left nut it isn't organic." Billy kept his back to the foreman's office as he studied the vending machine. "And if it has more than a drop of protein, I'd gnaw off my right one. After they mix it up, they turn on the conveyer belt and pour it into cardboard containers. Halfway through, sirens and bells go off and they stop the belt to change containers from ones marked *Infant* to ones marked *Toddler*. Same stuff near as I can tell. I told my daughter-in-law if they gave it to her free she wasn't to feed it to my grandbaby."

Conner's pulse sped up. Now they were getting somewhere.

The gears on the vending machine gave out an *errrrk* as Billy punched a button and a package of peanuts dropped into the bin below. "I gotta get back to work before that A-hole in the window reports me to my boss."

A familiar voice boomed through the room. "Conner! Conner you SOB, where are you?"

He spun around in time to see Lefty Bob, his head swiveling from side to side as he raced through the factory.

"Over here in the break room. What's the matter?"

Lefty Bob's black hair gleamed with rain and his shirt stuck to his skin. "What's the matter? You're about to become a father and you sit here drinking lukewarm soda like you don't have anything better to do."

Conner pulled out his phone again. "I don't have any messages."

"Are you kidding?" Billy finished off the peanuts and tossed the bag in the trash. "You see all these cement walls? They're reinforced. And those machines and equipment? This is a dead zone. You're not going to pick up a signal in here."

Noooo! The metal chair crashed to the floor as Conner leapt to his feet. "I've got to get home and pick up Jeannie."

Lefty Bob put a hand on his arm. "Slow down. I don't think we can make it in this weather. I nearly stalled out a couple of times and it's getting worse every minute. You know that tropical storm that was supposed to hit Mexico and die out? It picked up speed and did an about face. It's headed straight toward us. Don't worry about Jeannie. Noah's already picked her up and she's safe at the hospital. We might have to wait here."

"I'll walk if I have to. She's not going through this alone." His heart pounded unnaturally. How much help would he be to Jeannie if he had a heart attack now? At least she'd know he tried.

Billy gave a chuckle. "Then it's a good thing I'm here. I happen to have an eighteen-wheeler named Elle Mae parked outside. No lousy hurricane can stop Elle Mae."

Noah paced the narrow waiting room. Comfortable chairs, magazines, flat-screen TV, all gave the area a relaxing feel.

Relaxing was the farthest thing from his mind.

All the other husbands/expectant fathers were with their wives while Jeannie was alone. Should he go in with her? He was a friend. Did that count?

The nurse had called him *Mr. Crawford* when they rushed in and he'd been too flustered to correct her.

No, he wasn't a husband or a father. Would he ever be either of those? He shook off the thought. He didn't need that black cloud over his head. The one outside was bad enough.

If he could be sure what Jeannie wanted him to do, he'd do it. Instead, he paced some more.

Rain beat against the roof. Somewhere a floor below, a piece of patio furniture or a potted plant slammed into a wall. The lights flickered and went out for two seconds before the emergency generator came on and bathed the hall in a weak yellow glow.

The usual noises of the hospital halted, leaving only the sounds of the storm.

Wind roared, rattling windows and threatening to shatter the glass like tissue paper. It was two o'clock in the afternoon, but it could have easily been two in the morning. A black void waited outside.

He stopped to peer out, but saw only the reflection of his own worried face.

Face it, Conner wasn't coming. No one could make it through that downpour.

Jeannie must be terrified. He had to get in there with her. If he knew where *there* was.

A nurse came through the automatic doors marked *Do Not Enter.* She glanced around the empty room and her eyes settled on him. "Mr. Crawford?"

What was the right answer in a case like this? He took a deep swallow and prayed he was right. "Yes."

"They're prepping your wife for surgery. There's a dad's changing room in there." She nodded beyond the forbidding doors. "Put these on and join her in suite number twelve."

She handed him a stack of blue scrubs, shoe covers, cap, and mask before disappearing.

His heart threatened to escape from his chest and run

down the hall on its own. Surgery? What the Hell was wrong? He sneaked a last glance at his phone. No bars. No signal. No message from Conner. Had anyone even told him?

The *push to open* button on the wall stared at him accusingly, but he hesitated. He dreaded the look on Jeannie's face when he walked into that room instead of Conner. She would be so disappointed.

He lifted his hand as the sound of running footsteps filled the hall. A dripping wet Conner, Lefty Bob, and a small man wearing a khaki uniform and steel-toed work boots flew around the corner.

Noah hit the button and the door *whooshed* open. He held out the bundle to Conner. "Changing room's in there. She's in suite twelve being prepped for surgery. Hurry."

Conner never slowed down. He grabbed the clothes like a football hand-off and kept going, shouting over his shoulder, "Lefty Bob will explain it to you."

The doors *whooshed* shut, cutting off anything else Conner said. Noah turned toward the other two men, waiting.

Lefty Bob shrugged. "Jeannie's been having some kind of trouble with her blood pressure."

That was it? That was all the explanation he got? That's what Conner couldn't bring himself to tell him for the last two weeks?

The little guy with *Billy* stitched over his uniform pocket spoke up. "Her blood pressure has been creeping up for the last week or so and they were worried about preeclampsia. Not too unusual for first time moms, but when it happens, the baby has to come out, *pronto*."

Who was this man and how did he know about Jeannie's problems while he didn't?

"She's been in kind of a *Catch 22*. She needed to exercise to keep her blood pressure down, but the baby was slow to develop and needed more time so she had to stay still. This morning she realized she'd put on several pounds overnight and developed a migraine. Sure signs of preeclampsia. But at the same time, this storm brought on labor and that's bad."

"Why is that bad if she needed to have the baby right then?" He didn't know who this Billy guy was, but he seemed to understand the problem better than Lefty Bob.

"Labor can last hours, which she doesn't have, and it can raise her blood pressure which is dangerous for her and the baby. She needs a C-section."

Lefty Bob hit him with a blistering stare. "Conner was on the phone with the hospital all the way over here, but he had trouble getting any information. Seems her husband was already here in the waiting room."

Shit. He knew whatever he did would be wrong.

He had already been unnerved from the harrowing drive through the storm, and that was before he learned about Jeannie's tenuous medical condition. If he'd understood the urgency would he have driven faster, taken more risks, put both Jeannie and the baby in additional jeopardy?

A chill enveloped him. He could have killed them both.

Lefty Bob had just finished describing the dangerous drive in Elle Mae and Billy had filled him in on the information he'd shared with Conner when the double doors *whished* open again.

Conner stood there, grinning like a fool. "Jeannie and the baby are fine. It's a girl, six pounds two ounces. Doc says waiting those extra days made all the difference."

Was it possible to do surgery that fast? He'd barely caught

his breath.

Lefty Bob shook Conner's hand and slapped him on the back at the same time. "I should have bought you a cigar. Anyway, what's the little darling's name?"

Why hadn't he thought of that? Because he was still picturing them washed away, floating down the bayou.

Conner sat beside him and placed a hand on his shoulder. "There are two things I've been supposed to ask you for the last week. But things kept happening to interrupt me. Now Jeannie's told me to take care of it or not come back into the room."

A noose tightened around his chest and he held his breath. He'd faced down drug dealers without blinking, but worry about Jeannie and the baby had him in knots.

"First, will you be the baby's Godfather? We both trust you to be there for her if she needs you."

Noah's voice cracked as he answered. "Of course, I'd be honored." The thought that his friends trusted him with their baby's welfare made his heart swell.

"And second, if it's alright with you, we'd like to name the baby Elisabeth, after Betsy. Jeannie didn't want to without asking your permission first. She said to remind you she had known Betsy longer than you. In fact, she introduced you."

He nodded, unable to speak past the tears caught in his throat. Maybe all news wasn't bad news.

Or was it?

What would it mean to have Betsy's namesake living and laughing and growing and being loved? Could he bear to hear her name called? To know what he'd missed?

He could for Conner. And for Jeannie. For two people who had walked every step of the path with him.

Jeannie was right. She had known Betsy longer. He'd resisted every attempt at being matched with her teacher friend. He didn't believe in blind dates. Something must be wrong with a woman who had to be pawned off on a stranger.

Then Conner had asked him to be his best man and Betsy was Jeannie's maid-of-honor. They'd butted head several times over preparations, but he'd secretly admired the way she stood her ground with him. Not to mention he was intrigued by the way her curls bounced when she walked.

At the reception they had danced and he couldn't keep his eyes off the creamy skin exposed by her one-shouldered lavender dress. She'd taken a little convincing—a *lot* of convincing—but they were married three months later.

If he hadn't been so stubborn, they could've had more time together.

He'd make it up to her by being the best damn Godfather any baby ever had.

CHAPTER EIGHTEEN

NOAH STOOD ON his back stoop—his *World's Best Uncle* coffee mug clutched in one hand—while Sweet Pea made certain no cats or squirrels or strangers of any type had intruded on her territory during the night.

The entire city seemed to be covered by a dome of uniform gray. From time to time, the sky spit out fat drops of rain. The wind had settled into a steady breeze with only occasional gusts as a reminder that Mother Nature was still in charge.

His eyes felt like they'd been sandblasted. He'd spent half the night in a bar across the street from the hospital with Lefty Bob and Billy. They drank beer and waited for the wind to die down and the water to recede while Billy regaled them with stories about the perils of piloting a big rig through Houston traffic.

The little guy should have been a stand-up comedian.

Meanwhile, he'd been in shock and mostly stared into space. Hell, he was still in shock. Conflicting emotion raged through him.

He was pissed Conner hadn't told him about Jeannie's condition.

He was relieved he hadn't known about Jeannie's condition. He'd have been as nervous as a cat at the dog pound.

He was deeply touched they had named the baby after Betsy.

He was worried about how he'd react to hearing Betsy's name attached to another person.

Mostly he was mentally and physically exhausted. Good thing it was Saturday and he didn't have to deal with any assholes. His yard was a soggy mess of leaves, broken branches, and pine needles. He didn't want to look too closely at a tangle of debris that might have once been a bird's nest. He'd clean it up tomorrow after the ground had time to dry out.

Today, he'd stay home, relax in front of the TV, and make up to Sweet Pea for not feeding her until well past midnight. Maybe take her for a walk, play toss with Mr. Squeaky Man, and enjoy a nap with her curled on his chest.

A perfect weekend, even if the day was half gone already.

He took a sip of his coffee and spit it into the flowerbed. It had gone cold while he was staring into the past.

Sweet Pea scooted past him, her job complete. The backyard was safe from intruders. Not a squirrel or the yellow tabby next door had dared to venture in overnight.

He let the screen door swing shut. Conner was fine. Jeannie was fine. Betsy was fine—he smiled at that thought—and on Monday he'd get to work. Solve this case so he could take some needed time off for himself.

Thirty minutes later, he unhooked Sweet Pea's leash and eyed the TV. It was Saturday. What were the chances?

He settled into the sofa and grabbed the remote. Kiddy

show. Kiddy show. Infomercial. All news station. Where were the sports?

He flipped past golf—he'd just gotten up, and wasn't ready to go back to sleep—and landed on some sport he hadn't seen before.

Parkour? What the fuck? He'd never heard of it.

Men were racing down an obstacle course made to look like a war-torn city. They ran, they jumped, they bounded off one object onto another, swung from bar to bar, leapt over obstacles.

The first guy fell and possibly broke his ankle. The second guy slipped despite some type of special glove and was disqualified. The third made it all the way to the end.

Noah was just getting interested when his cell rang.

"Daugherty." Noah didn't take his eyes off the screen. He already knew the next guy was in trouble. He didn't have enough speed pushing off the wrecked car. He'd never make it to the window ledge.

"This is Cooter."

Who? Oh, yeah. The bartender. "Yes, Cooter. Did Kelly contact you?"

"She stopped by for her money. I tried to give her your number, but she wouldn't take it. Said she was going to grab her things and run. She was hoping to stay out of trouble."

Damn. She was already in trouble. Didn't she see that?

"Thanks for letting me know. If you see her again, remind her I'm trying to protect her, not mess her up." That's all he could ask the guy to do.

"Yeah. About that. I wouldn't have called you since she wasn't interested, but I remembered what you said about her being in danger. Guess who's sitting here at the bar? Junior Redden and he's not in a good mood. Claims his girlfriend betrayed him and left him to rot in the can. Says he needed a beer to get the taste of jail out of his mouth. I'd offer him a free one to slow him down, but I'm well known for never giving *anyone* a free beer."

Noah had his shoes on before Cooter stopped talking. He tried Kelly's cell while he retrieved his weapon from the cabinet above the refrigerator. A canned voice reported the number was not in service.

Had her battery died or had Junior cancelled the contract?

If Junior nursed his beer, it might take him twenty minutes to finish. If Noah raced, it would take him thirty minutes to reach the trailer park.

If the manager, Dewey, delayed Kelly, she'd still be there when Junior got home.

Any way you looked at it, someone was in for an unpleasant surprise.

Lola raced over streets wet from last night's storm. Water ran along the curb-line but only backed into streets in a few spots. Good thing he'd sprung for the heavy-duty tires.

Noah had checked the traffic report before he left home. Bayous across town were full but flowing, allowing drains to do their jobs. A couple of underpasses leading to Land of Lost Pines Trailer Park were blocked and he'd planned his route accordingly.

Charlotte wasn't a biggie as hurricanes go, only a category two, but strong enough to do some damage around town and drop a lot of rain. Fortunately, she had moved out quickly and was now bringing that moisture into Arkansas. She'd probably reach Tennessee by tonight.

While no blue showed through the solid layer of clouds, patches of the gray sky had lightened into something that offered no color at all.

The air itself seemed washed clean as if for a fresh start.

But he was headed to a place even a hurricane couldn't wash clean and a fresh start was more of a last chance.

The sign identifying Land of Lost Pines had disappeared along with most of the residents' nameplates. A plastic lawn chair had been lifted up, carried to the middle of the road, and sat back down as if standing guard over the entrance.

Half under a double-wide, a child's pink riding toy lay upside-down and mangled, one wheel spinning in a sudden gust of wind. A tree limb thick as his wrist protruded from the roof of one trailer as if it had grown from a seedling straight through the residence and out the top. Other limbs littered the ground.

Several of the mobile homes had windows shattered, some covered with plastic or plywood, others gaping open, waiting for their owners to return.

Noah couldn't blame those who had evacuated to a safer spot. He wouldn't have wanted to spend yesterday in an aluminum coffin perched on cinderblocks. Fortunately, none seemed to have been blown off their tenuous foundations.

He eyed the ruts in the crushed-shell street leading into the trailer park. Several cars had passed recently. One of them would have been Kelly's. Was Junior's another?

Lola held steady, never skidding, as he eased her through the muck toward the end trailer. Kelly's distinctive Honda was parked with its trunk open and facing the door. Junior had pulled his truck sideways, blocking her exit.

Noah parked Lola to one side so she was hidden by their

neighbor's home and crept forward, keeping out of Junior's line-of-sight. Raised voices floated past him while he was still ten feet away.

"You bitch! I spent a week in that hell-hole because of you."

"I did exactly what you said. I told those officers you never came inside. You saw a stranger trespassing and digging through the dumpster so you tried to stop him." Kelly's voice held a note of panic. Good, maybe she'd believe him about being in danger.

He inched closer, mud sucking at the soles of his shoes. A dog barked but no one seemed to notice.

"You shouldn't have talked to that fucking cop in the first place. I told you to stay away from him."

"I didn't tell him anything." Kelly was yelling now. "Only what we agreed. That you were asleep beside me all night. I thought that would make him go away before you got home and he tried to question you."

"What did I tell you about thinking on your own? Leave that to me and do what I tell you."

"I'm sorry. It won't happen again." How many domestic arguments had he witnessed over the years? They always followed the same pattern. First the yelling, then the fear, finally the pleading. Which meant he needed to get her out of there fast before violence broke out.

Noah avoided the steps and slipped under the porch railing near the back of the trailer. One board groaned with his weight and he froze. Junior must not have heard. He never stopped yelling.

"You bet your ass it won't. I threw you out once and I'll throw you out again. Come back and I'll call the cops on *you*. And don't think you're taking anything with you. I paid for all of this shit. Drop it and walk out of here the way you came in—half naked and broke."

If Kelly agreed to leave, Junior would have to come outside to move his truck and he'd be exposed. Nothing to do but hide and pray Junior didn't spot Lola.

Noah spun around and saw a line of muddy footprints leading to the door. Now what?

"Those are my things. I'm working. I gave you my paycheck every week."

Nooo. Leave while you can, Kelly. I'll take care of Junior when he's outside. He hugged the side of the trailer and watched them in a mirror on the far wall. Junior had hold of Kelly's arms and might harm her if he rushed in now. He had to wait until there was a space between them.

"If you turned over everything you made, you're the worst waitress in the history of time. Where've you been stashing the rest of your tips?"

Junior dropped Kelly's arms and grabbed her purse, upending it on the sofa and pawing through the contents.

Noah readied his Glock and took a step toward the door. He wasn't going to be caught without a weapon this time.

Before he could get inside, Junior backhanded Kelly with a loud *slap*, sending her reeling against the coffee table and onto the floor. He stood over her, shaking a wad of bills in her face. "What have you been doing, giving blow jobs in Cooter's back room?"

"You know Cooter wouldn't stand for that. I cashed my last paycheck."

"Cooter would stand for it just fine if he was first in line. As for a paycheck, you wouldn't pull down this much if you worked twenty-four hours a day the whole time I was gone. This proves you can't be trusted. You've been holding out on me and I'm gonna have to kill you for it. I won't have a backstabber out there who could turn on me at any minute."

Noah eased inside and pointed the Glock at Junior's head. "You're under arrest. Lock your hands behind your head."

Kelly picked that moment to kick out with both legs, connecting hard with Junior's groin. Junior let out a scream like a cat being tortured.

He stumbled back and into Noah, whose muddy feet skidded out from under him. The two men went down in a tangled heap.

A stack of one and five dollar bills flew into the air and rained down on them. Kelly began grabbing the cash and stuffing it into her bra.

"You fucking bitch." Junior moaned and clutched his genitals. He tried to sit up and reach for Kelly. She stopped gathering the bills long enough to grab a lamp and smash it over Junior's head. He collapsed, crashing into Noah and flattening his nose.

Noah had one thought before darkness overtook him.

Why had she done that? Did she think she was helping or was she planning her escape?

CHAPTER NINETEEN

"I'M GETTING TIRED of cleaning up your mess." The tall deputy was the same one who'd rescued Noah when he and Junior were pinned on the bridge.

The guy had laughed at him that day and was laughing almost as hard this time. "By the way, how many stitches did you get in that leg? We had an office pool. I bet fifteen."

The shorter deputy leaned into Noah's face. Remnants of a meatball sandwich speckled his uniform shirt. "I'm the one who had to climb into that dumpster and retrieve your weapon. I'm torn between wanting to win the pot with my guess of seven stitches and hoping you had to suffer with several more."

Noah held the bag of frozen peas to his bloody nose. If he put the bag down, he might have to hit someone. "I saw this man strike a woman and threaten to kill her. What was I supposed to do, wait outside to see if he changed his mind?"

"Too bad the woman isn't here to corroborate your story. Speaking of which, weren't you supposed to stay away from her, and him?" The deputy nodded toward Junior. "And this place, until some legal issues were resolved?"

"Fucking yeah," Junior yelled from his seat on the sofa. "He's obviously got a hard-on for me because I'm suing him. You should let me go and arrest *him*." He held out his wrists, handcuffs now swapped for the length of electrical cord Noah had used to tie him up.

That tacky lamp had come in handy twice now. He'd like to use the cord one more time. As a garrote around Junior's fat neck.

Noah dropped the bag of peas. His nose had quit bleeding and was completely numb. He couldn't even smell Junior's prison stink.

There was no doubt about it. He was screwed seven ways from Sunday. Normally, a cop's word had more weight than a low-life creep accused of setting his parents on fire, but that didn't hold true with Junior suing him and Kelly nowhere to be found. Add to that, he'd been specifically told not to contact her. Yet he was naming her as his witness.

He might as well start filling out the papers for his resignation. Lieutenant Jansen couldn't save him now.

With enough money, Tom Meyers might be able to pull some legal shit and save him from jail. Without, he'd better make friends with Junior because they were likely to end up cellmates.

Lola bounced over potholed roads and Noah didn't bother to slow down, although the jolting could start his nose bleeding again at any time. So what? His shirt and face and life were already ruined.

Ahead, the sign for Cooter's stood out like a beacon. His mouth was as parched as a bag of lint and the only thing he could taste was dried blood. A cold beer would hit the spot.

Hell, he wasn't on duty. Might never be again.

He parked Lola, jumped a two-inch deep puddle, and headed for the door when he spotted the rear bumper of a faded blue Honda hiding behind a bush in back of the bar.

No. Way.

He slid inside, being careful not to let the screen door slam behind him. Ceiling fans rotated at sloth-speed, stirring warm air, but not much else.

Kelly had her back to him and a tray of empties in her hand when he spoke into her ear. "Shiner Bock, please."

The bottles *clinked* against each other but didn't fall as she jerked around.

A bruise was forming on her cheek where Junior had hit her, but that wasn't what surprised him most when he got a good look at her. Kelly had always been a well-endowed woman. Now she overflowed her tank top. He didn't have to wonder where she'd hidden the money.

Her eyes darted toward the back door as if she might run. He had to stop her before that happened. "Calm down and get me my beer. I'm not going to arrest you." Could he? No one had taken his badge or gun. Yet.

He slid into the nearest chair and placed his hands on the sticky table, palms down. No threat to her or anyone. Two other tables were occupied, the nearest by two men in work shirts and boots, more interested in the TV than anything else.

The second table contained a lone, middle-aged man staring into his beer as if it held the secrets of the universe.

Kelly took the overloaded tray to the bar and returned with his Shiner, slamming the bottle onto the table so hard foam spewed out the top. A waste of good beer.

"Look, I appreciate that you protected me from Junior. Or should I say you distracted Junior while I protected myself. And that's just it. I've been protecting myself since I was eleven years old. I don't need your help. I can't afford to get messed up with the police."

"You can't afford not to." Shit. He came off sounding like Clint Eastwood when he was trying for Morgan Freeman. His beer waited, cold and inviting. A bead of moisture rolled down its side. He took a sip, stalling while his temper cooled.

The taste was Heaven in a bottle, washing away the sweat and dust and blood.

"I'm guessing you're afraid of Junior." He expected her to nod, but she shrugged instead. "You should be. He doesn't need you anymore and you can only hurt him. You're on record spouting everything he told you to. If you die now, it stands. If you live, you might retract your statements or get tripped up on cross-examination. He. Can't. Afford. To. Let. You. Live."

Was he pushing it? No. He'd seen the look in Junior's eyes. By running away, Kelly had turned herself into an albatross around his neck. It was bound to happen sooner or later. Maybe she knew it and that's why she ran.

She gave a miniscule shake of her head. "You don't understand. I can handle Junior. At least I could before you burst in and ruined everything. I need him as much as he needs me. Without him, I have nothing. Literally. Only what's on my back right now."

She must have seen him glance at her cleavage. "Yeah. I

know. I have some cash. It comes to a little over $300. How long do you think that will last? When Junior was arrested the first time, I didn't like the idea of staying at his place alone because of that pervert, Dewey, but my mother called. She needed help with my little brother. He has autism and I've done more to raise him than anyone. Normally, I wouldn't set foot in her house, but my stepfather was on a fishing trip and she wanted to use the time to get her bunion operation. So you see, I wasn't running away from Junior, I went home to help my brother."

Noah used one foot to push out a chair for Kelly. She glanced at Cooter as if for permission before sitting.

"You can't stay at your mom's until this is settled?" He'd never understand families. He'd kill for his, and had, while others wouldn't offer a hand to their own child.

"That's what I'm trying to tell you. My stepfather started abusing me when I was eleven. Not much at first. A pat on the butt, an *accidental* brush as he passed. By the time I was fifteen, he'd graduated to outright groping."

"Did you tell your mother?"

"She said to lock my door if I was worried. I did, then spent the next year listening to him rattle the knob every night. I was sixteen when I came home from school and discovered he'd taken the knob clean off. Told my mother it was broken. I scooted my dresser in front of the door that night. It killed me to abandon my little brother, but I moved out the next day. Haven't been back since until last week. Big mistake. He came home from fishing a day early, saw me, and started screaming and cursing. I grabbed my purse and ran. Didn't even have shoes on. So don't ask me how I could lay next to Junior when I've had years of practice sleeping with one eye open. Now I can't go back to the trailer. I've got no clothes and no place to live. I'm screwed all the way around."

Shit. Everybody had a story and most of them were worse than his.

She reached across the table, snagged his beer and downed it in one long gulp. "Got any suggestions?"

"We can't straighten any of this out until you tell the truth. You've got to call the sheriff's department and offer to give them a statement detailing everything that happened starting with the night you passed out and including both the day I came over and today when he hit you and threatened to kill you. It would probably be best if you stayed in a motel tonight until we're sure Junior will stay locked up. After that, you can live in the trailer or anywhere you want. I'll make sure Dewey doesn't bother you and I'll help you get your things back from your mother's."

"Why do you think I moved in with Junior? I'm only seventeen! I'm not old enough to rent a motel room or an apartment without an adult. Believe me, I've tried."

Holy shit! His stomach twisted into a Gordian knot. Thoughts whirled around in his head like Charlotte's winds had last night. First one then another fought its way to the front of his brain. The most inappropriate led the way.

Girls didn't look like that when he was in high school.

As a minor, she couldn't legally grant him access to Junior's trailer.

Hell, he'd just given a drink to a minor. He could lose his job.

He'd probably already lost his job. He could be arrested.

Why hadn't Earl discovered any of this?

Everything he learned from her was fruit of the poisonous tree and couldn't be used.

Junior was going to walk.

Could he threaten Junior with statutory rape as leverage against his lawsuit?

He'd have to hire Tom Meyers to get him out of this shit.

That could take all of Betsy's insurance money. Then what would he leave Rachelle?

He pressed his palm into the table to calm himself. The wood was sticky from spilled beer. Every sound and smell in the room was heightened. "Is your mother's married name Manus?" With all the questions he had, why the fuck had that one popped out first?

"No, her name is Sandy Cronin."

Now he had a chance of finding Kelly if she disappeared again. His subconscious was working even if his conscious wasn't.

"I was sleeping in my car when I met Rory Manus. He was in his fifties, but a nice guy."

Yeah, I bet he was nice as pie. A fifty-year-old guy hitting on a sixteen-year-old kid with no place to live.

"He promised to send me to nursing school like I'd always wanted so I could learn to take care of kids like my brother. We got married. Well, sort of. Not in a church or anything, but common law. He told me it was just as real if I started using his name."

Okay. That explained at lot. No wonder Earl couldn't find a record. And if Kelly was married, she was an emancipated minor. She could let him into Junior's trailer.

He was off the hook. And Junior was back in deep shit.

"I was already registered in nursing school and the first semester paid for when Rory got killed in an accident at work.

His kids took all the insurance money and anything else of value. Called me a whore and said we weren't really married because I didn't have anything on paper. Dewey threatened to kick me out of our trailer unless I gave him a blow job every month with the rent. Since I couldn't pay the rent at all, he wanted a lot more than that. That's when Junior offered to let me move in with him."

Yeah, that Junior's a real prince.

A wave of acid climbed up Noah's throat. He hadn't liked Dewey the first time he set eyes on the trailer park manager. Now he planned to make it his life's work to see the old guy paid. If Kelly would testify, he could charge the man with attempt assault or blackmail or something. Conner could figure out what would work best.

Noah's heart dropped five inches. Conner was on leave and wouldn't be helping with anything for six weeks.

He took a deep breath filled with stale beer and burnt nachos. He was on his own, but he could fix this.

"Nothing's changed. Go right now and talk to the sheriff. Tell him everything. Don't elaborate. Don't make up anything. Don't hide anything. Tell the absolute truth. Tell them about Dewey, too. Maybe they'll arrest him."

A board creaked and Noah felt a presence looming over him. Cooter.

"If they don't arrest Dewey, I'll have a talk with the guy. He'll never bother you again. Until then, I have a cot and a shower in the back room. The door has a good strong lock. You'll be safe until you find a place to live. There's only one problem. This is a bar. You can't work here if you're not eighteen."

CHAPTER TWENTY

NOAH SANK INTO the sofa and flipped on the TV. The Parkour tournament was over and the Astros were playing the Yankees. Not interested.

He flipped the channel. Soccer. Definitely not interested.

He flipped again. Golf. Maybe. He could use a nap. Nothing had gone right for him since he got up this morning.

His knuckles were raw and scraped. His nose throbbed. He'd cut the inside of his cheek and it felt like a chunk of skin was dangling, waiting to be ripped off. One tooth ached and might be loose.

Kelly had agreed to call the sheriff but he didn't completely believe her. He was either out of trouble or in worse trouble than before and he wouldn't know which until Monday.

If he fell asleep and woke up again, would it count as a new day?

He'd stretched out and lifted Sweet Pea onto his chest when his phone vibrated, indicating an email. He eyed his cell, sitting on the coffee table. To reach it, he'd have to move the dog and she was asleep.

Five minutes later he cursed and reached for his phone. Sweet Pea gave him the stink eye, but Jeannie was out of surgery less than twenty-four hours and Betsy in NICU. Not to mention the guilt he felt over Kelly's situation.

He couldn't ignore any message.

Conner's name on the *from* line caused him to sit up.

The subject line read *Beneficial Products,* but he opened it cautiously, as if it could bite him. Several paragraphs of single-spaced text and a numbered to-do list waited for him.

In the text portion, Conner had summarized the case and everything they knew at this point. Noah leaned his head back and closed his eyes.

Conner had used his first day as a father to bring the murder book up-to-date.

Noah sent him a quick text. *What are you doing working?*

Jeannie and Betsy asleep. If I get up or turn on TV I wake them.

The sight of Betsy's name in Conner's text made Noah's heart skip a beat, but he kept going. *You should sleep too. While you can LOL.*

Can't. Too nervous. Keep watching them breathe.

They OK?

Great! Betsy color good, eating, out of NICU. Home tomorrow.

I'll stop by and bring you supper from Mamma Mia's. What do you want?

Anything w/o garlic. Hard for baby to digest.

What? They wouldn't be feeding it to the baby, she was nursing. Oh… He hadn't thought of that. So many things he didn't know about babies. Would he have learned?

Conner made one last parting shot. *Don't forget to check the to-do list.*

Noah bit back a sarcastic reply. Most of the items he'd thought of himself, but one or two surprised him. *Will do. Rest if you can. I saw the crappy plastic sofa they gave you.*☺

He rubbed Sweet Pea's tummy absently while staring at the TV. *Fuck golf.* He wasn't tired, just bored and restless. He'd drop by the office, print out Conner's report, insert them into the murder book, clean up his emails, and be ready to hit the ground running first thing Monday morning.

Who knew? Maybe something lurking in his emails would be what he needed to solve the case.

The sight of Conner's empty desk steeled Noah's resolve. He needed to buckle down and get this case wrapped up. Someone was picking off people like ducks in a carnival shooting gallery.

He wove through the empty desks to his corner of the room, eyeing a splash of color that didn't belong. What the fuck? Someone had taped a pink message slip onto his computer screen.

R.J. Perry from the Chronicle had called twice asking for an interview. Fuck that. Not if the guy tied him to a chair and threatened him with a Taser. His jaw tightened as he wadded the scrap of paper and tossed into the trash can where it hit with a *ping* that should have been satisfying but left him cold.

Now what? He couldn't keep Perry at bay forever. The guy would find a way to corner him. If he didn't, the TV vultures would and that would be worse.

He had to solve this case *now*, while he still had a job.

He clicked on his emails and realized it might already be too late. A message from Internal Affairs glared back at him. If he opened it and learned he had been put on leave, that was it. Game over. He couldn't keep investigating.

His hand hovered over the *delete* key. Best to leave it unopened and plead ignorance.

Instead, he'd bring the murder book up-to-date and stall any complaints from the big boss.

Who was he kidding? He didn't give a shit about the book or the Chief. He just couldn't stand the idea someone might get away with murder because he'd screwed up.

If he was on his way out, he'd leave a step-by-step trail for the next detective to follow. Maybe a fresh set of eyes would find what he'd missed.

He printed out Conner's report and added it to the growing murder book along with reports for the Gwinn and Spencer autopsies he'd found on his desk. No surprises there.

Forensic accounting had found the money trail, weaving its ugly way through several off-shore accounts from Beneficial Products into Dr. Graham's greedy hands, but so what? All those people were dead and couldn't be prosecuted.

And the one who'd done the killing was still a mystery.

That left the to-do list. He grabbed a pen from the papier-mâché holder Iris had made him for Christmas. If he checked off the items as he completed them, he could tell himself he'd accomplished *something* worthwhile.

He grabbed the list and stuck it in his pocket on his way out the door. Time to get out of here before someone saw him.

If the Chief's golf game had been rained out and he needed

an excuse to get away from his wife for an hour, he could pop up at any minute. One look at Noah's swollen nose and any chance of bluffing his way out of trouble was as gone as yesterday's storm.

Sunday morning was a new day in many ways. The blue of the sky was even more startling when contrasted with the last four days of dismal gray. A few puffy cotton candy clouds floated past in the lingering breeze. A regular Chamber of Commerce day, the last thirty-six hours forgotten except for debris littering the soggy ground.

Noah stood in the backyard and took a deep breath, enjoying the clean scent of the fresh air.

If he could breathe, the swelling in his nose must have gone down enough not to be noticeable. Right?

He hopped into Lola and headed out. He had one stop to make before picking up Rachelle.

With Junior Redden in jail and Kelly cooperating, that left him with only two open cases on the books.

If he could close one of those today, first thing Monday morning—assuming he still had a job—he'd be able to concentrate on the one involving multiple murders. Then he'd be free.

Free to take off work for several weeks.

Free to clear his head from all the negative thoughts he'd had lately.

Free from spending his days around scumbags and lowlifes.

Trey Delafield's mother had already waited three weeks for her son's death certificate. He could have waited until tomorrow to tell her about the M.E.'s conclusions, but that didn't feel right.

Not for her and not for him.

He'd have wanted to know as soon as possible, wouldn't she?

He pulled Lola into the driveway of another McMansion. Was this his month to rub shoulders with the rich and famous? If so, he was ready to get back to his normal clientele—the poor and obscure.

He'd barely switched off Lola's engine when the front door opened and LaVonne Delafield bounded out. She wore a gleaming white tennis dress and gripped a high-end racket in one hand. A navy visor held back her ash-blond hair.

Hardly the picture of a grieving mother.

Noah clamped his jaw so tight his teeth hurt. What a waste of his day off. If she hadn't seen him, he'd have turned around and let her wait another day.

"Detective Dougherty, is that you? I didn't expect to see you on a Sunday. Come in. Come in." She held the door open and motioned him inside.

He concentrated on taking slow and steady breaths, letting the anger flow out with each exhale. He was here. He might as well do his job.

The inside of the house was cool and dark. He took a deep breath. It didn't smell of anything—not food, not pets, not kids, nothing. The complete absence of smell or sound or sign of life.

A ghost house.

He would have gone insane within ten minutes of living here.

Mrs. Delafield's tennis shoes made no sound as she crossed the marble entryway and sat on a leather sofa. "I'm so glad you weren't ten minutes later. I'd have missed you. I've stayed in this house, pacing, picking up pieces of imaginary lint, fluffing unwrinkled pillows until I thought I would scream. This morning my sister absolutely insisted I go out with her for a game of tennis. I knew it was a mistake. That I should wait in case you called."

He lowered himself next to her, one hand admiring the plush leather. "We finally got a report from the Medical Examiner and I wanted to deliver it to you personally. Trey definitely died from an overdose of heroin, but the M.E. feels it was accidental, not suicide."

Would that make her feel better? Her son was still dead.

"How could that happen?" Tears marred her perfectly applied make-up.

"The dose he used was unusually pure. He wouldn't have expected it to be that strong."

She rubbed her temples. "It was so stupid, really. He had his wisdom teeth out and the dentist gave him oxycodone for the pain. When I visited him in rehab, he told me the minute that first pill hit his bloodstream he was hooked. He felt like he was enough for the first time in his life. I never knew what he meant. He was enough for me. Thank you. Knowing he didn't do this on purpose won't bring him back, but it will allow me to remember him without the anger."

Back in Lola, Noah gave himself a mental head-slap. He'd done it again. He jumped to conclusions. Judged someone by first impressions without digging deeper. He'd been in Homicide too long to make those rookie mistakes.

He couldn't speak for the dead if he wasn't listening to what they said.

Noah was still angry with himself as he neared his sister's house. He'd had a chip on his shoulder for weeks. Months, if he was honest. Time for that to end.

He had two cases down and two to go. He wouldn't make the same mistakes again. Even jerks like Madlyn Gwinn and Craig Spencer deserved his best.

Rachelle ran out of her door before he had the engine switched off. A purse the size of Rhode Island was slung over one shoulder, a shopping bag in one hand and an enormous pink gift-wrapped box in the other. "Let's go before Frank changes his mind."

"Why would he change his mind?"

"He told the girls he would take them out to dinner and buy them a surprise. They think it's a Lego set. When they find out they're going to Academy for fishing rods, it won't be a pretty sight."

"Maybe they have Disney princess fishing poles."

Rachelle gave him a withering glare. "He'd be better off with Elektra or Buffy the Vampire Slayer."

He'd at least *heard* of Buffy. He had no idea who Elektra was. Better change the subject while he had the chance. "What've you got in the box?"

She held up first the shopping bag, then the box. "Some baby stuff from Emma and Iris and a gift for Betsy. It's a sort of sling so you can hold the baby next to you but still have both hands free. What did you get them?"

"I'm picking up dinner for all four of us from El Mariachi. Beef, chicken, and shrimp fajitas, refried beans, Spanish rice, and guacamole." He'd given up on Manna Mia's. Everything they had contained garlic.

"You didn't get them a baby gift?"

Was he supposed to? Hell, the dinner was costing a fortune.

She rolled her eyes. "At least you didn't order anything with garlic."

How did everybody know these things but him?

Noah didn't answer, just turned into the nearest drug store. He came out five minutes later with two enormous plastic bags of disposable diapers.

She reached over with her index finger, pulled open the corner of one bag, and shrugged. "That'll do."

He let a smile play around the corners of his mouth. Things were looking up.

Rachelle stared straight ahead, watching the world go past, reminders of Charlotte evident in downed limbs and twisted signs. "Are you going to tell me what's wrong with your nose or keep pretending nothing happened?"

Damn. He'd been sure no one would notice.

Now he'd have to explain it to her, and to Jeannie—and to Conner.

CHAPTER
TWENTY-ONE

J EANNIE LOOKED ONE hundred percent better than the last time Noah had seen her. Her color was back, the bloating was gone from her face, and her body looked like a normal woman instead of someone who might explode at any moment. She walked gingerly, but her smile was warm and genuine.

"Noah, Rachelle, I'm so glad to see you. Conner's driving me crazy. Hovering over me like a mother hen." Her hug melted that hidden corner of worry he'd been guarding since he saw her whisked away at the hospital.

Conner came in, holding Betsy like he'd been taking care of babies all his life.

Noah panicked when his partner tried to hand him the pink-wrapped bundle. She was so tiny. What if he held her too tight and broke something? Or too loose and dropped her?

Rachelle saw her chance and swooped in. "I'll take her." She had Betsy in her arms, *oohing* and *aahing* and making baby sounds while Noah was still trying to figure the logistics of taking the bundle from Conner.

She took her eyes off Betsy long enough to glance at Jeannie. "How much does she weigh now?"

"An even six pounds when we left the hospital. She lost down to five and a half, but is already starting to gain it back."

"She lost weight? Is she sick?" That icy spot in Noah's gut flared up again.

Conner placed a reassuring hand on his shoulder. "All babies lose weight after they're born. The way Jeannie was retaining fluid, we're lucky that's all she lost. She's eating like a champ and gaining fast."

For one insane second, he was relieved he and his Betsy never had time to become parents. If he wasn't up to the stress of childbirth, how would he handle a stubbed toe or first date?

He glanced at Conner, eyeing his baby with a love that was palpable across the room. No, he'd have managed, given a chance. He'd have read the books, and studied the films, and gone to the classes. Learned what they could eat and how to change diapers.

Hell, he'd been mother, father, and big brother to Rachelle since she was a teen. He'd learned how to French braid her hair, helped her pick out a prom dress, and walked her down the aisle.

Although, these days she spent more time mothering him.

"What smells so good? I'm starving." Jeannie smelled pretty good herself. An aroma he associated with mothers: part talcum powder, part baby milk, part love, part overall contentment.

"Betsy's not the only one around here who's eating like a champ," Conner stage-whispered.

Jeannie laughed and slapped him on the arm. "You can carry the next one. Then we'll see who's worked up an appetite."

Betsy slept in a cradle-swing while they ate, but stirred as they pushed back from the table.

Conner kissed Jeannie on top of her head. "Why don't you two ladies take Betsy into the other room and relax while Noah and I clear the table and clean up the kitchen?"

"Sounds like a plan. I want to hear how Emma and Iris are doing." Jeannie patted him on the cheek. "While you're at it, maybe you can get Noah to tell you what happened to his nose. I'm sure whatever story he gave Rachelle is a crock."

"Told me he was stung by a bee while working in the yard this morning," Rachelle piped up. "And I believe the stork delivered this baby, also."

They'd eaten off paper plates, so Conner boxed up the leftovers and stored them in the fridge while Noah stuck the glasses in the dishwasher. Five minutes to gather his thoughts before his partner started in on him.

"You want to tell me what happened?"

Wrong. Less than five minutes. "Junior Redden." He might as well admit it. Conner would know if he were lying.

"I figured that much. Weren't you supposed to stay away from him and anything to do with his case?"

"The bartender called to warn me Kelly had gone to the trailer to get her things and Junior was headed that way with a mad on for being left in jail all week."

"And it never crossed your mind to send the sheriff's department over to protect her?"

Actually, he had considered it for one brief moment, but they might not have made it a priority and they would have left without an argument if Kelly said she didn't need any help.

"It was my responsibility. She already had a hard life and I screwed it up worse. Because of me, she doesn't have a job or a place to live. Junior wants to kill her. Well, he wanted to anyway, and that was before she hit him over the head with a lamp to save my sorry ass after I burst in when he threatened her. Now I have to wait until Monday to find out if she'll clear my name. I think she will but I'm not sure. That doesn't count the fact that she's seventeen and a minor and couldn't legally give me permission to search Junior's trailer that first time although she's been married—maybe—so she might be an emancipated minor. We could threaten Junior with statuary rape either for real or as a bargaining tool if she's willing to testify, but why would she? And this whole thing is such a mess, I'm not sure even Tom Meyers could straighten it out."

Wow! He hadn't expected that to all spill out in one breath. He must be more worried than he'd realized.

"Kelly Manus is seventeen? What are they putting in the water these days?"

Noah glanced at Conner's face and laughed. After all the crap he'd dumped on his partner's shoulders, that was his first comment?

He poured soap into the dishwasher, closed the lid, and sat on a kitchen chair. "So what do you think?"

Conner took the chair across from him and stretched out his legs. "You may have left out a few pertinent details in that recitation, but, here goes. I'm not sure how someone can *not know* if they were ever married, but that aside, we don't need anything from inside that trailer. The dumpster was on public land and whatever was found in there is admissible evidence."

"Not according to the trailer park manager. He says the

dumpster is on private property and I was trespassing."

"Fuck the trailer park manager."

Had Conner actually said that? He must be taking this seriously.

"The bandages were in the trash. You tossed it, you lost it. That's police work 101. Of course, the lab report isn't in so that might be a moot point."

"Yeah, I had a couple of lab reports on my desk yesterday, but several are still missing, including that one." Damn. He hadn't meant to admit his life was so dull, he willingly went into the office on a Saturday.

Conner ignored him. "It'll be tricky, but a case can be made that you going over there was exigent circumstances. You're the one who understood the situation. Still, using statutory rape as a bargaining tool might be the best way to go. It doesn't matter if she's been married before. She isn't married to him and she's underage. As for you ruining her life, what a load of rubbish. Junior Redden did that, along with a series of poor choices she made on her own."

Kelly hadn't chosen to have a stepfather who abused her or a mother who didn't protect her, but yeah, she had made some poor choices.

"Jeannie's mother will be here in the morning. She has to stop by the kennel first and board her dog. They aren't open on Sunday. I should be in the office by noon."

"What are you talking about? You're off duty for six weeks."

"I don't like to leave things unresolved. My mother-in-law will be here for the next ten days. If Kelly admits she doesn't know whether Junior left during the night, and if the lab finds traces of drugs in her blood, that case is finished."

Noah opened his mouth to object, but Conner shook his head. "It's as wrapped up as we can make it. Anything else is for the lawyers to decide. You worrying about who'll say what won't make a drop of difference. I figure Jeannie and her mom will be talking so much, they won't even notice I'm gone for two days."

Conner was right. He'd been chewing on his problems with about as much success as an ant with a bone. It would work out how it was meant to work out. If necessary, he'd hire that overpriced, overdressed, smooth-talking lawyer to clear his name.

He almost smiled. Seeing Junior Redden try to face down Tom Meyers might be worth the cost.

Either way, his part in the Redden murders was finished. There was only one case left he cared about. "Okay, we've got two days to figure out who keeps bumping off Beneficial Products employees. And yes, I'm counting Rodney Graham as an employee. He took their money and did their dirty work."

CHAPTER TWENTY-TWO

THERE WAS A time, before Betsy died, when Noah dreaded Mondays. Not anymore. For the last eleven months, he'd been happy to see the conclusion of the weekend. To have somewhere he needed to be. People who depended on him.

Today was different. He was actually excited to go into work.

The Beneficial Products murders were about more than just three homicides. Make that four. The R&D guy's car crash was in another county, but still tied to the others. That company had—at the least—been screwing around with baby formula.

Add to that, this would be his last chance to work with Conner for the six weeks. Maybe forever.

Lola seemed to know her way downtown, almost driving herself. Conner wouldn't be in until after lunch so Noah checked his email for any reports that hadn't come on Saturday.

At the top of the list was the lab report on the bandages retrieved from The Land of Lost Pines dumpster. The blood was definitely Kelly's and contained a heavy dose of the same pain medication Junior had been prescribed for his bad back.

After a dose like that, she wouldn't have woken up if a troupe of monkeys had run screaming through the trailer breaking dishes. Certainly not if Junior slipped out long enough to murder his parents.

The ADA assigned to the Redden case was a first class weenie. Afraid to charge Junior while he had an alibi. Well, he didn't have any excuse now. Junior's flimsy alibi had developed a king-sized hole and resulted in possible additional charges.

One call to the DA's office and Junior's indictment was back on the books. Another call to the jail ensured he wouldn't be released before the paperwork went through.

He didn't have any way to help Kelly, but he could ease her mind. He called the bar and Cooter answered.

"This is Noah Daugherty. Is Kelly around?"

"Yeah, she's in the back. I've hired her to clean the bathrooms, mop out the place, and wash the dishes. It's not much, but it comes with a free hamburger and all the fries she can eat. Hold on. I'll get her."

Cooter set the receiver down with a *clunk* and heavy footsteps thudded away from the phone.

Hell. Waiting tables in a bar and living with Junior wasn't much, but cleaning bathrooms and sleeping on a cot in the back room was worse. It wasn't his fault, but that didn't make him feel any better.

Kelly's footsteps were much softer. "Hey, Noah. I stopped by the Sheriff's station yesterday and told them the whole story. That Junior knew who you were before he attacked you and that he threatened to kill me. I even said I asked you to come out Saturday. I might have stretched the truth a little, but I sort of expected Cooter would tell you where I was. Hope that gets you out of any trouble I caused."

Damn. Now he felt even worse. "You didn't have to do that, Kelly, but it's definitely appreciated. I know things are tough for you now, but I have news that might help."

"Funny you should say that. This isn't so bad. I kind of like being on my own. Taking care of myself. I'll be eighteen next month so I should be able to find a job. Cooter says I can stay here until then."

"Well if you want to go back to the trailer, Junior won't be getting out any time soon. Lab tests proved he drugged you the night his parents were killed. The DA has filed murder charges against him plus the assault charges for hitting you."

"I went back there yesterday and picked up my things. I don't ever want to see that place again. Too many memories. Most of them bad."

He'd barely disconnected when another email popped up on his computer. This one had *Beneficial Products baby formula* in the subject line.

His hand trembled as he clicked *open.*

The first time he read it, his mind wouldn't accept what he was seeing. He took a deep breath, closed his eyes, and counted to five before reading it a second time.

According to the county lab, Conner's Beneficial Products carton of baby formula contained low-grade powdered cow's milk cut liberally with wood pulp, cornstarch, talcum, and a few chemicals he couldn't pronounce.

Holy Crap! They'd fed that stuff to babies? Noah's stomach cramped and he resisted the urge to throw up. What if Conner had taken it home for Betsy?

What about parents who *had* given it to their children? Sick children.

He sucked in a lungful of air, trying to fill the hollow space in his chest. That poison needed to be taken off the market, fast. Lieutenant Jansen, the Chief of Detectives, and the Chief of Police were all in a meeting at City Hall. He couldn't get through to them if he tried.

And if he did, they'd want more information before taking steps.

Think. Think. Think. Madlyn Gwinn had to know. She was the CEO. In order to turn a failing business around, she hadn't just cut personnel. She'd cut corners.

The guy in the car crash. He was head of R&D. Research and Development. He was probably the one who figured out what products to use.

Craig Spencer. As head of accounting, he would have shopped around for the cheapest suppliers. Even if he wasn't aware *exactly* what those shipments contained, he'd discouraged Brandt Kittrell from buying it so he knew it was useless, if not dangerous.

What about Rodney Graham? No one at Beneficial Products would have risked telling him what was going on. He was a hired gun. Paid to use his name and position to hawk a product he obviously knew was inferior.

Okay, whose grieving relatives should he contact?

The R&D guy. He'd been divorced, so it was unlikely anyone knew his secrets. Wade Gwinn. A joke. Tom Meyers, Esq. would never let him close to the grieving widower.

Rodney Graham. Not worth talking to his beneficiaries, although his nurse might be another story.

That left Evie Spencer. Had Craig told her anything? From what Noah had gathered about their relationship, not likely. However, anything was possible. And he had an excuse to visit her and find out. It was right there on Conner's to-do list.

Question Evie Spencer about the pool cue bridge.

Noah tried for his best smile, but Evie Spencer wasn't buying it. She didn't say a word, just pivoted and trudged toward the back of the house, leaving the door half open.

She hadn't slammed it in his face or told him to leave, so he followed her inside. He found her at the kitchen counter, pouring him a cup of coffee. The digital clock over the oven read 9:48. He'd skipped breakfast in an attempt to clear his desk before Conner got in. His only coffee so far, one cup of brown sludge from the vending machine.

He took the cup and nodded his thanks. "How are you doing, Evie? Do you need anything?" That sounded lame, even to his own ears.

"My husband back?" She perched on a barstool next to the counter and he copied her.

Yep. He'd started off on the wrong foot, as he so often did.

She must have forgiven him. She took a sip of coffee and said, "I'm hanging in there."

And she seemed to be right. Her color was better. Her shoulders didn't slump. Her eyes held signs of life.

"How's Joey handling things?"

"I swear there's a smart little boy hiding in there somewhere. I told him about his dad. He's sad. I can tell. But he copes better with the house quiet."

Noah looked around. The house *was* quiet. "Your family's not here?"

"No. They swore they'd help me take care of everything. Then they beat feet out of here as soon as the memorial service finished and they found out I'd probably be broke before this whole thing was over."

He took a sip of his coffee. Hot. Strong. Just the way he liked it. "Why do you say that?"

"With Madlyn gone, and Stefan Hueber from R&D gone, and Craig gone. Not to mention Dr. Graham. I don't see how Beneficial Products can continue to operate."

Little did she know what shit was about to hit the fan.

She played with her cup, not looking at him. "At best, it'll be years before they're back up to strength. I've got Craig's life insurance, and I'll be eligible for social security, but if the company goes under, I'll lose his 401(k) and my health insurance and his company retirement and his year-end bonus."

Ripples. Every death caused ripples.

"That little bitch at the front desk has already called to ask for his company car back along with his company credit card. I hadn't planned to use it, but now I'm tempted to go out and stock up on food and supplies for Joey and anything else I can think of."

He couldn't tell her to go ahead. Odds were some schmuck from a bankruptcy firm would show up and ask for the money back. But he sort of hoped she did it. She hadn't killed her husband and her life was about to get a whole lot worse because some dickwad had.

She pinned him with a stare worthy of a predatory jaguar. Maybe she had more inner strength than he gave her credit for.

He'd been making that mistake a lot lately. A fatal flaw in his chosen profession.

"Have you figured out what happened to Craig?" she asked.

Ahh. That was the question, wasn't it? "We're working on it. I wondered if you had any ideas or if Craig ever said anything about Beneficial Products that might help us."

"Craig had two talents. He was a whiz with taxes. I swear, he knew the tax code by heart. He read the latest manual at night like a mystery novel. Plus, he was a slash and burn accountant. Companies hired him to find ways to cut production costs. And he did it better than most because he used logic and didn't consider the human consequences. He never talked much about his work—he knew I didn't completely approve—but lately he'd clammed up entirely. He didn't like whatever was happening at that company, yet he was making more money than ever and we needed it for Joey."

"And you don't know what the company was doing that bothered him?"

"He never said, but I suspected he was finally beginning to develop some empathy for the people who got laid off. We have neighbors who lost their jobs and had to accept something with less pay and worse hours. Does that help?"

Not really. From everything he'd learned so far, it didn't look like an angry worker was responsible for this string of murders. "You never know. Every little bit helps."

They both drank their coffee in silence before Noah broached the subject he'd used as an excuse to drive over here. "I was wondering about something. Did you ever own a pool table?"

"No, we already had two kids and Joey on the way when

we moved into this place. Besides, Brandt Kittrell had one in his garage. That was when he was married to Sophie. Our kids played together all the time. None of us had much money, so on Saturday nights we'd cook outside and play a few games of pool. Craig loved the game because it's based on math and angles. He'd never played before but was soon sweeping every match. Brandt didn't much like that. Things got tense for a while. Craig never did have enough sense to be a gracious winner. Plus, Brandt lost a pretty good job with an oil company and had to scramble to make ends meet. We were making more money just as he was making less."

Yeah. Chelsea Kittrell had mentioned that Craig didn't score well in the *works and plays well with others* column. But that didn't account for the other deaths.

Evie's eyes got a faraway look. "Sophie caught Brandt in an affair at work, which is what caused him to lose his job. She left him and took their kids with her. Candace and Heath, our older kids, went off to school and Joey doesn't play with other children. Brandt married Chelsea. She used to race motorcycles—I guess she never lost that need for competition—and Craig told him that because she occasionally won money, he should call it a business and could deduct all her expenses from their taxes. Voila! They were best friends again. I think he sold the pool table to buy nursery equipment. Still, those were good times. Thanks for bringing up happy memories."

Yeah. He was full of cheerful tidbits. Just call him the good news fairy.

"I heard your sister couldn't move down here for a couple of years. Have you had any luck finding anyone to help with Joey?"

"It seems nobody wants to live in a converted garage and

take care of a forty-pound kid who still wears a diaper. Not for the money I can afford to pay. I don't need help twenty-four hours a day. I was thinking about putting up a sign at the junior college."

"I happen to know someone who needs a place to live. She's used to taking care of her disabled little brother. Maybe the two of you could work out some type of arrangement."

Evie's face lit up and she grabbed Kelly's number out of his hand.

Maybe he was the good news fairy after all. About time something positive came out of this terrible mess. Heaven knows, it had ruined enough lives.

Time to meet Conner and find *someone* to arrest.

CHAPTER
TWENTY-THREE

Noah almost laughed. He'd never before seen Conner with bags under his eyes. "How's it going, bro? Baby doing okay?"

Conner put his face in his hands and bent almost to the desk. "How could someone that tiny make so much noise? And what's the deal with the all-nighter? She slept so long yesterday afternoon I went in twice to make sure she was alright. Then at midnight she decides it's time to party. I've never been this happy for the peace and quiet of our office."

Noah glanced around. Lefty Bob had an unwilling suspect cuffed to a chair beside his desk, yelling about his innocence. The new guy cursed at a paper jam in the printer. Earl's phone rang endlessly at his empty desk. The Lieu stomped through the room radiating his displeasure at his meeting with the big bosses.

This was peace and quiet?

"What about Jeannie? I hope we didn't tire her out yesterday."

Conner didn't look up. His voice was barely audible. "We

had to call the doctor this morning. Seems the baby wasn't nursing vigorously at first and now Jeannie has a clogged milk duct and one engorged breast. She's using hot compresses and Betsy is eating better now so she should be fine by morning."

Noah *really* didn't want to talk about Jeannie's breasts. He didn't even want to think about them. But Conner was his partner, and you did what you had to do. "Is she in pain?"

"Ever get a blow to the balls when you were playing sports? How'd you feel the next day? Only she has to keep using it if she wants to get better."

Ouch

Two bloodshot eyes peered at Noah over folded hands. "I don't know whether to pray this case lasts all week so I can grab a nap at my desk like Lefty Bob does on occasion, or hope we wrap it up by quitting time because I can't pace the floor all night singing lullabies and get up for work in the morning."

Conner, singing lullabies? Poor Betsy. Sure, the man liked music, but that didn't mean he could carry a tune. The child might be scarred for life.

Time to put him out of his misery. "I have some information that might be of help in closing this case."

"Daugherty. Crawford. My office." The Lieu's voice boomed across the room.

Every. Damn. Time.

How was he supposed to get any work done when he had to report in every two minutes?

He pushed back from his desk and stalked to his boss's office. Conner was a little slower, but followed suit. The room smelled like stale coffee and the ridiculous concoction the Lieu rubbed on his head in hopes of halting his receding hairline.

Jansen leaned forward, hands on his desk. "What do you have to say for yourself?"

About what? There were so many things he could be in hot water for. If he guessed the wrong one, he was facing double trouble.

The Lieu pointed at Conner. "Your own union fought for Family Leave and you show up here three days after your wife gives birth? You want to screw this thing up for every man on the force?"

Conner was the one in a bind? A cool breeze of relief swept over Noah.

"I plan on taking my full leave, sir. I have a few things I need to clear up and this seemed like a good time while my mother-in-law is here to help out."

As far as Noah knew, Conner got along well with Jeannie's mother, even liked the woman. Jansen was another story. He was well known to despise his mother-in-law. He'd go out in the field to supervise a traffic ticket to avoid her. "Alright, then. See that you don't dawdle around here too long."

"No, sir. A couple of days should do it." Conner glanced at Noah for support.

Jansen didn't give him time to answer. "Don't think you're out of the woods, Daugherty. What's this I hear about you getting beat up by Junior Redden—*again?* Legal specifically warned you to stay away from him, his girlfriend, and that dump they call a home. Witness tampering is no joke. "

Noah stuffed his hands in his pockets. His nose was itching, but he didn't dare call attention to it. He'd studied it in the mirror while shaving and the swelling seemed to have gone down, but it was still tender to the touch. "Wasn't my idea, sir. She called and asked me to come out and help her. When I got there, Junior was slapping her around. I've been told she's meeting with the DA today, ready to spill everything she knows. That should get me off the hook with Legal."

"So I heard." Jansen settled back into his leather, ergonomically designed chair.

If his boss ever got promoted, Noah was going to steal that chair and leave his hard plastic one in its place.

"You're damn lucky." Jansen put his feet on his desk and the chair conformed perfectly to his movements. "The DA's got some leverage. He's going to offer the creep a walk on the assault and statutory rape charges if he forgets about suing you and the department."

"You can't let him do that. With Kelly's testimony, Redden doesn't have a leg to stand on. We should slap him with everything we've got. You never know what will stick."

Jansen ignored him and kept talking. He was the boss. He could do that. "Won't take any time off his sentence, but prison life's hard on convicted rapists. So, it's been what, ten days? And you've solved the one case you already had solved—"

"Plus the Delafied case."

Conner shot him a questioning look.

"The M.E. ruled it an accidental overdose. Might be nice to know who sold him the dope, but for now, it's off the books." Okay, so that was another instance of closing something that wasn't actually a homicide, but it still counted.

The Lieu glared at him for interrupting. "But the bodies are stacking up on the Gwinn homicide. Have you narrowed the field of suspects? I understand she fired a lot of people."

"We don't have a specific person of interest, but we're getting close. The thing is, I don't think it has anything to do with the workers she fired. I received this report from the lab a couple of minutes ago. I was about to bring it in to you." Noah handed one copy to his partner and another to his boss.

Conner's face blanched white as the paper he held. Jansen's turned red and he started to sputter. "What the hell is this stuff supposed to be?"

"Baby formula. Created especially for sick infants."

"Where did you get the sample?"

"Conner bought it at the dead doctor's office. We have to get out there and stop them. This stuff is still on the shelves. Parents are buying it as we speak."

"Hold your damn horses. I want this poison off the market as much as you do, but we have to go about it the right way. Was it entered as evidence at the time?"

Shit, they'd screwed up on that one. "No, sir. At the time we were still throwing darts to see where they landed. Trying to figure out a direction for the investigation."

Jansen didn't look too angry. He'd been here before. "I'll notify the mayor and pass the problem off to the DA. Let him handle it. Can you imagine the lawsuits if we checked a container someone from the doctor's office had contaminated for revenge? We'll have to test samples taken directly from the factory."

What a load of crap. They knew one carton contained a dangerous substance. Shut it down. Pull it off the market until they were sure. They'd done that with pain killers and those were for adults.

Jansen held the lab report in one hand and reached across stacks of paper for his phone with the other. "I'll get right on this. It won't take but a day or two, I promise. Meanwhile, get your asses out there and find out who's killing off the people capable of giving us a straight answer."

Noah didn't have to be told twice. He scooted out of the Lieu's office and back to his desk. This time Conner almost passed him.

"I don't like this one bit." Conner didn't often get frustrated. When he did, he picked at his thumbnail.

Noah glanced at his partner. His cuticle was starting to bleed.

"I don't blame you. I want that stuff off the shelves yesterday. The boss has a point though. It's not up to us. This has to be done right. Let's finish this case and get you home to Jeannie and Betsy. I give you my word. If nothing happens in the next forty-eight hours, I'll bring that fucking company down myself."

Conner must have believed him. He dropped his hand into his lap and left his thumb alone. "So where are we going to start on this case? You seem to have learned a lot since we last talked. Have any suggestions?"

"I've got an idea. It's a little far-fetched, but I'd like your opinion on someone. He's had a couple of run-ins with Craig Spencer, but he seems too weak, too spineless, to have murdered four people. The thing is, I've recently realized people can be tougher than they look. It's a twenty minute drive. I'll keep my mouth shut so you can take a nap on the way over there."

Conner didn't have to answer. His yawn said it all.

The big cop, Daugherty, had been at Evie's house all morning. Was he closing in or floundering? Either way, that fat witch wouldn't be any help.

She didn't know a thing. But only because she didn't *want* to know anything. She'd buried her head in the sand all the way up to her useless ass.

As if having a sick kid was enough of an excuse. Had she ever worried about other people's kids?

They'd had a sick kid once and they never caught a break. Nobody came to their aid. Nobody looked out for them.

Karma really was a bitch. One mistake in a lifetime of doing the right thing and what happens? Everything good in the world is snatched away. Circling down the drain before your very eyes.

While the rest of the world watches and grows fatter.

To hell with that. Sometimes Karma needed a little boost. The odds were even now. Well, not even, but better. There were still several names on the list. Those who would never get their just desserts. Never pay for what they'd done.

Only one name untouched, unscathed, left a pang of regret. One name that should have topped the list. One person who had physically done the dirty work. One worker bee who had scoured the world for the cheapest products. One lost soul who would in time taste the fires of Hell.

A name not easily come by. Found only when the Spencer home emptied for that joke of a memorial service. As if anyone that evil should be lauded.

Luckily, Craig was as sloppy with the security on his home computer as he had been six months ago. When this search for the truth started.

All that information available at the touch of a finger if you knew the password.

Candace.

The one child he cared about. The only one who took after him instead of Evie.

Six letters, one capital. No numerals or signs. Weak. Like

him.

And that led to another name. Darius Breeden had escaped his punishment. So far.

Too bad his name hadn't come up earlier. He'd certainly earned the right to go first. But that first day at Craig's computer had been a shocker, with emails and price points and delivery versus manufacturing costs and rational discussions about lives lost and the cost of settling lawsuits out of court. The time had sped by in a blur and suddenly Evie was coming in the back door leaving barely enough time to slide out the front.

Madlyn Gwinn's name was on the company website along with Stefan Hueber, head of R&D. Darius Breeden had slipped by until too late, unnoticed, invisible. Lucky for him then, but time had run out now.

Maybe that was best. Let him live to face the vitriol that would rain down on his head for the rest of his days.

Because all this filth would come out soon, and no one involved would ever be clean again.

But that begged the question: Did the scales in Lady Justice's hand weigh the death of those who committed evil for the sake of monetary gain as heavily as the death of those innocents who perished due to their greed? Did one outweigh the other leaving the scales balanced? Would the punisher receive the same punishment as the punished, no matter how much they deserved their fate?

Daugherty might not have all the pieces to the puzzle. The who might have escaped him, but surely he'd latched on to the why. He wasn't that stupid.

Otherwise, why was his shiny black truck parked at their curb?

CHAPTER
TWENTY-FOUR

"WE'RE HERE."

Conner opened one eye. "Where's here?"

He tried to glance around, but while the nap had done wonders for his energy level, it had also given him a king-sized crick in his neck.

"Brandt Kittrell's house. He lives next door to Craig Spencer. They didn't get along and Craig made more money than he did."

"Not the strongest of motives." Noah had said it was far-fetched, but this was downright flimsy.

"He once owned a pool table and had a sick kid who used Beneficial Products baby formula which Craig wouldn't give him for free."

"Getting warmer."

"Living next door gives him easy access. That's motive, means, and opportunity. The golden trifecta."

"Almost there. What about Madlyn Gwinn and Rodney Graham?"

"I don't think he knew her personally, but her name is easy to find. It's on the company web page. And Graham was the doctor who prescribed the contaminated formula."

"Bingo. Let's talk to the guy." He glanced at the one-story white brick house. Two cars filled the driveway and a blue medical equipment van was parked in front of them. "What are all these cars doing here?"

"Don't know. They weren't here this morning."

Conner rolled his neck to one side until he heard a loud *crack*. Better. "We're not going to learn anything sitting outside." He opened Lola's door and stepped onto the curb.

The grass was thick and spongy under his feet. The recent rain had left it so green it looked painted. Noah had told him about his interview with the Kittrells, so he thought he was prepared.

He was wrong.

Brandt Kittrell was a drab-looking man. His hair fell somewhere on the color chart between light brown and dark blond. His eyes looked like dabs of mud. With blondish brows and lashes that faded into his face.

A slight beard shadow and worry lines around his eyes coupled with sagging shoulders and a rumpled shirt left the only fitting description as *defeated*.

Noah's voice was hushed, as if not wanting to disturb anyone in the house. "Hey, Brandt. This is my partner, Conner Crawford. We'd like to talk to you for a moment, if you have time."

Conner held out his hand and received a limp handshake in return. Noah wasn't usually so gentle—pushing his way inside was more his speed—but everything about the man and the house screamed illness, as if they were literally crossing death's door.

"Only for a minute. Hospice is setting up some equipment for Chelsea."

One step inside and Conner noticed the medicinal smell. Almost like the hospital, but without the hope.

Brandt led them through the darkened living room where pieces of an unassembled hospital bed littered the floor. A workman in blue coveralls matching the van outside studied a set of instructions.

I hope that's easier to put together than Betsy's crib or Chelsea will be sleeping on the floor.

In the hall, a box-like machine roared. A clear plastic tube snaked out of the machine and looped and coiled its way into the kitchen where it ended in a nasal cannula supplying oxygen to Chelsea as she sat at the table, drinking tea.

"Look who's here. Noah came by with his partner, Conner. They want to talk to us for a minute. Do you feel up to it?"

No, we want to talk to your husband. Alone. Noah had said the woman was sick, but he had no idea she was this bad.

"I do if you'll turn down the flow on this stupid machine. I can't hear a thing and it feels like it's going to blow the back of my head off."

Brandt almost tripped over his own feet as he ran to accommodate his wife.

"Sorry about all this." Chelsea waved a hand toward the living room. "Brandt always overreacts. I had a little accident last night. Fell out of bed when I got up to go to the bathroom. I just need to remember to dangle my feet for a minute and get my balance instead of jumping out of bed and running off in the dark. Now I feel like a prisoner. He watches me so close, I can't even go next door to visit Evie alone."

Hurried footsteps preceded Brandt into the room. His eyes flew to Chelsea first as if making sure nothing untoward had happened to her while he was gone. "That feel better, honey?"

"Yes, thanks."

"So what did you need from us?" He glanced at Noah. Conner sat back and observed.

"We're trying to get a clearer picture of Craig Spencer. I understand you had a couple of run-ins with him."

Chelsea snorted. Hard to do with a plastic cannula in her nose.

Brandt's face turned serious as if he were testifying in court and wanted to get his words exactly right. "I think you'd be hard-pressed to find anyone who hasn't had some type of run-in with Craig. We certainly had our ups and downs over the years. The thing is, he could be a real asshole." He glanced at Chelsea in mute apology for his language. "But, it took me years to figure this out; he didn't do it on purpose. He simply didn't know any better."

She nodded and the tube dangling down her chest danced. "According to Evie, Craig came from what we call today a *dysfunctional family.* Back when I was growing up, we called them *trailer trash,* or maybe assholes. His parents had no idea how to deal with a kid whose IQ doubled their's combined so they ignored him. He kind of raised himself. Consequently, he never learned manners or how to deal with people."

"Right." Brandt's head bobbed. "One day he'd do something so rude and thoughtless, you were stunned. The next time you saw him, he'd go out of his way to help. Craig was tall and good-looking and while not rich when they moved here, obviously competent. What my dad called an up-and-comer. Now honey," he glanced at Chelsea. "I know Evie's your friend, but you have to admit, she's not a beauty."

He reached across the table to squeeze her hand and she squeezed back. Conner had seen his parents do the same thing. No offense meant, none taken. Did he and Jeannie have secret signals they didn't realize they sent? Someday would Betsy remember and smile?

"At first, I wondered why he would marry someone like Evie. Within a few weeks, I wondered how he got someone as sweet as Evie to marry him. But once you understand him, it's easier to shrug your shoulders and think *that's just Craig.* I guess I'm saying it's possible someone could hold a grudge against him."

The workman dropped a bed railing in the other room and it hit the floor with a *clang* that reverberated through the house. Brandt flinched as if someone had stuck a knife in his back.

"You didn't have to know Craig personally to hate him. He was a numbers guy. He figured out exactly the speed he had to drive to get the best mileage out of his car. And that's how fast he went. Day, night. Rain, sun. Rush hour or Saturday afternoon. Freeway, or dirt path. Didn't matter to him. That's the speed he drove."

Conner leaned forward and spoke for the first time since they'd entered the house. "Do you know anyone *specifically* who held a grudge against Craig or Beneficial Products?"

"No. Evie mentioned to Chelsea that they were belt-tightening over there. Letting a lot of people go. But that was always the story when Craig took a new job."

"I'm sure Noah's already asked you this, but sometimes people forget things. Did you see or hear anything unusual the night he died?"

"I was at work. Didn't learn about it until the next day."

"What about you, Mrs. Kittrell?"

Brandt answered for her. "She was a little stronger then. I could leave her alone. Before I went to work, I helped her into bed. I made sure she had a book, the TV remote, a glass of water, some fruit or crackers as a snack and her pills. She'd read or watch her programs until the news was over, then take a sleeping pill. She wouldn't have heard a sound."

Conner suddenly realized what had tipped Noah to Brandt Kittrell. Like Kelly Manus, Chelsea wouldn't have a clue what her husband did after she took her sleeping pill. But that was a double-edged sword. She couldn't accuse him, but she couldn't alibi him, either.

Conner closed his memo pad as he and Noah started for the door. Noah stopped suddenly, snapped his fingers, and swung around.

Damn, that man was overacting. He'd blow everything if he kept that up.

"Evie mentioned you used to have a pool table."

Conner watched Brandt's face, but the man didn't blink. If the question worried him, he gave no reaction. "Yeah. We used to have some great Friday nights with Craig and Evie, shooting a few games. That was before I married this wonderful woman." He gave his wife a weak smile. "Sold it to make room for Chelsea's motorcycle. You can leave a car outside, but not a bike. Later, we sold the bike to furnish the nursery."

Only on the last line did his head droop.

"You wouldn't have any of the accessories, would you? I need to buy a gift for a friend with a new pool table. Cues or bridges or, what'd they call that triangle thing to hold the balls?"

"A ball rack. No, that all went with the table. I'm sure you can find some used ones on Craigslist."

Every word, every move replayed in Conner's mind. Brandt Kittrell might just be a better actor than Noah, and his partner had gotten in a lot of practice over the years. But then psychopaths were supposed to be masters at that, weren't they?

Conner didn't utter a sound for the first ten minutes of the drive back to town.

Noah glanced over to see if his partner had gone back to sleep. No, his eyes were open and staring straight ahead. He sucked on his lower lip in a move Noah recognized as deep concentration.

Another three minutes and he couldn't stand it any longer. "So, what do you think of Brandt Kittrell?"

"He's definitely a conundrum. He seems empty, as if life has seeped out of him like a deflated balloon, yet he's very protective of Chelsea. He would never do this for himself, but for his wife? Maybe. If the murders happened after her death, I wouldn't doubt he wanted revenge. While she's alive? Only if he thought it would bring her peace."

An invisible fist punched Noah in the chest. Lola jerked to one side and he overcorrected, swerving from one side of the road to the other. Luckily, traffic was light heading into town.

Conner's head snapped around. "What?"

"Pothole." His voice cracked but he kept driving.

Conner's description had hit too close to home.

On her deathbed, Noah's mother had begged him to find his

father's violin. The one a drug-dealing mugger had killed him for. Noah found the culprit, shoved him, grabbed the violin, two bottles of pills for her breakthrough pain, and ran. Only later did he learn the thief had hit his head, causing his brain to swell, resulting in the man's death.

The police called it a drug deal gone bad. Noah called it the worst mistake of his life. His sister suspected when she found the violin hidden in his closet, but Betsy was the only one who knew the truth. And all because he wanted to bring his mother peace.

Was that what Brandt Kittrell was doing?

"See that you don't hit any more potholes. I'd like to make it home alive." Conner seemed calm, but Noah knew better. Sometimes he thought his partner was psychic.

"Do we know what Brandt Kittrell does for a living?" Conner flipped through pages in his spiral memo pad, putting them back on track.

"Only that he's on the night shift and it's not as good a job as the one he had before he messed up and started screwing somebody at work."

Conner hauled out his iPhone and started punching buttons. "Let me text Earl. Maybe he can find out by the time we get back."

Probably not. Earl was good but slow, and they were pulling into the parking garage now.

As they entered the office, Noah could see Earl, his nose six inches from the computer screen. The man was in serious need of new glasses. Conner started toward him. "I'll see if the computer whisperer has found anything."

"Go ahead. I'll check us in with the boss. I've got to leave in five minutes. I have an appointment to get these stitches out." They had pulled uncomfortably since the day Junior Redden drug him and the pallet attached to his leg across a dusty garbage dump. Now they itched like a mother and he wouldn't miss his appointment to nab Jack the Ripper. If the doc wasn't in, he'd do the job himself.

He was at his desk, making sure the doc wasn't running late when Conner slapped a folder down hard enough to make any loose papers fly. Noah grabbed the sticky note with the doctor's phone number and jerked his head around to see his normally cool, calm, profanity-hating partner, his face a dull red, his eyes smoldering, his chin jutting out far enough to stop traffic.

"The son-of-a-bitch works as a night security guard for fucking Beneficial Products."

Noah sat in the black leather Herman Miller office chair Betsy had bought him as a housewarming gift. He'd slipped into shorts—any fabric touching his new scar felt like spiders dancing up and down his leg—and rested his foot on his desk.

Tomorrow was going to be a bitch. The doctor had given him a numbing cream, but only after forcing him to sit through a lecture.

You keep getting into fights, one of these days it'll be something I can't fix.

The human body is a fragile machine. Don't treat it like a punching bag.

You're not a kid anymore. How long do you plan to keep up this foolishness?

I'm getting tired of patching you up.

Your body's starting to look like the zipper department in a fabric store.

Keep it up. I don't care. I've got three kids to send to college. Blah, blah, blah, blah.

Did everyone think he did this on purpose? First Conner, then Rachelle, now the doc. It wasn't like he enjoyed getting knifed, beat-up, shot at. Maybe someone should talk to the jerk-offs who kept trying to kill him.

Aww, fuck. Might as well call Conner and get it over with. One more lecture today and he'd be done.

He wasn't disappointed.

"Did the doc happen to mention what might have happened to you with an open wound rolling around in garbage and rat pooh? You could have lost your leg."

Next time he'd ask the perp to hold off a minute until they could find a sterile surface. That should go over well.

A change of subject was definitely called for. "How's Jeannie? Her breast feeling better?" It felt so wrong to ask that.

"Much. Still tender but improving. She should be well by morning."

"What happened after I left? You find out anything about Brant Kittrell?" Sweet Pea jumped into his lap, looking for any treats that might be available. Noah found a Cheetos nub hiding behind his keyboard and gave it to her.

"According to the guy in charge of scheduling, he worked the nights Madlyn Gwinn, Craig Spencer, and Rodney Graham died. Stefan Hueber suffered his fatal car crash on a Sunday. Brandt didn't work that day."

"We need to concentrate on the Gwinn and Spencer homicides. Those are our best bets. Hueber's car could have been tampered with at any time prior to his last race and proving exactly when the drugs were put in Graham's scotch might be tough. Any good defense attorney could blow smoke all over those two cases." He pictured Tom Meyer with his white hair and expensive suits. His air of superiority. He'd make a fool of that underage, underpaid ADA.

"I agree, but the lab says the roofies were in Graham's ice, not his scotch which makes it harder to claim any other night except the one he died. As for the Gwinn case, bad news. The video gurus cleaned up the tape and swear no one entered or left her complex through the front gate between ten thirty that night and five forty-five the next morning. Are you on Facebook?"

What? Hardly. That was an asinine question.

Conner didn't wait for his answer. "Stefan Hueber was. All kinds of photos of him grinning like an idiot next to that papier-mâché car he tooled around the track in. Guess where he stored it when he wasn't racing? In his garage at home. Where he didn't have security cameras. Less than two miles from the Kittrells' house."

"Has Brandt ever worked as a mechanic? Would he have any idea how to sabotage a car?"

Noah listened to the click of keystrokes as Conner checked his computer. "Nothing listed on his resume."

"Okay, so we start with Spencer. Once we have that one nailed down, we'll work on the others. Damn, I wish I could figure out how someone got to Madlyn Gwinn. Do you suppose she's a red herring? That her husband did her and Kittrell did the rest?"

"Are you thinking Gwinn's death set him off and he used it as a red herring to take out the others?"

"Except that Hueber came first." Sweet Pea gave up begging, circled twice, digging her toenails into Noah's thigh, and settled down for a nap.

"That one's still listed as unknown. Could have been an accident."

"You're the one who hates coincidences."

"I know, but they have to exist. Why else would someone have made up the word?"

Noah would have pulled his hair out but there wasn't any point. It wouldn't help. "Let's meet someone from the security company at Beneficial Products first thing in the morning. I want to know exactly what Kittrell does. Where he's stationed, what areas he covers, if he has to clock in, if anyone sees him during his shift, and if there are any security cameras."

CHAPTER TWENTY-FIVE

NOAH PINCHED THE bridge of his nose. Maybe if he counted to ten. "So you don't know what Brandt Kittrell did at night."

"I showed you what he did. He came on at seven and clocked in on the factory floor. He took the passkey and the clipboard from the officer going off duty. They went over anything suspicious that happened on the last shift, who, if anyone, was in the building, and if anyone or anything was expected. Then the eleven-to-seven officer left and he took over. He patrolled the building and grounds until I relieved him at three and we went through the same routine. He was allowed to sit in the company break room from eleven-thirty to twelve for lunch and he had two fifteen-minute breaks whenever he felt the need."

"But what did he do once he was alone?"

The security guard sighed, exasperation coating his face. "He patrolled the outside grounds and the inside, including the offices and factory floor. He changed directions at least once per shift at random times. More often if he saw or heard anything suspicious. He recorded any unusual happenings on this clipboard, a copy of which is given every day to our supervisor and this company."

The man was short and skinny and fourteen years old if he was a day. His uniform was several sizes too large and drooped on nonexistent shoulders. He wouldn't have frightened off a flea.

"And you know this how?" Noah was trying to stay calm. Honestly he was. But the stupidity of some people never ceased to amaze him.

"I taught him myself. He followed me for one week before he was allowed to work on his own."

"Our officers are very well trained." The business-suited executive from the security company looked out of place tramping through the weeds surrounding Beneficial Products. He probably had never been in the field in his life, dispensing his overrated knowledge from a desk chair in an air conditioned office.

Two steps behind him, Conner chuckled as he made notes on his memo pad. Noah took a deep breath and immediately started sneezing. Heat, dust, pollen, insects and a chain link fence with more holes than Swiss cheese. Anyone could come in or out unnoticed.

Conner took pity on him and stepped forward, placing a hand on the kid's shoulder. "No one doubts your dedication. We're simply asking; once you finished training Brandt Kittrell and he began to work alone, how do you know he followed instructions? Does he have to punch in from time to time during his shift? Are there security cameras on the inside or outside of the building?"

The COO spoke up, having finally found a subject he actually knew about. "He punches in and out when he starts and finishes his shift and for lunch but not for breaks. His lunch time is a suggestion only. He can move it up or back by half an hour. We wouldn't make him run from the far end of the building to get there in time."

How thoughtful of you. "Okay, that covers the time clock. What about security cameras?"

Noah had addressed the question to the company official, but the security officer answered. "There are a few scattered around. One facing the parking lot, one in the back, one in the factory, and a couple covering the executive offices."

A slight blush covered the kid's face. "Sometimes in the middle of the night, if I get lonely, I wave to the camera. I like to think somebody in the home office is watching and waves back. Makes me feel safer."

Was he for real? He was so young he probably had to call his mother if he was coming home late. No one was watching him. He was on his own. God help him if anything happened.

The company exec coughed and mumbled, a hand over his mouth, "About that, we may need to talk. Later."

Yep. The cameras were for show only. Not connected to anything. Why was he not surprised?

Noah glared at the useless, overweight company stooge, sweating in the sun, a coating of dust on his wingtips, his soft hands hanging limp. "Before this day is over, send me all of Kittrell's time sheets and logs for the last three months. Don't make me get a subpoena."

Lt. Jansen stood outside his office, his arms crossed over his puny chest, his wooly eyebrows knotted into an almost unbroken straight line. "Got anything to report? The brass is banging on my door and the way you two keep avoiding giving me updates, I'm tempted to let them have you."

"Almost there, boss. We've got the guy, we're just trying to wrap him up with a bow." Noah couldn't blame the Lieu. They had been negligent in keeping him in the loop on their progress.

"What'd ya have on him?"

"He had a sick kid who used the formula and later died."

"That's good, but if the kid was already sick, why would he think the formula caused it?"

Conner flipped pages in his memo pad as if every word was sworn testimony. "He worked at Beneficial Products as a night security guard. He'd have seen the bags with Chinese and Russian writing. Also, he lives next door to Craig Spencer, once owned a pool table, and Dr. Graham prescribed the formula."

"Getting better. You find any connection with the Gwinn homicide? That's the one I'm getting the most heat about."

Figured. Everyone was equal, but the rich were more equal than most. "Haven't got that tied down. Once we prove one case, the others will fall into place." But only if he could figure out how Kittrell got into that gated community without being seen.

"What else do you need and how long will it take to gift wrap the sucker?" Jansen's eyebrows eased a quarter inch.

"Waiting on the guy's time sheet from his job." Noah glanced toward his computer. They could get started on it if the Lieu would let them get back to work.

"Do you need a subpoena?"

"Naw. His boss sees the wisdom in sending it without one." Surprising what a little blackmail could accomplish. If the worker bees discovered the security cameras were phony and no one was keeping an eye on them, even that dedicated young security guard might decide to put his feet up for a short rest every once in a while.

"Let me know if you need a stern phone call to light a fire under his butt."

"Will do, boss. Thanks." Sometimes he forgot Jansen was on their side. "You got anything about keeping that formula off the shelves?"

"It's working its way up the chain of command. I had a call an hour ago from someone in the Chief's office asking if I was sure about the allegations. I said I trusted my men. Did they trust the county lab?"

Noah bit back his impatience. He had promised to leave that side of the investigation to those in charge. He only hoped they worked as hard as he and Conner did on their portion of the job.

Noah worked the phone while he waited for his least favorite security company to email a copy of Brandt Kittrell's time sheet and log book. Meanwhile, he still had one open case on the books.

His best suspect had disappeared before he and Conner could question him. Reports surfaced occasionally of sightings in Oregon or Detroit or Canada or Thailand or, his favorite, Playa Del Carman. He'd pressed for a ticket to the resort city to search for the guy but Jansen had threatened to put him on night shift if he didn't quit bothering him.

At least once a week he called the guy's family and, on the off chance his parents didn't want to turn him in, he called their neighbors. He yawned while talking to a ninety-year-old woman who spent her life looking out of windows and claimed Noah's calls were the highlight of her week, but, "No, that no-good Hendrix boy hadn't showed his ugly face."

Conner used the wait to check Kittrell's driving record. During the time of the murders had he gotten any speeding tickets? Parking tickets? Used his EZ Pass on the tollway? Had a wreck or fender-bender?

When Noah's computer *dinged* with an incoming email, he almost cheered.

About damn time.

He printed off two copies of Kittrell's information so both he and Conner could get to work. He also printed a calendar for the same time period so he could make notes, look for a pattern. Or spot something that didn't fit in his usual pattern.

For someone who didn't sound thrilled about his job, Kittrell was pretty conscientious. He generally clocked in six to ten minutes before his shift started, giving him a chance to go over the logbook with the departing guard. Once he was only one minute early, but never late.

Clocking out followed roughly the same pattern. As for his lunch breaks, while the time varied by fifteen minutes, he stuck to the suggested schedule.

According to the M.E., Spencer died between eleven forty-five and twelve thirty.

On the night of Craig Spencer's murder, Kittrell clocked out for lunch at twelve twenty-seven and back in at twelve fifty-four. Shorting himself by three minutes.

Even at night, with no traffic, he couldn't have made it home in less than twenty minutes. Add to that another five minutes to get out of the building and to his car plus time to get into position and kill Spencer and he would have missed Dr. M's estimated time of death on the far end by an hour or more.

The doc could be off, but not by that much. Spencer could have gotten home later than Evie remembered, but the doc swore other factors backed up her recollections.

That still left the eleven forty-five estimate on the front end. Hell, Kittrell could have turned around and left directly after clocking in.

Or could he?

Noah glanced at Conner. His partner was deep into reading the same report. He chewed on his lip and made notations on a legal pad, giving off a tuneless hum as he worked.

The logbook was a jumble of scratched notes and formal reports. A notation of *kids necking in the parking lot* was followed by *coyote in back lot.*

What the fuck? A coyote less than a mile from downtown Houston? Kittrell must be seeing things. It was probably a big tom cat, or a dog. Maybe he should keep an eye on Sweet Pea at night, just in case.

The log of employees on site was more formal. Madlyn Gwinn and Craig Spencer often worked late. On the night of his murder, Spencer was the last to leave the building. He signed out at four minutes past seven, putting him home exactly when his wife remembered.

Copies of other forms were stapled to the log. Not often, maybe twice a month, deliveries were made after hours. When that happened, Kittrell signed for them.

A small shiver raced down Noah's spine. They had him. He could protest he never looked at the bags of ingredients kept in the factory storeroom. But here was his signature on a delivery from China. And another from Russia.

He dug through the invoices looking for the date of Spencer's murder. There it was. Four fifty-pound bags from Taiwan signed by Kittrell and Conner's favorite eighteen-wheeler driver Billy Bowman. And time stamped eleven forty-eight.

Noah flipped back and forth through the pages, searching for something he missed. Anything. He checked the notes he'd made at the autopsy and the ones he'd jotted on the makeshift calendar.

He glanced at Conner who had quit humming and now drummed his fingers on the desk.

He didn't want to say it. He couldn't. So Conner had to.

"Brandt Kittrell couldn't have killed Craig Spencer."

CHAPTER
TWENTY-SIX

NOAH DROVE WHILE Conner dug in his billfold for the crumbled slip of paper he'd used to scratch down Billy Bowman's number. The truck driver answered on the first ring and Conner put his phone on speaker so Noah could hear.

Billy's squeaky voice hadn't gotten any deeper since Friday. "Hey there, new papa. How's the parental life treating you? Jeannie and the baby doing okay?"

"You think Jeannie would let a little thing like major surgery slow her down? She and her mother hardly let me get close to Betsy. They're going to spoil that baby. That was supposed to be my job."

"You'll have the next eighteen years to do that. You infringe on your mother-in-law's cuddle time and you got big trouble down the road."

Enough chitchat. Time to get down to business. "I've got a little trouble right now."

"Have anything to do with Beneficial Products?"

"You got it right on the first guess."

"Figured you'd run into difficulty when I hadn't seen any headlines by this morning."

He wasn't too happy about that either. "In all your trips to that factory, you make any friends?"

That should be an easy *yes*. Billy made friends everywhere he went.

"More acquaintances than friends. Most everybody's been let go except those who are so desperate for work they don't care what the company's up to. Guys over there are scared to say more than two words to you."

"Either of those two words ever have anything to do with the time clock? I was wondering if there was any way to fiddle with it. Finagle a little extra time for lunch or if you were late. They'd never tell me, but they might talk to you."

"Yeah, right. Those guys live and die by that clock. They never take more than twenty-five minutes for their half hour break. And that includes running up and down the stairs to punch in and out. I've seen them tear out of there leaving half a bag of chips or a cookie which I feel is my due for having to clean up their mess. If they knew how to work the clock, I'd of seen 'em do it."

"Once again you have my undying thanks. You'll see that headline soon. I promise."

Would he? That promise seemed a little shaky right now.

Noah kept watching him as he recorded the highlights of his conversation with Billy in his memo pad. "Keep your eyes on the road. I'll write, you drive."

"I don't have to watch the road. I've made this trip so many times, Lola knows the way by heart."

"What do you expect to find on this trip that you didn't all those other times?"

"I have no idea unless Evie admits she killed Craig or that her timeline was way-the-hell off." Noah took a quick peek at the road.

Lola did seem to know the way on her own, but Conner would just as soon Noah did his share of the navigating. "We both know that isn't going to happen. Evie loved her husband, even if he was a jerk. And she's much worse off without him. As for the timeline; she only backed up what the doc already knew. Face it. The time clock proves Brandt Kittrell was eating lunch at Beneficial Products on the nights Craig Spencer and Madlyn Gwinn were murdered. The only one he could have killed is Rodney Graham and that's a stretch."

"Well, we've got to do something. Maybe she can suggest a new suspect. Rodney Graham didn't have anybody who cared enough about him to help us and Tom Meyer won't let us near Wade Gwinn. She's our only hope."

Lola pulled in front of the Spencer home and Noah stomped toward the door, ignoring Conner as if saying the truth out loud made this his fault.

He already had one child to take care of. He couldn't babysit Noah as well.

Kelly Manus threw the door open before they had time to knock. "Noah! Conner! It's great to see you. Come in."

She wore faded jeans and an oversized T-shirt. Her face glowed under no makeup and her hair swung back and forth in a ponytail. All in all, she looked like a normal seventeen-year-old girl. If it hadn't been for the distinctive Honda sitting in the driveway, he wouldn't have recognized her.

Noah must have been as surprised as he was. He sputtered his first few words. "It's uh…you're um… Nice to see you too, Kelly."

"I'm glad I have a chance to thank you personally for getting me this job. It's going to be perfect. I can go to school Monday, Wednesday, and Friday and still have time on weekends and evenings to help Evie with Joey. On Tuesdays and Thursdays I can take care of him while she runs errands or help her take him to doctor appointments. And I have a *huge* room all to myself."

She bounced on her toes while talking, excitement spilling out with every word. "Plus," she lowered her voice as if it were all too good to be true. "She's paying me *and* feeding me. Have you ever heard of anything so fine?"

A seven-day work week and always on call? Probably against child labor laws, but better than anything Kelly had experienced. Conner motioned down the hall, anxious to get this over with. "Sounds great, Kelly. I'm happy for you. Could we come in and talk to Evie for a minute?"

"She's giving Joey his breathing treatment." She pointed to the worn sofa Evie's family had occupied on their first trip. "Have a seat and I'll send her out."

Kelly had been there one day and the house already smelled better. As if a window had been opened and fresh air let in. Or Brice Palmer's family let out.

They waited in silence five minutes before Evie shuffled out, rolling down the sleeves of a tent-like caftan. She settled herself in a threadbare chair and nodded to each man. "I saw you pull up through Joey's window, but I couldn't leave him right then. I also saw you at Brandt and Chelsea's earlier. Are you actually thinking he'd kill Craig over a case of hurt feelings?"

Noah had been the one who dealt with her the most, so Conner leaned back and let him continue. "No, ma'am. We went over to Beneficial Products and checked his time card. He couldn't possibly have killed your husband. He was definitely at work during the time frame in question. We wanted to let you know so you wouldn't have any worries in that direction."

"I wasn't worried. Brandt is the kindest, gentlest man I've ever met. He has too much empathy to put anyone else through what he's about to experience. Now that you've wasted this much time, you can get to work finding the real killer."

Nice to know her true feelings on the subject. Would have been even nicer if she'd told them at the start, but they'd have to investigate no matter what she said.

Conner stepped in before Noah could argue. "You've had time to think about this. Can you suggest anyone who had a personal grudge against your husband?"

"I doubt it was anyone who knew us personally. Have you checked the people who lost their jobs when the company downsized?"

"We have, but we may need to go over the list again. Give them a closer look." Earl had telephoned most of them, but getting a feel for someone over the phone was tough.

Noah leaned forward, elbows on his knees, and spoke to Evie. "I see you were able to arrange something with Kelly. I hope she works out for you."

"That girl is a Godsend. Joey already loves her. I feel guilty about paying her so little, but I'm afraid to spend a penny until I have Craig's insurance in my pocket. I don't know about his 401(k). I'm not sure I'll ever get it, but I told his snooty secretary

I'd bring his credit card and company car in when she had the papers ready for me to sign. That way I'd only have to make one trip. The second I get that check, if I ever do, I'm going to deposit it in one bank then transfer it to another before the company folds. They still don't have a CEO. No one wants that thankless job."

Conner had an old uncle who declared women should stick to sewing and baking because their brains weren't wired for money matters. He made the bank the executor of his will and the bank president promptly invested in a shaky real estate deal and lost his aunt's inheritance.

After listening to Evie Spencer talk, and hearing Noah's story about the ex-plant-foreman's wife Sarah, he was more certain than ever the world would be better off if women ran anything of importance.

On the drive back to the office, Noah was the one in deep thought. Conner hated to interrupt him, but he'd had enough. He was missing Betsy's first days.

"I'm not coming in tomorrow unless something breaks. We're back where we started on day one, without a decent lead to follow. Call me the minute you find something and I'll be right in. Until then, I'm on leave."

"You're right. We don't have a lead worth shit. You might as well stay home where you can actually do some good. I only have one thought that keeps circling around my mind; I was wrong about Evie Spencer."

Noah? Admitting he was wrong?

"She's not worse off with her husband dead. It may take her a while, but she'll be fine."

So, the two dummies were at it again. Going first to one house, then to the other, then back to the first.

Like watching a ping-pong match.

How many miles had he put on that poor truck? It sat next to the curb, big, black, menacing. Like the raven from a Poe poem. Or was it more like a vulture, hovering, waiting for something to happen? Ready to swoop in at the first opportunity.

He might as well be driving on a treadmill for all the progress he'd made.

Not a single victim was worth the effort. Each and every one a murderer.

Getting exactly what they deserved.

Reaping the seeds of their deadly harvest.

If only there were some way to know for certain all this destruction would cause the Evil Empire to fall. The Fatal Factory to implode in the dust of its own poison.

The names of those responsible written large for the entire world to see.

The mighty brought down, their legacy tarnished beyond redemption.

Time would tell.

Time, fleeting time, the most precious commodity of all.

CHAPTER TWENTY-SEVEN

NOAH MET EARL and Danielle at the children's hospital. Each week the harsh fluorescent lights and hospital aroma hit him like a punch in the gut. Each week he swore he'd be prepared next time.

Each week he wasn't.

He recognized about half the kids from their last visit and the one before. Others were first-timers, their parents big-eyed with worry.

A few he'd seen occasionally over the months he'd been playing here. They came, went home, and came back, sicker than the last time he'd seen them. Their parents simply looked tired, drained.

The trio mixed up the songs from week to week, trying not to give the exact same show for the kids, doctors, nurses who were there week in and week out. When they finished their regular set, they started down the hall, playing a few songs geared to older kids.

He'd called Rachelle to find out what was popular with teenagers although how she was supposed to know, he wasn't sure. She listed a few from popular movies.

He printed off the sheet music, made notes about arrangements, and emailed it to Earl and Danielle. Amazingly, it seemed to work without the benefit of formal practice.

Kids he'd never seen before stood in the door of their rooms, hospital gowns held closed with one hand, IV pole held with the other. All this time, and they'd never given a thought to the older kids, separated from their friends, missing school, missing the chance to become independent.

When he passed the room where Madison had been last week, he slowed. The light was off and the room empty. Did that mean she had gone home in time for her algebra test?

He sent up a prayer she wouldn't become one of the frequent flyers, returning over and over again, each time thinner and weaker, until they disappeared.

As usual, he was restless when he got home, unable to put those pale faces out of his mind. He brought in the mail, put out the garbage, played tug with Sweet Pea, and searched for something to watch on TV.

He channel surfed, landing on one program for two minutes before moving on to the next. Where was that contest he watched last Saturday? He needed to watch strong, healthy athletes run and jump and swing from poles and fall and break something that would heal in a matter of weeks.

If they were injured, it was their own doing. Not some mysterious universal plan.

He gave up, watched one inning of Astro's baseball, and called it a night. Not that it did much good. He tossed and turned until Sweet Pea deserted him and moved to another room.

His dreams would have sent Dr. Freud running for help. *Cirque de Soleil* played in his head all night, complete with clownish costumes and strange, haunting music.

He awoke in a sweat and had to splash cold water on his face. He needed to either come to grips with seeing sick kids or find another place to volunteer.

He couldn't keep up this torture.

The *creak, creak, creak* of the rocking chair lulled Conner as much as it did Betsy. The house was blessedly silent. Jeannie was asleep. His mother-in-law asleep or reading. Betsy's eyes drooped lower and lower.

Five more minutes and she'd be out. And he could go back to bed.

The early morning sun painted her yellow room with a warm glow.

Hard to believe all this peace came at the expense of a long night full of crying, fussing, refusing all attempts at comfort.

Six pounds of terror wrapped in a pink blanket and smelling of love.

He'd wanted a baby, sure. But he'd had no idea how wide his heart could open. How a happy *gurgle* could wash away all the ugliness of the world.

Her eyelids closed. Two more minutes. Was he the champ or what? He slowed the rhythm of the rocker, ready to ease to his feet.

His phone rang.

Betsy's eyes sprang open. Her lips puckered. She drew in a

deep breath. A shrill wail cut through the room. Sleeping Beauty disappeared and the Demon of the Night returned.

He tried to rock faster while fumbling in his pocket to silence the offending cell phone, but it was too late. She-who-must-not-be-disturbed was *up*.

"There's a special place in Hell for those who wake a sleeping baby."

Noah whispered as if that would solve the problem. "I'm sorry. I can call back later if that will help."

And wake her a second time? "What is it, partner? I'm supposed to be off duty until we find some evidence that will crack this case open. I doubt that has happened overnight. Unless somebody else died."

He jerked forward, startling Betsy and increasing the volume of her cries. "That's not it, is it? Nobody else died, did they?" Could he stay back and play patty-cake while more people were murdered?

"The body count has remained the same, but I've come up with an idea. I need you to come with me and look at something. Tell me if I'm crazy."

"Can't you explain it to me over the phone?"

Conner stood and paced across the room, jostling Betsy against one shoulder. At the far end of the room he pivoted, ready to head back where he started. Standing in the nursery door, Jeannie glared at him, her hands on her hips. "Give me that baby before you scramble her brains. If Noah has an idea how to solve this case, get out there and help him. When you're home with us, I want your mind here, not wrestling with those murders."

She took Betsy from his arms and the crying diminished to

a few hiccups. "More than that, I want any of those monsters left who put babies' lives at risk for profit put away in a deep, dark hole where they can't contaminate the world any longer."

Conner lifted the phone he'd let drop to his side. "Pick me up in an hour."

"Sleep well?" Noah asked. The silent treatment was killing him.

Conner refused to look at him. This was going to be a long day. "I slept very well from ten thirty to midnight and again from two until four fifteen, thank you very much. I may have dozed a little around five thirty. You?"

"About the same." Conner wasn't the only one who was sleep-deprived.

"Want to tell me about it?"

Conner was starting to thaw, but now Noah had his back up. "No. I'd rather show it to you and let you make your own decisions."

They drove for five minutes before Noah broke down and tried to smooth things over. "How's Betsy?"

"Now that everyone else in the world is awake? She's asleep. That's why I was waiting for you outside. In case you decided to ring the doorbell." Conner offered a half-smile. "We're not going back to Carrelton Street, are we?"

"Not yet. First we're headed someplace a lot fancier but every bit as rotten."

He'd barely finished talking when they pulled up in front of Madlyn Gwinn's exclusive enclave. He punched a number into a keypad beside the wrought iron gates and they swung open, allowing them inside.

Lola's tires whispered *shhhhh* as they crossed the flagstones to the Gwinn townhouse. Ahead, red barrel-tile roofs contrasted with the oatmeal stucco walls, each townhome worth millions, but indistinguishable from its neighbor.

Wade Gwinn paced in front of his garage, fish-belly white legs poking out from khaki cargo shorts. It was mid-summer. Didn't the guy ever get out in the sun? He owned a pool for goodness' sake, and only painted in the mornings.

The minute Noah turned off Lola's engine, he started toward them, gesturing with the cell phone in his hand.

"My lawyer says I have to let you in, but I don't have to talk to you. In fact, he'll cut me loose if I do. I'm supposed to call him if you even *try* to question me."

"We don't need to talk to you, Mr. Gwinn. You don't have to be here. We just need you to let us into the backyard." Wade Gwinn had been a prick when they thought he was guilty and he was still one as they tried to prove they were wrong.

Of course, he didn't know they were on his side—maybe. Unless Conner said his idea was crap. In which case he was back on the list.

Wade stayed true to his word. He didn't speak one syllable as he led them through the house.

Noah took a quick peek into the kitchen as they passed. Empty wine and liquor bottles spilled out of the overflowing trash. Dirty glasses cluttered the counter.

Wade himself had lost weight but it hadn't done him any favors. The skin on his face drooped as if it were made out of wax and was starting to melt in the hot sun.

Ripples.

"You can let yourselves out when you're finished. I'll be up in my studio, working."

"How's the painting going?" He shouldn't ask, but for some reason, he actually wanted to know.

Wade shook his head, a bewildered look on his face. "It's changed. All black and navy and blood red slashes. For the life of me, I can't seem to get my old style back. I may lose what few followers I have. But for now, at least, that's what I paint. I may have to sell this house. Madlyn's insurance company is being a bitch about issuing me the payment and her bank accounts are frozen. This place is too big anyway. I rattle around in it. But don't know where I'll find a studio with better light."

He clamped his mouth shut with an almost audible *snap* when he realized he was blabbering. "I'll leave you to it," he mumbled as he turned his back.

More ripples.

Noah swung open the French doors to the patio. Crime scene tape littered the ground while leaves floated in the once azure water of the pool. Had Wade let the pool boy go along with the maid, or was the guy too traumatized by the sight of Madlyn's naked, bloated body to return?

Two more people out of work.

And the ripples continued.

"What is it you wanted to show me?"

Conner wanted to get to work and get out of here and Noah couldn't blame him. "Back here."

The two men crossed the miniscule yard to the back corner.

"What am I supposed to be looking at, the cable post?"

"Have you ever heard of something called *parkour*?"

"Don't think I have."

"It's a form of exercise first developed by the military using obstacle courses in training for guerilla warfare in urban settings. They run and jump and climb and crawl and swing off things."

"Have any of our suspects been in the military?"

"Not that I know of." Had they checked Wade or Brandt Kittrell's records?

"I suppose you're wondering if someone could run, spring off the cable post, and land on top of that wall. Assuming this fictitious person managed that tricky maneuver and didn't overshoot, landing in the junkyard behind and breaking his neck only then to be eaten by vicious guard dogs, he'd still have half a mile to walk on a surface narrower than your foot with overhanging bushes and tree limbs. Impossible."

"Not if her foot was half the size of mine and she had a gold medal for balance beam in the World Gymnastics Championships."

"Are you insane? How many years ago was that? I can't think of a person we've interviewed who's in worse physical shape. She's literally on her deathbed."

"She is now, but what about two weeks ago? Evie Spencer said this came on fast once she stopped the treatments."

Conner jammed his hands into his pockets and pivoted toward the house. "I still think you're crazy, but I guess we have to check it out."

"About those dogs…"

"Yeah?"

"I'm not that sure they exist. Could just be a couple of empty food bowls and a jumbo-sized dog house."

Conner rolled his eyes. Always the skeptic. "Speaking of jumbo-sized, didn't we see a couple of piles of rather large dog poop?"

"Plastic. Saw some exactly like them last weekend at the pet store when I was replacing Sweet Pea's favorite squeaky toy."

CHAPTER
TWENTY-EIGHT

LOLA MADE HER way back to Carrelton Street with little help from Noah. He and Conner had just stepped out when he saw Evie Spencer and Kelly loading Joey into her van.

"Are you looking for me, Detective? I'm supposed to meet Craig's secretary at his office in thirty minutes. She has the paperwork ready so I can access his retirement fund. You'd be surprised how fast they can move when they're worried about what you might know. I need to get over there while I have Kelly to drive the company car and before they change their minds."

Good for her. The way things were going, she'd better get that check in the bank fast.

Noah hadn't been planning to ask her anything, but she could clear up a few issues. "I won't hold you up more than a couple of minutes but I do have some questions you could help me with. Can you give me a timeline for Chelsea's illness? How long since she's been well enough to get around on her own, drive a car?"

"Chelsea? Really? That's not possible. Her health's been bad for months. She's dying, not going around killing people."

"I'm sure you're right, but we have to write this stuff down. Show what everybody was doing, when. Eliminate them so the DA won't be blindsided during trial."

"Well, like I told you, it wasn't a straight line. When she had chemo, she'd be sick as a dog for days, gradually improving as the week went along. There were days she couldn't get off the sofa and others when she'd pop over here for tea and a visit. Sometimes both in one day. When she finished her last treatment, she got better for a while, then worse. This last spell came on fast. I could see her going downhill by the day, the hour."

"When was the last time you saw her drive?"

"Not for a month or more. Craig thought he saw her pulling out of the subdivision a week or so ago, but that was ridiculous. She's on morphine. She's not allowed behind the wheel."

Sure, and anyone who killed four people would never break a traffic law.

"Craig swore it was her little baby-blue Fiat. I said maybe Brandt was driving, but it was late and he should have been at work. Besides, Brandt hates that car. It's a stick shift and he can't get out of the driveway without killing the engine. Craig was worried he had skipped out of work to check on Chelsea so he called the plant and Brandt answered so he must have been mistaken."

Conner looked up from the notes he was taking. "Her battery would have been shot by that time, anyway."

Evie gave a humorless laugh. "I doubt that would have stopped her. With the way she used to fix that motorcycle of hers, a dead battery would be child's play."

A light began to form behind Evie's eyes as they grew bigger and bigger. She sagged against the car and Noah grabbed her arm before she went down. "Nooo. Not Chelsea. Not my best friend. I knew I was going to lose her, but not this way. Not her memory, too."

Brandt blocked the half-open door. "You have to quit bothering us. Chelsea's not doing well today. She's been in a lot of pain. I gave her some morphine and she just got to sleep."

Hospital smells spilled through the opening. Noah could see pill bottles sitting on the coffee table next to the sofa Chelsea had been lying on the first time he saw her.

He hesitated, torn by memories of his mother, suffering with breakthrough pain her doctor couldn't control.

Until he'd killed a man to bring her some relief.

Should he allow Chelsea to die in peace?

No. He'd killed by accident. She'd plotted and planned, causing her victims as much pain as possible. They deserved justice and their families deserved answers.

Brandt was as much a victim as Craig and Rodney and Madlyn and Stefan Hueber, but he couldn't let that stop him.

"We don't have to come into the house right now, but we'd like to see Chelsea's car. Is it in the garage?"

"Sure, but it hasn't been moved in at least two months."

Noah didn't say a word, just waited until Brandt shrugged. "I'll get the keys."

He closed the front door and disappeared. Noah and Conner waited in the driveway until the garage door began to *screech* and inch upward. Inside sat a pale blue Fiat with a black top, not as dusty as Noah expected.

Shelving circled the walls. While one area held lawn supplies and fertilizer, the other side held repair equipment and parts for the now-sold motorcycle. Noah strolled toward that section and began examining cans of brake fluid and wrenches. He lifted a pair of size small gloves.

Was that a faint dusting of stucco on the palms? No point in him trying to decide. The lab would know for sure. He pulled a plastic evidence bag from his pocket and slid them inside. With all the forensic shows on TV these days, juries were no longer satisfied with circumstantial evidence, no matter how overwhelming. They demanded concrete facts, backed up by test tubes and scientific reports given by witnesses with impressive degrees.

Conner tried to slip behind the wheel of the little blue car but had to move the seat back before he could get inside.

Noah glanced at Brandt, waiting at the door that led into the laundry room and shuffling from one foot to the other. The guy was six foot three if he was an inch. A little taller than Noah and three or more inches taller than Conner.

His partner wedged himself in, his knees nearly hitting the steering wheel. He pressed down on the clutch and turned the key. The motor started with a roar. He let it run for a minute before switching it off and climbing out.

Noah stood with his hands in his pockets, breathing in exhaust fumes, motor oil, dust and despair. He should have been happy to wrap up this case. Instead, he was just sad.

"We need to come in, Brandt. I think you know why. I'm sorry, but we'll have to wake Chelsea. She has some questions to answer. I've already called my boss and a patrol officer. They'll be here any minute."

"Can we wait till they arrive? Let her sleep these last few minutes?"

Noah shook his head, but Conner folded his memo pad and placed it in his pocket. "Sure. Why don't we sit in the kitchen? I could use a cup of coffee."

Brandt released the door, allowing it to swing open. He pivoted on one heel and trudged toward the back of the house, his shoulders slumped until he was half his normal height.

The ripples never ended.

"Chelsea?"

The voice was familiar. She opened her eyes but it took a moment for the room to quit spinning and her vision to focus.

That big cop. Maybe he wasn't such a dummy after all.

"Can you hear me?"

"Yes." She felt her lips move—they were so dry they cracked—but didn't hear a sound come out.

Behind the cop was the other one. The one with suspicious eyes that took in everything. Brandt, sweet Brandt, was off to the side, his face pale, tears streaming down his cheeks.

The one thing she regretted. He'd already suffered so much. And now she had caused him more.

If he'd been more of a man, stood up for baby Aaron, none of this had to happen. But no, he'd refused to sue that evil company. That would cost him his precious job. As if a job was worth more than his son. And the resulting investigation might send his friend Craig to jail. His friend, who would surely never have let their baby die if he knew what was going on.

So he sat back and did nothing except worry about the bags delivered from foreign countries. It was all up to her, like everything in their marriage.

Up to her to drop hints to that shrew wife of his that he was having an affair.

Up to her to seduce him in the first place.

Up to her to ask Craig to find him a job.

Up to her to avenge Aaron.

And now, up to her to pay the price.

Brandt pushed his way forward and raised the head of her bed. He smoothed a soothing balm onto her lips and held a straw to her mouth for a sip of water. So cool, so comforting to her parched throat.

She tried again. "Yes?" The word came out a *croak*.

"Did you sabotage the breaks on Stephan Hueber's race car?"

She nodded.

"You need to answer out loud for the record." The cop held up a recording device.

"Yes." The word sounded stronger. She felt stronger saying it. Telling the world what she'd done. No more hiding. No more sneaking around after dark.

"Did you hold Madlyn Gwinn under water in her hot tub until she drowned?"

"Yes. The bitch," she added.

"And Rodney Graham?"

"He was supposed to be Aaron's doctor. Instead he murdered my child."

Her throat was closing again. She motioned to the cup of water and the cop held it to her lips. After she'd managed a few sips, he started again. Relentless.

"What about Craig Spencer?"

"I spent more time in that house than he did. Whenever Evie left, I'd go over there and check his computer. The fool had his password written beside it but half the time he left it on. Easy to find out what that company was doing. Lots more people you can prosecute if you're willing to. Check the folder marked *Weight Training*."

Somewhere in the back of the room Brandt choked out a sob.

"How did you cause him to drop a barbell on his throat, killing him?"

They hadn't figured that out? Maybe they were dummies after all.

"I unlocked the window in his garage, opening it enough to get my fingers under, but not enough for him to notice, then watched from my bedroom until the light came on. I went out my back door so no one could see me. After he'd completed a dozen reps and I knew he'd be too weak to recover, I used our old pool bridge and knocked his elbow out from under the weight. He saw me. He realized what was happening and that no one would help him. Just like Aaron."

That was the most satisfying death of all. He knew them personally. He understood why he deserved to die.

"We have a recording, but my partner had been writing down everything you've said. Are you willing to sign it?"

"Yes." The word ripped out of her throat. Perhaps the last she'd ever utter.

Her husband's voice came out strained and high. "She's under the influence of morphine. You can't use any of this in court."

Poor Brandt. Still trying to stand up for her. Too little. Too late.

Her eyes couldn't focus on the words so the thin cop read them out to her. She nodded and reached for a pen, scribbling some illegible loops on the bottom of the page.

The big cop lifted her wrist and clicked something cold and metallic on it then fastened the other end to the bed rail.

She tried to find Brandt's face in the crowded room, but her eyes drooped shut.

Her time had come.

CHAPTER
TWENTY-NINE

"WHAT DO YOU mean, you can't arrest anyone?" Noah felt his voice take on a hard edge. Not the best way to deal with his boss.

"We haven't found anything on anyone's computer that is in the least bit incriminating."

"Have you tried Craig Spencer's home computer? A little bird told me he had the password taped to the desk beside it."

"Rumor has it, a warrant is in the works." Lt. Jansen didn't look any more pleased about the situation than Noah. The case had been moved up the chain of command. Out of his hands.

"Won't Evie give permission?"

"She's gone to her brother's lake house in the hill country. No cell phone service. Your teenage friend is living there, but we learned our lesson from that debacle with her boyfriend's trailer and won't be asking her permission. The justice department is better off with a warrant anyway. Then there's no question when it comes to trial."

Evie might have needed a quiet place to grieve in private. Then again, she could be stalling while she moved Craig's retirement funds someplace safe. Or protecting his reputation for the sake of his children. Either way, kids were getting sicker every day that poison was on the market.

Would anybody ever come to trial for anything? Chelsea was dead. Madlyn, Stefan, Craig and Rodney were dead. Who was left to prosecute?

"What about the company, Beneficial Products. Can you do anything about them?" Another day had passed and nothing was on the news about the recall of their baby formula.

"The factory was empty. The mixing vats, the blades, the assembly line, the floor, the storeroom. All scrubbed clean. Not a grain of product. Not a speck of dust. They claimed it was routine sanitizing between batches."

"Did they check the stuff on the shelves? Wasn't that contaminated?"

"Maybe, but the big wigs had decided to start with the factory first. Now they have to go to different stores and suppliers, buy some product off the open market and start the testing procedure all over again. It could take a week."

Some of those kids might not have a week. He'd made promises.

Was his word as useless as the guarantee of purity stamped on the cartons of Beneficial Products baby formula?

Jansen studied him over half-rimmed glasses. "Stay out of this, Daugherty. It's well above our pay grade. I can't protect you from those in power."

Noah stomped back to his desk. A storm churned his insides to mush, making Charlotte seem like an autumn breeze. He'd sent Conner home, assuring him he'd take care of the loose ends. Now what? Call his partner and say he lied?

Could he look at little Betsy, knowing other kids were in danger?

He had a lot to make up for if he wanted to join his Betsy in Heaven. At one time, he'd counted the bad guys he took off the streets hoping for the magic number of forty nine misremembered from an old Sunday School lesson about forgiving not seven times but seven times seven.

Then he'd Googled the quote and realized the Bible said seventy times seven and 490 was more than he could accomplish in a lifetime, much less the fourteen months he'd given himself because he'd promised his sister and Conner's wife he wouldn't make any major decisions until at least a year after Betsy's death..

October was fast approaching. Whether he decided to implement his plan or stick around to watch his nieces and godchild grow, he had to live with himself and his decisions.

A new pink message memo was taped to his computer. He stuffed it in his pocket and left the building to make his call.

Noah settled onto his sofa, fed Sweet Pea one last Cheetos nub, and opened the newspaper.

FEDS RAID LOCAL COMPANY. PRODUCTS PULLED FROM SHELVES.

The headline screamed from the front page of *The Houston Chronicle*, but it was already national news. There was no stopping it now. The public outcry had become an avalanche.

The Feds hadn't released the contents of Beneficial Products supposedly organic baby formula, the one made especially for fragile infants, but Noah's formerly least favorite reporter had managed to pry the list from a secret informant.

Every batch was different.

While some contained talc, others used chalk. Some had flour instead of cornstarch. Some didn't have any real milk at all, but used something called rice milk or, worst of all, almond milk with no warning label for kids who were allergic to nuts.

One thing they all had in common: copious amounts of sugar. After all, what good was it if the kiddos wouldn't drink it? Mom and Dad wouldn't buy a second carton.

Noah could picture Craig Spencer or Stefan Hueber or one of their toadies—Darius Breeden? His name had appeared several times—searching the world for the cheapest ingredients. The thought made his stomach turn.

How many kids had been endangered while he stumbled around looking at disgruntled employees or pissed-off spouses?

He folded back the paper and followed the story on the next page. New names appeared every day.

Names of those who knew and did nothing.

Names of people he hadn't come across in his investigation. Who might have walked away unscathed. Whose only punishment was their name besmirched.

After all, had any laws been broken other than mislabeling a product? What was the punishment for that, a fine? No invitation to the mayor's inauguration?

Their friends and family would know. Would that make any difference? Or were those the type of people who would only look down on them for getting caught?

At least they might not be asked to sit on prestigious boards in the future. Not much of a reprimand for putting the lives of innocent children in jeopardy.

He'd done his part. The rest was up to the lawyers, with a little help from public opinion.

Hunter Lassen's wife, Sarah, called to thank him but he claimed to be out of the loop. Learning about it through the newspaper like everyone else. She didn't sound convinced.

He propped his feet on the coffee table and Sweet Pea snuggled in his lap after realizing there were no more Cheetos nubs waiting for her.

There was talk R.J. Perry might win a Pulitzer Prize. Good for him. He deserved it. As long as he respected their confidentiality agreement.

The DA had made noises about forcing the reporter to reveal his source but countless angry letters to the editor caused him to drop his efforts in that direction. Some of those letters had initials he recognized as fellow officers.

Jansen had hemmed and hawed and made veiled threats but Noah kept his mouth shut and nothing happened. They both agreed it was a good time for Noah to use his accumulated leave.

He'd already been to the local home improvement store and bought the supplies to build a deck in his backyard. They would be delivered tomorrow. When it was finished, he planned to throw a large party and invite not only his family, but some of the neighbors he only nodded to on his nightly walks with Sweet Pea.

A new Disney movie opened next week and he'd ordered three tickets online, ready to surprise Emma on her birthday.

Frank planned to take him fishing on Saturday. Maybe it wouldn't be too bad. Rachelle seemed happy he was making the effort.

Tonight, he was invited to Conner's for dinner. His mother-in-law was cooking. In a couple of weeks, after she left and Betsy was a little bigger, he'd offer to babysit and let them go out for a few hours.

All in all, life was good. Or as good as he deserved.

ACKNOWLEDGMENTS

Writing a book can be a lonely endeavor, but not when you have friends who help you and offer inspiration along the way.

My children, Ron and Angela, have always been my staunchest supporters. Without their encouragement, I would never have managed to keep going when things got tough.

All of my family—Karen, Jason, Andrew, Sam, Caroline, and Bode—along with my friends—Jan, Shawnna, Christie, Delma, Jami, and many more—have made this trip not only possible but enjoyable.

Carla Rossi and Kimberly Dawn, you made the process easier and better in every way

Thank you to the members of Northwest Houston RWA, Kiss of Death RWA, Houston Northwest Medical Center Auxiliary, my fans and supporters, and to you the reader.

Dear Readers,

I hope you enjoyed this book as much as I enjoyed writing it. If you did, please consider taking a moment to leave a review. Authors live and die by reviews. Reviews don't need to be long. A single paragraph works better than a long retelling of the story. Just say what you liked about the book. How it made you feel. Did it offer heart-racing excitement or heart-tugging emotions? Did the characters come to life? Were you invested in the outcome? Did the villain give you the creeps?

If you are interest in seeing what else Noah and Conner are up to, check out the rest of the books in the Seasons Pass series. Remember: Murder is always in season.

WINTER SONG

Homicide detective Noah Daugherty is on a mission: solve cases, lock up murderous scum, and get on with what's left of his life. He's on the clock, and his time is steadily ticking away. His path leads him to an icy Houston street, where a car has careened out-of-control and crashed, its driver, a beautiful young socialite, is dead. All the clues lead straight to her husband, but Noah's intuition screams the case is more than meets the eye.

Not willing to give up until he solves this cold-blooded murder, he finds the unthinkable . . . a hitman no one saw coming, with a chilling personal agenda that now targets Noah.

Can he solve the case and save himself before winter is finished singing her song?

SPRING SHADOW

Homicide detective Noah Daugherty finds purpose in solving the most horrendous of crimes. The last thing he wants is to babysit some spoiled country singer, but that's exactly what his lieutenant demands.

Posing undercover as a member of the singer's band, he makes it his mission to protect her from a stalker whose ominous threats have become increasingly personal. As things heat up, she hides a piece of her past that is key to solving the case, ashamed of the part she plays.

Can Noah unearth the painful truth before spring casts its dark shadow?

AUTUMN SECRETS

The harvest moon has arrived and homicide detective Noah Daugherty is drawn into one final, harrowing case when the search for clues leads him to the middle of a killing field. Desperate, he enlists the help of a woman from his past. Together they discover a serial killer, hell bent on reaping his own depraved version of social sanitation.

As Noah continues his urgent search for justice, the demented madman seems to stay one step ahead, taunting him and threatening everyone he holds dear.

Can Noah put a stop to the killing, or will he be buried along with autumn's secrets?

Check out my website at: www.SusanCMuller.com

Or join me on social media.
Facebook: Susan C. Muller, author
Twitter: @SusanCMuller

Sign up for my newsletter to learn about new releases and to be eligible for prizes. http://eepurl.com/cibhMn

Love reading? Join my review crew for ARCs (Advanced Reader Copy) of my latest novels.
https://goo.gl/forms/BW55alj8iSjAjCCB2